Originally from France, Jocelyne Rapinac is a modern languages teacher who has lived in the US, Switzerland and the UK with her husband James. *Freedom Fries and Café Crème* is her first novel.

Freedom Fries
and
Café Crème

Freedom Fries
and
Café Crème

Jocelyne Rapinac

Gallic Books
London

A Gallic Book

First published in Great Britain in 2012 by Gallic Books,
59 Ebury Street, London, SW1W 0NZ

A CIP record for this book is available from the British Library
ISBN 978-1-908313-00-3

Typeset in Fournier MT by Gallic Books
Printed and bound by CPI Group (UK) Ltd, Croydon, CR0 4YY

2 4 6 8 10 9 7 5 3 1

To James

Special thanks to James, Jane, Kat, Yvonne and
all of you who made me believe in my writing and cooking.

This book is also dedicated to all of you who work very hard
in a kitchen trying to please the palates of so many of us!

January

The Height of Good Taste

'To eat is a necessity, to eat intelligently is an art.'
François, Duc de La Rochefoucauld,
1613–1680, French writer

'Papa, what's a New Year's resolution?'

Armand, reading and sipping his coffee, was a little taken aback by this sudden question. He got up from the comfortable sofa and turned up the flames of the gas fire until he could feel an agreeable warmth on his face. Then he settled back down, inviting Juliette to sit beside him ...

A few minutes later, she seemed satisfied with her father's explanation.

'Have you made one, Papa?'

'Well, er, let me think about it ...'

The little girl was all ears.

'I promise I'll tell you later, Juliette.'

'OK, Papa! Then I might make one myself.'

Juliette was always so conciliatory.

January and its New Year's resolutions! And what *were* Armand's, since, for once, he was feeling rather satisfied with his life? He simply wanted to go on trying to be as happy as he could, and to keep certain habits that he believed were good for him and Juliette.

Would a relationship actually contribute more to his happiness? Or would it simply be a call of the flesh, since he felt no lack of companionship or affection right now? And he had hardly been able to trust anyone after what Han had done to him and Juliette.

On the other hand, there was Liana, whom he'd met at Brenda's New Year's Eve dinner party. How attractive, friendly and witty she was. Even though they'd been seated at a table with other people, the two of them had managed a good bit of subtle flirtation throughout the evening, while enjoying Brenda's exquisite festive dinner.

Much of their flirting had been based around the sensual enjoyment of the food – the aroma, the deliciousness and beautiful presentation of dishes – and the sweetness of the champagne had helped oil the wheels.

They'd been having such a very good time … until Armand had had to leave when his mobile phone rang to remind him it was late and he should return home.

'So soon?' said Liana, disappointed, feeling that the spell of the evening had been broken.

Armand muttered a vague excuse, but his face showed his regret.

'Anyway, it was very nice to meet you, Armand!'

Liana was smart enough to see she couldn't say anything to detain him, and though she could imagine many scenarios that would explain his sudden departure, she didn't ask.

'I hope I'll see you again,' she added, summoning her self-confidence. After all, they'd established a bond through their conversation and their shared love of gourmet food.

'I hope so, too,' Armand replied sincerely.

He left, thinking that he would definitely contact Brenda to learn more about Liana, and possibly to ask her for Liana's phone number.

Actually, Brenda had called Armand the day after to tell him that Liana had asked for *his* phone number.

Women nowadays do take the initiative, don't they? And why not? thought Armand.

That had been a few days ago and Liana hadn't called. Not that Armand really expected her to, but one never knew. He hadn't called her, after all. Even if he'd felt very attracted to her – he had never enjoyed such sensuous dining with anyone before – he was a little afraid he might be disappointed if they met in other circumstances.

Snow was falling slowly, bringing an atmosphere of peace to the neighbourhood.

It's hard to believe we're in Manhattan, mused Armand, watching the snowflakes drifting down. As his mind wandered back to Liana and New Year's Eve, Suzanne Ciani's piano music, playing soothingly in the background, added a little melancholy note to his mood.

Later on, Armand knew, he would have much less time to relax since Rick and Carla, his employers, would be back.

He turned from the window to look at Juliette. She was drawing a very colourful picture to give to Rick and Carla. The couple were portrayed with outsized smiley faces, standing beneath a dark, slim Eiffel Tower, and with a big sun shining in the background.

Juliette was really into her drawing, the tip of her little

11

tongue pressed against her upper lip in concentration. Even her teachers were amazed, and happy to see that, unlike many of her peers, she did other things besides watching TV or playing computer games.

Armand walked around the spacious, overly decorated apartment to check that everything was in order before Rick and Carla arrived. The cleaning lady was just finishing and he was satisfied that the place had never looked better.

Three strident buzzes from the doorbell.

'Papa, they're back!' Juliette ran to the front door.

Yes, Rick and Carla had returned. Although it was their home, they always rang the bell to announce their arrival since Armand and Juliette lived in. 'It's a question of respect,' they insisted.

The door opened on a pair of smiling, artificially tanned faces. Tony, the apartment block concierge, was behind them, pushing their abundant luggage on a trolley.

'Hello, Rick and Carla. Welcome home! You look great,' Armand greeted them.

'Yeah,' Juliette confirmed, animated, jumping up and clapping her hands.

'*Bonjour, tous les deux*, so good to see you! And to be home!' Carla and Rick said almost in unison.

They skipped into the living room, took their coats off, sat down on the big white sofa and sighed with pleasure. Juliette immediately seated herself between the new arrivals. The three of them giggled with delight. Rick and Carla admired the picture Juliette had drawn for them. It would be added to their significant collection, as they were the lucky recipients of most of Juliette's artwork.

Armand told Tony where to leave the luggage. Then the concierge departed with a contented smile, showing Armand the bottle of Armagnac that Rick and Carla had given him.

Carla sought out the presents she and Rick had brought for Juliette: a beautiful vintage doll and a French book.

'I'll call her Armande, after Papa.'

Rick, Carla and Armand smiled because that's what the little girl called all her dolls.

'We had a nice, peaceful time with my parents over Christmas,' Rick said. 'They send their regards. The Paris trip was—'

'We had a blast!' Carla burst out.

'Yes, what a wonderful trip!'

'Too much food and drink, though! You'll need to get us back on the straight and narrow. Anyway, it's good to be back.'

They both looked sincerely at Armand and his daughter.

'And you? How are you doing, Armand, and little princess Juliette?' Carla asked.

Armand told them that everything was fine.

'Any exciting news? How is your family?'

'Just give me a few moments to fix you some drinks and I'll tell you,' Armand replied, getting up and going to the kitchen.

Even if the kitchen still felt a little too clinical to him – more like a laboratory than a place to prepare food, owing to its cutting-edge designer style – Armand was more

13

comfortable there since he'd humanised it with antique culinary equipment and jars of aromatic herbs. The first time he'd seen the kitchen in which he was to do much of his work he'd felt as out of place as poor Monsieur Hulot experimenting with the ultra-modern appliances in his sister's kitchen in *Mon Oncle*. But, since Armand had brought his influence to bear, the kitchen looked and functioned much better, with a rather eclectic mix of styles that Rick and Carla found so chic.

Armand returned with a vegetable cocktail and a tray of mini blinis, and gave a brief account of his holiday. His mother and sister had come for a visit, which was a big event for them, since neither travelled frequently as they didn't have much money and were continually busy with their small strawberry farm in Quebec. They'd really enjoyed New York – it was only their second visit – but who wouldn't like this wonderful city, especially when they could stay with Armand in this huge, fabulous apartment on the Upper West Side?

'How was Brenda's dinner party? Did you meet anyone, er, interesting?' Rick enquired.

Armand was perfectly aware that Rick and Carla wanted him to meet someone, but he also knew they would be devastated if he left them.

'I'm saving that news for later,' he told them. 'I'd rather hear about your trip first.'

'Yes, me too!' Juliette added enthusiastically.

Rick and Carla loved it when Armand and Juliette showed an interest in their lives, which they themselves believed to be so exciting, though Armand actually found their lifestyle a bit too tiring for his taste, and Juliette, a young girl, was still easily impressed.

The couple didn't really know where to start, and their story was a little jumbled and confused, but Armand and his daughter listened patiently.

How very relaxed and re-energised Rick and Carla look, Armand thought, gazing at the couple chatting effervescently, even if they've just spent seven hours on a plane. Since they flew business class on Hexagone Air it certainly ought to have been relaxing.

Suddenly Rick got up and turned to his wife.

'Carla, why don't we go have a quick shower? Then we'll be ready for dinner.'

'Sounds good to me!' Looking at herself in the big mirror above the sofa, she added, 'Oh, yes, I definitely need to freshen up.'

They disappeared to their gigantic, immaculate, elegantly tiled bathroom, giggling like teenagers.

Armand admired how happy the couple were. Even though he was only thirty-one, he was convinced he'd never be in such a beautiful relationship.

Armand had a high regard for the integrity of Rick and Carla's affection. He had never seen anything like it, except in romantic films. Was it because they had met when they were in their early forties, and already knew a good deal about life? Did the fact that they didn't have any children have something to do with it?

Love always looks more glamorous when you live in a big, beautiful apartment, and when you never have to think about money and trivial chores, reflected Armand cynically, while going back to the kitchen to prepare a delicious but healthy welcome-home dinner.

'… And happy New Year!'

Exceptionally, Armand and Juliette were to have dinner with Rick and Carla in the dining room to celebrate their return. Armand laid the table with Carla's best tableware, the dishes were inlaid with tricolour pearls and the cutlery was encrusted with semi-precious stones. It was a little too rococo for his taste, but Carla liked it.

Armand and Juliette usually had their dinner in the kitchen before Rick and Carla ate theirs after they'd come home from work.

Since they hadn't seen each other for a couple of weeks, the evening's discussion was to consist of:

1. More details about Rick and Carla's exclusive luxury culinary and cultural tour, staying in an exclusive world-class hotel in Paris

2. All the new healthy food and drink Armand had discovered while they were away

3. Rick and Carla's resolutions for this New Year

4. The week's to-do list, starting tomorrow morning at six fifteen sharp – the toughest transition for Armand after two weeks of morning laziness

Rick and Carla sat down at the dining-room table, refreshed by their shower, still in a festive mood.

The dining room's imposing baroque clock struck twice: it was only 4.30 p.m., but in view of Rick and Carla's jet lag it seemed wise to have an early dinner.

'Home sweet home,' crooned Rick, kissing Juliette on her forehead.

The little girl sat in her place with the new Armande doll on a chair to her right. The happy couple were clearly ready for dinner as well. Armand went over to put on some music, which Rick and Carla always insisted on while they were eating. Armand was still in the mood for Suzanne Ciani's relaxing piano notes.

'Dinner smells divine!' Carla enthused. 'I'm starved!'

'After everything we ate on the plane!'

'It was very good, actually …' she admitted.

Well, I hope so, since you were in business class, Armand thought but didn't say.

'… and I don't know why, but I always have such a big appetite when I'm in the air!' she added with that naivety that suited her so well.

I would too if I were being served champagne non-stop, and a gourmet meal, maybe with foie gras, Armand reflected a little enviously.

'I'm sure I put on at least four pounds! Armand, I'm counting on you to help me regain my figure!' she continued.

'Of course! That means veggie cocktails and more stomach exercises!' Armand smiled. *Well, it is part of my job, isn't it?*

'We ate very well most of the time, but we missed your cooking, Armand,' Rick said, visibly enjoying the soup. 'This is delicious – a new recipe?'

'Sort of,' Armand answered vaguely.

'To be added to your book? Have you worked on it, since, after all, you have had some time off?' Carla enquired.

'Well, you know, with my mother and sister visiting ...'

'But they were only here for a week, weren't they?'

Armand was not going to tell her that, besides spending time with Juliette, he had lounged in the most comfortable armchair in front of the fire, reading books, watching silly comedies, or – on a less agreeable note – just staring out of the window and dwelling on bitter memories from the past and worries for the future.

'Leave him alone, Carla. Armand needed some time off,' said Rick, winking at Armand, knowing full well what he'd been through. Rick, too, was writing a book – had been for almost ten years now – with the curious title of *It's Unfortunate that Socialism Will Never Flourish in America*.

Carla thought that Armand's book would be far more interesting than her husband's because people would rather read and talk about good food and recipes than politics, especially nowadays.

'I really love this soup!' Rick repeated, trying to keep the subject away from books.

Armand appreciated Rick and Carla complimenting his cooking. He was always grateful for the praise, since, when he was growing up, his family had rarely had anything positive to say to him.

'Wait until you see the *dernier cri* pieces I brought back from Paris,' Carla told him. 'They'll give you some great material for your book. I also thought about a few titles on the plane. I couldn't read, and the only movies were tiresome commercial ones.'

Rick and Armand exchanged glances: Carla would never change. When she had something on her mind it was hard to stop her. *Why doesn't she just write the book herself?*

Suddenly Carla stood up, blew out all the candles except one, and turned the lights off. Juliette asked what was going on but Armand took her hand and told her not to be afraid. The melancholy piano music in the background added to the air of mystery.

But not for Rick, who was obviously in cahoots with Carla. He was chuckling quietly.

'Go on eating, and describe your sensations,' Carla ordered gently, her tone serious. 'The aroma, the texture, the flavour of what you're putting in your mouths.'

Armand found all this a little odd, even if he was used to the occasional eccentricities of the couple.

'OK,' Juliette replied, more relaxed now, and definitely more amused about this little game than her father.

Kids always think that life is fun, Armand mused. Why does that have to come to an end when one grows up? Although adulthood didn't seem to have stopped the fun for Rick and Carla, who were constantly cheerful.

'Of course, *you* know what ingredients are on your plate, Armand, but Rick, Juliette and I will try to guess what they are while we eat in the dark.'

The three of them in turn shared their observations about the soup.

After a few minutes Juliette grew tired of the game. She couldn't identify all the ingredients, even though she did pretty well describing what she had on her plate. She whispered in her father's ear that she wanted the lights turned back on.

Finally Armand told everyone what the ingredients were.

After a few 'Oh, really?' and 'I knew it!' the lights were back on and the candles relit.

'You see, the most interesting meal we had on our Parisian trip was at the restaurant Sombre-Obscur, one of the *restaurants branchés* of the moment, where you basically eat in the dark,' Rick explained.

'Definitely a world-class restaurant!' Carla added.

Armand didn't really like these sorts of places. In his opinion they offered no atmosphere, besides having a similar corporate designer look, with no sense of conviviality – the way Rick and Carla's kitchen had looked before Armand had added his human touch – and they all served the same kinds of dishes no matter where you were in the world: experimental cooking, overly complex preparations and bizarre mixtures of ingredients that in the end denatured the essence of the food. The prices were also completely over the top.

Armand would have preferred an intimate local family restaurant, colourful and welcoming, where the menu was made from what was available that morning at the market and the cuisine was as authentic as its clientele. Unfortunately these little eating places were becoming increasingly rare everywhere in the world.

'And you'll never guess what we had for dessert!' Rick finished.

'The most expensive dessert in the world!' exclaimed Carla.

And, yes, it has to be expensive otherwise it can't possibly be any good, Armand thought.

'White truffle ice cream. Thirty euros a scoop!' Rick informed them.

'What? That's forty-five dollars!' shouted Armand.

'That's awfully expensive for white chocolate ice cream,' said Juliette, her eyes wide with surprise.

Rick explained to her what white truffles were.

The little girl made a face. 'Ice cream with mushrooms?'

'Was it good, at least?' Armand enquired.

'It was, wasn't it?' Rick turned to Carla dubiously.

'It was ... er, yes, it definitely was.'

That wasn't said with much conviction, Armand decided. It was apparent to him that Rick and Carla had simply played their preferred role of trendy connoisseurs because it was the wealthy people's thing to do, not because it was enjoyable.

Rick and Carla continued raving about Sombre-Obscur, where customers were supposedly able to develop their sense of taste and smell, and experience brand-new and exciting sensations while eating.

'It was a bit tricky to eat and drink neatly at times, but we truly could taste our food like we never have before. It was worth a try, wasn't it?'

'It was. Er, it definitely was.'

'You spent the whole meal in total darkness?' Juliette asked, somewhat astounded.

Welcome to the odd world of adults, Armand was

tempted to whisper in his daughter's ear.

'Just a few candles on the walls of the restaurant, that's all,' Carla explained.

'That seems a little creepy, doesn't it?' Juliette stared at her father with her big hazel eyes.

'It was very romantic, actually!' Carla replied, glancing languorously at Rick.

Romantic, my foot! Armand decided it was a silly idea because a big part of the delight in enjoying food is to see what you're eating. *If you want to taste what you have in your mouth without seeing the food, then close your eyes! This so-called innovative cuisine that mixes anything and everything together with no logic – no, thanks! And watching your companion enjoying food is also delicious … if indeed one has someone with whom you can share such pleasure …*

'I wonder if such a restaurant would work in New York?' asked Rick, cutting short Armand's thoughts.

'Why not?' Carla replied.

'Because we Americans aren't used to spending a long time sitting at a table smelling, tasting, sensing the food. Remember how long the dinner was? No, people definitely don't have the time here,' Rick concluded firmly.

'But people like us do, don't they?' remarked Carla. She wanted to believe that she and Rick had healthier eating habits these days, and that they lived better than their friends and acquaintances.

Armand brought in the main course and a salad.

'Ah, how thoughtful of you!' exclaimed Rick and Carla together, smiling appreciatively. 'For dessert, did you also make …?'

'Wait and see,' Armand answered, winking.

'I made the salad, and I put some colours into it!' Juliette informed them proudly.

'Like you always do in your pretty drawings.' Carla smiled fondly, being full of admiration for the little girl. She had felt attached to her since the day they met. 'It's beautiful! Artistic talent definitely runs in the family.'

'Talking about talent,' said Rick as he took a generous portion of the Divine Meat Pie, 'the afternoon we spent at the international Art in Food exhibition was simply fabulous.'

'All the works of art were made of food,' Carla explained.

'Really, really?' Juliette opened her eyes even wider.

'Oh, yes. There were miniature Christmas trees made of spinach meringues.'

'And they even had a fashion show with …'

'… a dress made of various shades of pasta …'

'… with jewellery made of dried fruit and beans, and hats made of bread.'

Rick and Carla continued with ever more extravagant descriptions. Juliette looked at the two of them as if they were aliens from the planet Food.

Armand was sure that his daughter was already thinking about the pictures she'd draw from all this.

I personally prefer the kind of culinary art that stands on a plate in order to delight by being eaten, and that satisfies the eyes and the taste buds. All this seems a little wasteful when you think about the many people who are starving in the world. But, once more, Armand kept his thoughts to himself.

'And the Petit Palais had a special exhibition of still lifes:

La table des peintres. Totally first-rate!' said Rick.

'I would have liked that. Wouldn't you, Papa?' asked the budding artist.

But Armand didn't have a chance to reply.

'Some of the paintings looked so incredibly real,' Carla added, 'that I felt like I wanted to plunge into them. I imagined myself sitting at the table wearing an elegant period dress, tasting the foods and drinks that were represented so beautifully, and being exhilarated by all the sensations of an idyllic vanished era.'

A silence ensued. Everyone was struck by Carla's images from the past, when people took time to eat, and enjoyed the company of their friends and families, and the outdoors, with a kind of simple nonchalance.

It was time for dessert. Armand opened a small bottle of champagne and poured a few sparkling drops into his daughter's glass.

'I see you also thought of the Winter Fruit Delight! Thank you, Armand!' exclaimed Rick and Carla.

'To a New Year full of good meals!'

'And healthy habits!'

'*C'est si bon, si bon si bon*', crooned Rick.

After dessert, Juliette was ready to go to her room with the Armande doll and her new French book. She said good night to them all after making them promise that they would tell her all about their New Year's resolutions the next day.

When Juliette had gone to bed, Rick and Carla gave Armand their first gift. They never failed to bring him and his daughter a few presents whenever they went on their travels. Armand wondered if they felt sorry for him because he couldn't afford trips like theirs. Not that he was at all interested in luxury travel – he personally thought it a bit superficial – though he did sometimes wish that he could see more of the world. But at least New York had a lot to offer.

The first gift was a thick book about *La table des peintres* exhibition, which Rick and Carla began praising for a second time.

Looking at them, Armand realised once again that he had never seen a couple get along so well: two married people who spent so much time together at the table, appreciating almost any kind of food, and constantly talking to each other. When he was with them he often felt as if he were part of the audience at a long and cheerful romantic play.

That made him think about Liana …

The way Rick and Carla had met was a good omen. 'Impress me with a meal you've cooked and I'll date you' was a new concept in dating. The gathering of single people took place at a renowned and upmarket cookery school. The participants needed to know how to cook, at least a little bit. There was a pre-selection of fifteen women and fifteen men. Each participant was asked to cook his or her favourite dish, and then display it alongside everyone else's on a long buffet table. Then everyone was invited to taste the dishes that appeared the most appetising. Carla literally fell in love with Rick's Winter Fruit Delight, and Rick with Carla's Divine Meat Pie. They found a little table for two away from the others and stayed until someone politely informed them that it was closing time and they were the only ones left.

Back to the reality of their hectic daily routine, Rick and Carla had had to face the fact that they didn't have time to prepare and enjoy the kind of meals they both loved because of their long working hours. Being extremely career-oriented, they spent their whole day working, eating only when they could spare a few moments. They were usually too tired to cook when they got home in the evenings: she, back from her law office; he, from the hospital.

The new couple needed to find a solution in order to be completely happy. They were desperately searching for the answer when a colleague of Rick's told him about the *Art de Vivre* show that was coming up.

Armand was exhibiting at the show, trying to sell his services as a good-and-healthy-life coach, his slogan being 'Too Busy to Cook? I Have the Solution!' Not that Armand was all that motivated by the idea at the time, but he was anxious to find a job, and he liked cooking. Why not, after all? Especially since he wanted a new start after Han's flight, and he was tired of selling holiday time-shares to people who didn't really want them.

Carla and Rick had hired him immediately: it was so fashionable to have a good-and-healthy-life coach, and a live-in one as well. This had suited Armand because he'd also needed a decent place to live for himself and Juliette, who was just a toddler then. Being Quebecois had been in his favour, Rick and Carla would later reveal, as they found his French heritage appealing.

The couple now flew to Quebec City at least twice a

year, 'for the remarkable food experience and romanticism without the jet lag', as they put it.

Since then, Rick and Carla had been eternally grateful to Armand, who had helped them lead more stable and less stressful lives. He did the shopping, cooked balanced and tasty meals, supervised their workouts in their gym room, and organised their social events.

Armand liked his job. An unusual kind of friendship had developed between him and his employers, plus he lived in a luxurious home – even if he found the furniture too modern and the many decorative objects a little too gaudy for his own taste.

'The *Tendance* show at the Grande Épicerie was also a lot of fun! So many trendy and sophisticated groceries!' said Carla, giving Armand a slender, elegant blue glass bottle with a white moon on it.

He examined the label and discovered the contents promised much.

After Armand had thanked them for all their gifts, he brought out a few of the food selections he had made. Another part of his job was trying to find the most fashionable, the healthiest and sometimes the most extraordinary food and drink: this was, after all, the height of good taste for Rick and Carla. They then went on to impress their friends and colleagues with Armand's discoveries.

'First, I came across some new tonic drinks from Africa made of hibiscus and baobab. They are supposed to be full of vitamin C.'

'Oooooh!' Rick and Carla said in unison.

'And here is a Brazilian rainforest superberry drink full of natural antioxidants, and Tepee Tea prepared by Native Americans, plus two tickets for the Salad Fashion Show, which will be held at Grand Central Terminal in April ...'

Rick and Carla examined the various items with keen interest, carefully reading through the exhaustive lists of ingredients.

Armand drew their attention. 'Now, it is New Year's resolutions time. You asked me to help you with your list, didn't you?'

'Indeed we did, Armand.'

Rick and Carla each took a pen and a slip of paper, as eager as two students that had returned to school after a long summer off. They began writing while Armand went to the kitchen to put the kettle on for their comforting evening drink: mint and liquorice herbal tea imported from France.

Tired but still in a positive mood, Rick and Carla had gone to bed early since they both had to be at work the following morning. Armand cleared the table, put everything into the dishwasher and finished tidying the kitchen, which he liked to be spotless every night before he himself retired.

He checked to see if Juliette was asleep. She was. She seemed to be at peace in her dreams, her new doll, Armande, at her side.

Armand went into his room and looked at the empty bed, just as he did every night. The sight of the lonely bed set him thinking.

What kind of life do I really have here? Am I only a

servant, after all? That was what his mother had once told him he was.

'Not a servant, a mentor. You're a new version of Jeeves for the new millennium; you're totally indispensable to Rick and Carla. That's rather chic, you know,' his friend Tom had told him, to make up for Armand's mother's mean comments.

It was true that Armand lived in a lovely home, in a good neighbourhood, in a great city. His little Juliette had a beautiful room and she lived contentedly. They both ate superbly every day. Carla and Rick were good for them.

When Han had shared his bed, there had been no peace and not much fun. They'd argued most of the time. The unwanted pregnancy only worsened the situation. Han had left the hospital the day after Juliette was born. Armand had heard she'd gone back to Taiwan, leaving him here, a father all by himself. He hadn't even tried to find Han in her own country. How could he trust her – or anyone else – after what she'd done to him?

Armand's mobile phone was ringing: *Unknown caller.*

'Hello, Armand? Hi, it's Liana. We met at Brenda's ...'
Women nowadays do take the initiative, don't they?

The sweet memory of their evening together was coming back to him.

'Yes, I remember. Brenda told me you asked for my number. How are you?'

'Fine, thank you. And you?'

As they started to chat they resumed the subtle flirtation they'd begun at Brenda's dinner party, even if there was no food and champagne to savour along with it.

'Tell me more about your job. I don't think I've ever heard of such a thing.'

'Neither had I before Tom, the friend I was staying with at the time, told me about this new trend of having a good-and-healthy-life coach. He said that a job like that could get me out of my difficult situation.'

'And with your knowledge of *savoir-vivre*, your logic and your cooking you could be very good at it,' Tom had encouraged.

'I was talked into it, even though I wasn't overly convinced it would work. But then what did I have to lose?'

'So you're a good-and-healthy-life coach! I hope you'll cook something for me one of these days. Actually, I like to cook as well ...'

They began talking about their favourite dishes.

'I find that sharing a meal with someone you, er, appreciate can be very comforting, very sensual,' Liana revealed.

Armand agreed, remembering the New Year's Eve dinner. He also thought how well sharing an interest in food had worked out for Rick and Carla.

Then Armand told Liana about Rick and Carla's luxury trip.

'Well, I've never heard of luxury culinary tourism before,' commented Liana. 'Of course, I couldn't possibly afford them on my salary. With such a high standard of living, being able to afford a live-in genius like you, exclusive culinary trips, I suppose that Rick and Carla are loaded?'

'Pretty much. Great careers – and no kids.'

'Who would want kids with a lifestyle like that? Kids cost so much these days, and they're so annoying!' Liana laughed in a way that Armand didn't appreciate.

Getting no reply, she continued, 'You mentioned that you were in a difficult situation before you met Rick and Carla.'

The conversation had definitely lost its carefree tone.

Armand then told her about Han.

'That's awful! I'm so sorry to hear that.'

'I'm fine now,' Armand said, more confidently than he expected.

Liana supposed that he must have a poor opinion of women after what had happened to him, but she tried to put that from her mind.

'So, you have a child!' she declared.

Silence.

'Why didn't you tell me at the dinner party?'

'Would you have called me then? Especially now that I know what you think of kids.'

When Liana hesitated, Armand left her no more time to answer.

'My daughter wasn't planned, but I really love her and I have to be responsible for her. It's not her fault if she has brainless parents. I want to be the best father I can for her. People aren't able to imagine how wonderful a child can be until they have one themselves.'

'Possibly ...' Liana said without much conviction.

'Oh, it wasn't easy at all being on my own, with no money. Anyway, Juliette is here now, and I like my situation with Rick and Carla.'

'I don't blame you.'

Armand had a feeling that Liana was probably less interested in him now.

'Well, listen, I'll see how busy my week ends up being and I'll call you,' she announced, confirming this.

Armand could sense the disappointment in her voice and he was annoyed, not because Liana might not be interested in him any more but because she didn't have the courage to tell him straight out it was because he was a father.

'If the fact that I've got a child bothers you, you should tell me right away,' he said coldly.

'I don't know, Armand. Up to now I've never even thought of dating someone who has a child. It's too bad because I really like you even if I don't know you very well. We appeared to be on the same wavelength over so much. The moments we shared at Brenda's were delicious.'

'I feel the same. But things seem to be a little different now, don't they?'

'My sister has been so indifferent to everyone since she thinks she created the Eighth Wonders of the World. And my nephews are such brats that I don't really have a very good experience of kids, you know.'

'But my Juliette is pretty well behaved.'

'I'm sure she is, and with such a beautiful name ... er, she can only be a good girl, can't she? And, er, with such a nice father ...'

After a little pause, Liana continued, 'I may call you again, Armand. I just don't know right now.'

'Fine, I understand.'

'Have a good night, Armand.'

'Good night, Liana.'

They hung up, each disappointed, not knowing what would happen next. But the special evening they'd spent together would remain engraved on their memories.

Armand looked at the gifts Rick and Carla had brought him. Then he went to the window. The sky had cleared and there was a striking full moon. He opened the blue flask of Eau de Lune, which was bottled under a full moon in the Alps, and was supposed to make your wishes come true if drunk on a moonlit night. After his conversation with Liana, Armand suddenly felt thirsty. He drank a glass of Eau de Lune and made a wish; he could be superstitious at times, after all, like his mother.

Afterwards he opened the bottle of cognac, for a last little treat before going to bed, and thought about what he had wished for. Armand's New Year's resolution was definitely going to be to make sure he and Juliette continued along their paths to happiness.

Four Recipes for Four to Celebrate the New Year

Armand's Yummy Soup

1 tbsp butter
1 tsp sugar
4 turnips, peeled and cubed
2 ripe pears, peeled and cubed
4 cups (1 litre) hot chicken stock
sea salt, ground black pepper and grated nutmeg
1 cup (250ml) milk
½ cup (125ml) whipped cream (optional)
chopped fresh dill, to serve

1. Heat the butter in a large saucepan. Add the sugar and turnips and sauté until golden. Add the pears and sauté for a further 2–3 mins. Add the chicken stock, bring to the boil and simmer for 10–12 mins, until the pears and turnips are tender. Add salt, pepper and nutmeg, to taste. Allow to cool slightly.

2. Transfer to a blender or use a stick blender to blend until smooth while gradually adding the milk. Reheat gently, then divide between four bowls and top with a spoonful of whipped cream, if desired. Sprinkle with fresh dill, grated nutmeg and black pepper.

Carla's Divine Meat Pie

This pie is usually made with the leftovers of
Thanksgiving dinner.

For the pastry:
1 cup (120g) self-raising flour, plus extra for dusting
1 cup (100g) oat flakes
½ tsp salt
120g butter, cut into pieces, plus extra for greasing

For the filling:
3 eggs, at room temperature
5 tbsp crème fraîche or cottage cheese
½ cup (125ml) gravy
sea salt, ground black pepper and grated nutmeg
250g cooked boneless turkey or chicken, cut into cubes
2 cups (200g) cooked stuffing (any kind)
½ cup (80g) raisins (optional)
1½ cups (175g) cooked fresh spinach or other greens
½ cup (60g) grated mature Cheddar cheese
Old Bay Seasoning or paprika

1. Mix the flour, oat flakes and salt in a large bowl and rub in the butter until the mixture resembles fine breadcrumbs. Add teaspoons of cold water until the mixture comes together to form a soft dough. Leave to rest at room temperature, covered, for at least 30 mins.

2. Preheat the oven to 190°C/375°F/Gas 5. Beat the eggs in a large bowl. Add the crème fraîche or cottage cheese, the gravy, a dash of salt, pepper and nutmeg and stir until combined.

3. Grease and lightly flour a 9½ in (24cm) pie dish. Roll out the pastry on a floured surface and use to line the dish. Lightly prick the base all over with a fork. Sprinkle in the turkey or chicken meat, stuffing, raisins and cooked spinach or greens, then spread over the egg mixture and sprinkle with grated Cheddar and Old Bay Seasoning or paprika, to taste. Bake for 40 mins, until golden. Serve hot.

Juliette's Colourful Salad

1 small red onion, thinly sliced
salt, for sprinkling
large bag mixed salad or fresh spinach leaves
½ cup (80g) dried cranberries
½ cup (100g) crumbled blue cheese (any kind)
1 apple, chopped
2 tangerines or 1 orange, pared and segmented, the
    segments cut into small pieces
½ cup (50g) shelled walnuts, roughly chopped, or
    Grape-Nuts cereal
small bunch flat-leaf parsley, finely chopped, to serve

For the dressing:
1 tsp Dijon mustard
1 tbsp balsamic vinegar
1 tbsp extra-virgin olive oil
2 tbsp grapeseed or walnut oil

1. Sprinkle the onion slices with salt and set aside for 10 mins. Divide the salad leaves between four bowls. Rinse the onion slices and dry on kitchen paper. Sprinkle the onion and all the remaining salad ingredients, except the parsley, over the leaves.

2. Make the dressing by shaking all the ingredients together in a jar with 1 tsp water. Pour over the salad, toss carefully, sprinkle with the parsley and serve.

Rick's Winter Fruit Delight

½ cup (80g) each pitted prunes, dried figs, dried
   apricots, dried cranberries and raisins
2 eating apples, chopped
1 orange and 2 tangerines, pared and segmented
1 bag (or 1 tsp) spiced or cinnamon tea, brewed in 1
   cup (250ml) boiling water for 10 mins
½ cup (50g) chopped walnuts
⅓ cup (60g) brown sugar
2 tbsp dark rum

Roughly chop the larger dried fruit and place in a saucepan with all the other dried and fresh fruit. Strain the tea and add to the pan with the walnuts and sugar. Simmer gently, covered, for 15–20 mins, until the mixture looks like compote. Remove from the heat and stir in the rum. Allow to cool, then refrigerate for at least 2 hours before serving.

Happy Hour *au Champagne, s'il Vous Plaît*!

*'In victory, you deserve champagne,
in defeat, you need it.'*
Napoleon, 1769–1821,
French leader

*'Chocolate is a perfect food, as wholesome as it is
delicious, a beneficient of exhausted power.'*
Baron Justus von Liebig, 1803–1873,
German chemist

Another very cold winter day … February: the time of year when people can be so depressed. There were only a few clients at the Zenith Bar that night … You couldn't blame people for not wanting to venture forth in such weather. Also, it was 14 February, and couples probably preferred a romantic dinner in the restaurant downstairs to celebrate Valentine's Day in style to sitting in the bar. I looked around and saw only two or three couples having pre-dinner cocktails, and a sprinkling of melancholy businessmen or -women looking all the more lonely for not having consoling cell phones in their hands, phones not being allowed up here.

I checked my watch. Strange … Anne-Sophie should have been here by now. She was always on time. She loved happy hour: two flutes of champagne for the price of one, and those delicious bar snacks! Since we'd met a few years ago, our Tuesday meetings had become a ritual not to be missed – even on Valentine's Day. We talked about this and that, we laughed, sometimes we cried. We had a great time.

Rather than worry, I decided just to relax in the comfortable warmth. I loved looking out at the lights of metropolitan Boston from up there, sipping my champagne, and listening to Pierre Hurel, who, to my complete delight, was playing the piano that evening …

Anne-Sophie's arrival put an abrupt end to my reverie. She plonked herself down in a chair and let out a deep sigh. She looked odd.

I couldn't help smiling, seeing her wrapped up in several layers of clothing. I might almost have said that she'd suddenly put on weight. She was holding a beautiful box of Cœurs Noirs chocolates – she knew I just couldn't resist them. A card that said 'Be my Valentine' was still attached to the box.

'Want them? They're yours!' she snapped angrily.

'Thanks, and happy Valentine's Day to you as well,' I responded, frowning. I was feeling a little confused here. 'But I don't have a gift for you, since you told me you think that Valentine's Day is only for couples.'

'I know, I know,' she replied impatiently, standing up.

I studied her as she sighed loudly again while laboriously removing her hat, gloves, scarf, heavy coat and wool cardigan, like an Egyptian mummy shedding its wrappings.

I wanted to laugh but didn't really dare, since Anne-Sophie seemed to be in one of her rages.

'And look at my hair. Awful! The air here is so cold and dry it won't stay in place! *Mon Dieu*, this dreadful climate! I can't stop shivering all the time; it's absolutely freezing!'

I didn't want to talk about the cold. I'd heard enough complaints about it lately.

Anne-Sophie sat down heavily, turned to look out of the huge bay window, and said nothing.

'Thanks again for the chocolates, but usually you reserve them for your Valentine,' I said eventually.

'I know, I know. Don't worry, I've prepared him some sweet treats for later tonight.'

A smiling and very attractive waitress approached. I'd never seen her before and decided she must be new.

'A glass of champagne, pleeease!' begged Anne-Sophie desperately.

She looked over the little folded menus to my side of the table. 'Oh, good, you've already got some appetisers!'

She had suddenly brightened upon seeing the food. She helped herself, chewing slowly, and contentment lit up her face.

Food is a comfort when you're upset, isn't it? For a while Anne-Sophie could forget her troubles while sipping her champagne and taking pleasure in eating. Neither of us spoke. We simply wanted to appreciate what we had on our plates and in our glasses, whilst listening to the piano music, and gazing out of the bay window. In the dry, clear air the view of the city lights was breathtaking.

At last Anne-Sophie was ready to tell me what had put her in such a rage.

'Guess who followed me up here with his stupid little *I'm really trying to learn about your rich and fascinating culture* expression on his face to wish me a happy Valentine's Day with this box of chocolates.'

'Spaulding?'

Anne-Sophie raised her eyebrows. 'How did you know?'

'Well, I didn't say anything, but I got the feeling that he wasn't completely insensitive to your charms when we saw him at your company Christmas party.'

'Really? It was that obvious? Anyhow, he just told me that he's crazy about me ... the nerve.'

'I guess the magical atmosphere of Valentine's Day gave him the courage to offer you some aphrodisiac food—'

'I'm married, and so is he,' Anne-Sophie cut in sharply. 'And you know that I think Valentine's Day should only be for couples.'

'Like it is in France.'

'Exactly. How I despise this profit-making, ultra-sweet and syrupy celebration where anybody can be a Valentine to anyone. It's so hypocritical.'

I wasn't going to argue. Having grown up across the pond, she would never understand how fun and special this day was for us in the States. I didn't tell her that I gave many Valentine cards to my co-workers, and that I received plenty in return. However, she might have had a point about the intense commercialisation of the occasion.

'If it's not true love, maybe Spaulding's just ready to have an affair,' I added. 'You know, a torrid adventure with a gorgeous Frenchwoman like you? How exciting!'

I giggled. But Anne-Sophie didn't.

Her scowl made me laugh even more. Finally, used to

being teased by me, she shrugged and continued her story. She told me that she'd informed Spaulding right there and then that he would be hugely disappointed; that she wasn't a sex addict, like most of the Frenchwomen he'd seen in movies. She'd also told him that he should be ashamed of wanting to cheat on his wife, the mother of his four children, and that in any case she wasn't going to leave a smart, gorgeous husband for a fling with a guy who looked stupid and had absolutely no taste in clothes (referring to Spaulding's habit of wearing blindingly white sneakers to travel home in after work with his bland, poorly cut grey pinstripe suit), and no idea about food. These two negative qualities always stopped Anne-Sophie from wanting to know anyone better.

She took a large sip of her champagne, then wolfed down two caramelised ginger garlic shrimps.

'Hmm, these are so good!'

Taking some more shrimps, she continued her story, which was really starting to amuse me.

'When I think that I used to feel sorry for him for his terrible clothes and dreary food habits, and I even thought he was a nice guy! Well, I was just trying to educate him in a way ...'

'Sure, with your wonderful French *savoir-vivre*,' I replied in a mocking tone.

'*Exactement, ma chère!* He could look rather fine with the right clothes on ... Anyhow, I took the chocolates for you – flavoured Cœurs Noirs, 75 per cent pure cocoa. You love them, don't you? And they're good for you, too.'

I knew about the aphrodisiac power of chocolate but I

was a little doubtful about the health benefits. I told Anne-Sophie as much.

She answered by showing me the box, as if that proved anything.

'With their high amount of cocoa? These are definitely healthy. You can trust me. I know.'

Right. The French know everything, and especially about food, don't they?

'Anyhow, I took the box of chocolates that Spaulding gave me and was starting to walk away, leaving him standing there like a vegetable, when I looked back and saw that his mouth was wide open. So I turned, ripped off the giant red silk rose that was attached to the chocolates, and stuck it in his mouth! I just couldn't resist. And then I left him there with the rose between his teeth!'

I burst out laughing, wishing I could have witnessed the scene. Anne-Sophie, although a typical well-mannered *bourgeoise Française*, full of principles, could be very funny and unpredictable with her moodiness.

'That wasn't too nice of you.'

'Maybe, but I believe it was the only way to make him aware that I'm not interested.'

'The poor guy may be feeling pretty miserable right now if he truly has feelings for you,' I said. 'We may even see him here soon.'

'Do you think so?' She looked around with a terrified expression, changing to relief once she was sure that there was no Spaulding in sight.

'I think he probably got the message,' I added drily.

After a minute, Anne-Sophie declared with a big

enigmatic smile: 'Well, it's not the first time that I've had to break someone's heart!'

'Right, I forgot: the undeniable charm of the Frenchies!'

She made a face and I was happy to see that her good mood was holding.

I sympathised with this Spaulding, in a way. He'd looked a bit insecure and strange to me when I'd seen him at the Christmas party. He'd been following Anne-Sophie everywhere, like a little dog, gazing at her constantly. Needless to say, his wife hadn't been at the party, and neither had Anne-Sophie's husband. I'd attended the event in his place, which was a real treat for me because the food was fantastic!

'Actually, you should have left him the chocolates. He needs them more than I do right now. They would alleviate his misery. You've told me about the benefit of chocolate in lifting depression.'

'He can get himself some more, can't he?'

I opened my box of Cœurs Noirs, put it on the tiny table, and the two of us admired the beautiful glossy heart-shaped pieces of dark chocolate. We sniffed with intense delight the aromas of cardamom, pink pepper, vanilla and bergamot. Spaulding might not have good dress sense but when it came to chocolates I took my hat off to him.

I was staring into the box of dark deliciousness, wondering whether to start eating them straight away or whether to wait. What a dilemma!

But before I had time to make a decision about this delicate matter I heard a voice I didn't recognise approaching the table.

'Hello! I'm Mary-Whitney Smith Monroe.'

44

We both looked up. Then Anne-Sophie gave a sharp cry of panic, nearly dropping the precious box of Cœurs Noirs.

'*Oh, mon Dieu!*' Her face had turned completely white. 'Spaulding's wife!' she whispered in my ear.

The unwelcome arrival was an ageing hippie type with an odd smile on her face. She was very tall, and skinny with it. She looked unhealthy to me, with her pallid complexion. Her abundant blondish hair fell shapelessly to her shoulders. She was wearing a long baggy dress under an overlong faded sheepskin coat. Both garments had seen better days.

I spotted Spaulding in the background, just leaving the room, the red silk rose in his hand.

Mary-Whitney pulled up a chair and joined us at our table without asking our consent.

'You're Anne-Sophie, aren't you?' she said sharply.

'Yes, I am,' answered my friend, not at all at ease.

Did Mary-Whitney know that her husband had a crush on Anne-Sophie, and was probably hoping to have an affair with her? Was that why she was here? Why else would she be?

'Well, I'll get right to the point since I don't have much time. Spaulding just told me everything. I came here straight after he phoned me while having a nervous breakdown in the restaurant foyer downstairs.'

'Was he really?' Anne-Sophie asked with a big sigh. Clearly she'd rather have been somewhere else.

'Yes, he was. Well, you see, I've been suspicious for a while. He finally confessed. You and I should have a serious conversation. Good thing that I have a quick mind

45

to think things over,' Mary-Whitney said with confidence and a wry smile.

Hello, I am still here! I'd have liked to add. *I could leave right now with my box of Cœurs Noirs, if I'm bothering you in any way!*

But it seemed impossible just to sneak out …

Had Mary-Whitney even noticed me? I touched Anne-Sophie's shoulder lightly.

'Let me introduce you to my friend Jessica,' she said, and I could hear just how edgy she was feeling.

'Hello,' I said.

'*Enchantée!*' Mary-Whitney answered vivaciously.

Does she speak French, then?

She started laughing loudly but I couldn't understand why. What was funny? The situation suddenly seemed very bizarre. I was still dying to leave but I knew I couldn't, having seen Anne-Sophie's *I am begging you to stay* stare. I put the box of chocolates safely in my bag. I didn't know exactly why, but it seemed like a good idea.

Without appearing to be at all embarrassed by my presence, Mary-Whitney announced: 'So, my Spaulding obviously has a crush on you, doesn't he?'

This sounded pretty direct to me.

'And I don't have much time to fight with you over him. I've got an important job, you know. Plus, I have four children, and a busy social life.'

An embodiment of the multi-tasking superwoman of the new millennium, I thought. There were just so many of them. How did they find the time and energy to cope with all their tasks and responsibilities? Well, sometimes they possibly didn't give enough attention to their husbands …

Still smiling strangely, Mary-Whitney went on, 'But Spaulding is my husband, and it's a role I still believe he's up to. I want him back. But ...' and she sighed '... it's certainly not the first time that he's been led astray by the power of feminine seduction.'

So why don't you take better care of your Spaulding and slow down the pace of your superwoman-of-the-new-millennium social life? I would have liked to ask her.

'His last extramarital conquest was a beautiful, sensuous brunette with gorgeous curly hair. He met her at his karate class.' Looking the speechless Anne-Sophie up and down, she added, 'Strangely enough, the complete opposite of you.'

Of you as well, by the way, I could have added.

Anne-Sophie is tiny but she's quite sexy and coquettish, with her blue eyes and her bobbed hair. I could see that, despite feeling very tense, she was trying to stay calm and polite, which demanded great effort. I didn't know how long she could take it, though.

'He wanted to have pasta every night!' continued Mary-Whitney.

'A drink, madam?' asked the pretty waitress, appearing at our table.

'Yes, a double Bourbon with ice, please!' Mary-Whitney replied at once.

'And for you, mesdames? More champagne?'

'We're fine right now, thanks,' I said.

'Pasta every night, you're telling me?' asked Anne-Sophie.

Mary-Whitney started laughing loudly again. 'Come

on – pasta! Carbs are very bad for you, everybody knows that!' she declared with conviction.

I was so tired of people counting carbohydrates.

'Everybody knows that you need some carbohydrates, like everything else,' I offered, 'but in moderation, of course …'

Ignoring my remark, Mary-Whitney didn't take her eyes off Anne-Sophie, who ventured, 'I understand that you have a problem with Spaulding. Let me reassure you that I haven't done anything … Believe me, I—'

'Charming French accent, very charming, dear. Keep it, it's lovely,' Mary-Whitney interrupted. And she started laughing once again.

Anne-Sophie preferred to keep silent. I knew how much she hated it when people told her that she had an accent, even if they found it charming. She had been trying to work on her American-English pronunciation, doing her utmost to obtain a 'ch'wing-gummy' American accent, as she called it. She hadn't been too successful. But we Americans, don't we just love the French accent? I know I do.

While I was distracted by this thought, the strange scene continued to unfold before me.

'I believe you, I believe you,' Mary-Whitney was saying, with a new burst of laughter.

This woman was truly dreadful!

'Well, after losing interest in the Latina prima donna and her pasta – my Spaulding didn't have much choice since she went back to her native Sicily – he started to wonder if he should buy a few Yves Saint Laurent or Karl Lagerfeld suits. Then he began learning French, this "extremely useful and beautiful language, which opens the door to the rich and fascinating culture of France", as he put it. He watched a programme on PBS called *French in Action*, in which the main female character never wore a bra under her ample top, and she was quite busty. The French can be so lewd!' And she laughed again.

Anne-Sophie and I said nothing.

'He was also talking about eating some bizarre food …' Mary-Whitney took a little note from her pocket and, smiling in that odd way again, she read it out with a terrible accent: '*Fwa graz, gojugere, paine deepice* …'

She threw the note on the table in disgust. I took it and read in silence.

Foie gras, gougère, pain d'épices. Gougère and pain d'épices were my favourite Anne-Sophie recipes.

I'm quite a Francophile but not a foie gras fan, since I know how the poor geese and ducks are brutally force-fed until their livers nearly burst.

With a devilish smile, as if talking about French food had suddenly given her more confidence, Anne-Sophie took up the note and read the list of dishes out loud, with, of course, the proper accent.

'Oh, excuse my French!' Mary-Whitney blurted out.

'Well, your husband is a colleague of mine with whom I've talked a lot about food …'

Was Anne-Sophie going to make a confession after all?

'Ah-ha! After *la cucina italiana*, calorific French cuisine! That's even better!' Mary-Whitney shouted a little too loudly. Some other customers – and they seemed to be more numerous now – turned to look at our table. They appeared to be interested in our little scene, particularly

49

since the pianist, who might have provided a distraction, or at least drowned out Mary-Whitney's voice, was away taking his break. I felt a little embarrassed.

Could it be that even if Mary-Whitney was the embodiment of the multi-tasking superwoman, she was really quite distressed by the awkward situation Spaulding had put her in? Were the peculiar smile and laugh merely her way of externalising her distress?

'You can easily figure out why he doesn't want to eat my Sunday tofu casseroles any longer. These exotic Italian and French dishes are more appealing to him – my Spaulding, who most of the time never paid any attention to what he had on his plate before he met the Latina prima donna, and now you. It seems to me that he really admires you two because you can do wonders with food.'

She stopped and inhaled deeply, as if needing oxygen to start up again, but then merely sat there, silent and pensive. She took a large gulp of her double Bourbon.

Anne-Sophie and I stared vaguely out of the window, hoping that she would simply leave.

'As if all that were so important. As long as what we eat is healthy!'

'Health is important for sure, but …'

But food also has to be appetising as well as attractive, as Anne-Sophie would have asserted. I could picture Mary-Whitney preparing her boring tofu casserole. I don't like tofu at all, even if I'm American and live in Cambridge, Massachusetts.

'You agree with me, though.'

'Yes, but—'

She didn't allow Anne-Sophie to finish.

'Then my Spaulding started to talk about the amazing home-made pastries you sometimes brought to share with your colleagues. Anyway, he needs to be careful with sugar, you know.'

Anne-Sophie and I were speechless. What next? Was Mary-Whitney going to sue Anne-Sophie because Spaulding's health was declining thanks to too much sugar from her cakes?

'Jessica?' Anne-Sophie whispered imploringly.

I knew that she needed some help here. Even if things had been smoothed over a little by the topic of food, I was still in a better state of mind than she, since I was just a spectator. I decided to do my best.

I turned to the asparagus-shaped woman and said in a serious tone as if I meant it, 'Mary-Whitney, why don't you tell us what we can do for you? You seem to have something on your mind. Otherwise you wouldn't be here, would you?'

'You're right.' Mary-Whitney looked at me with gratitude. 'I'm getting there.'

She took a sip of her Bourbon. 'Of course, Anne-Sophie, I wouldn't need your help if you moved back to France. That's what all the French do, once they've had enough of American food. Am I right?' She punctuated her question with a burst of laughter.

'Actually, I eat quite well here. There's a wide choice of ingredients, and I cook at home most of the time.'

'So no move back to your beloved France planned?'

Anne-Sophie shook her head.

'Not like the Latina prima donna going back to her

native Sicily, then?' Mary-Whitney pulled a sad face. No more horse-like laugh.

'No.'

Mary-Whitney seemed to be thinking. She had tried to warn off the little French lady, but that was clearly not going to work since the fault was all her Spaulding's. When she spoke again, I realised that she'd decided to work with the situation.

'Fine! What should I do now then? Have a French haircut, wear French clothes? Buy some healthy French food – if such a thing exists?'

'Of course it exists,' Anne-Sophie and I chimed in unison, both of us surely thinking about the fabulous French caterer that had opened the previous year in Central Square.

'But no takeout food – you'll have to cook yourself!'

And hopefully far more interesting stuff than tofu casseroles! Oh, please!

'But I don't have time to cook! I work late almost every night!'

Do you want to rescue your relationship or not? We're giving you good advice here, so take it or leave it!

The balance of power had shifted and now I was really starting to have some fun.

'But I always buy healthy takeout food, most of it made from whole grains and veggies. That's why we stay so thin in our family.'

But you're hardly the picture of health, I wanted to tell her, observing Mary-Whitney's uneven sallow complexion.

Mary-Whitney scrutinised Anne-Sophie's figure suspiciously. 'Look at you – even with all your scrumptious cooking, young French lady, you're still quite slim.'

Anne-Sophie smiled enigmatically once again, feeling a twinge of pride at being French.

'The French don't eat foie gras, meat and heavy dishes with sauce every day, you know,' I couldn't help telling Mary-Whitney.

I was tired of hearing my fellow Americans say they didn't understand how the French stayed so slim in spite of their rich, fatty diets. They didn't eat rich, fatty food all the time; they consumed a lot of fruit and vegetables, and they didn't eat constantly, either! But when they did, they sat down and ate slowly to appreciate what they had on their plates. I wanted to scream this vital piece of information at her, but managed to restrain myself.

'Really?' sighed Mary-Whitney.

Mary-Whitney's sighs had now taken the place of her strange smile and laugh. Since learning that Anne-Sophie intended to stay in Boston, Mary-Whitney's fighting spirit appeared to have waned considerably, maybe because she knew she was really going to need help to save her marriage.

'Then it's … er, well, I'm sure you've heard of the French red wine paradox,' Mary-Whitney ventured in a subdued voice.

'Yes, there was a show on TV about it a few weeks ago. Pretty funny, actually, don't you think?' I said, looking at Anne-Sophie.

Her brief fierce glance reminded me of a witch considering what kind of potion to prepare in order to poison the asparagus-shaped superwoman.

Mary-Whitney continued, 'Er, I don't know. I worked in France for six months, tried their food, drank red wine every day at lunch and dinner, like them, and gained around twenty pounds. Of course, I lost it all when I came back, thanks to the Slender Quick diet, and if—'

'It's in the genes,' Anne-Sophie declared, smiling. 'It's in the genes. And there's nothing you can do about it!'

'Of course! I don't see any other explanation,' Mary-Whitney agreed, letting out yet another big sigh.

'There is a further explanation,' I offered. 'It's not only genetic, it's what is actually consumed, and how the eating rituals are followed, so it's also cultural.'

'Of course. It's also cultural …'

But Mary-Whitney would probably never change her lifestyle. And why should she? To get her Spaulding back? No, he was the one who simply needed to stop his childish behaviour. But if he was really unhappy with Mary-Whitney there was little to be done.

However, the woman was a fighter.

'I'm afraid that I need your help, Anne-Sophie. Can you teach me how to cook healthy French food? I could perhaps cook on the weekends.'

I knew that at this point Anne-Sophie would have liked to shout a loud '*Ça ne va pas, non?*' But she was too flabbergasted by the question and still feeling rather proud to be French at that precise moment. Instead she remained silent, waiting to hear what was to come next.

'If I prepare the kind of food my Spaulding discovered thanks to you, I'll have a chance of winning him back, even if I do gain weight.'

Actually, your Spaulding might like it if you became a little plumper, I thought. It might remind him of his curvy Latina prima donna.

'I don't know about that …' Anne-Sophie mumbled.

'It probably seems surprising, but it's not that stupid an idea, when you think of it. I'll pay you good money for it,' Mary-Whitney added. She had clearly recovered some of the self-control a multi-tasking superwoman of the new millennium is supposed to have. 'And you could give me advice about a French-style makeover.'

'I don't want your money.'

That was the very answer I would have given myself.

'Well, think about it. Here's all the information you need to reach me: emails, home and work phone numbers, fax, cell phone … Just think about it.'

Mary-Whitney finished her double Bourbon, got up eagerly and left a fifty-dollar bill on the table.

'That's for the Bourbon and more champagne. Celebrate Valentine's Day on me!' And the asparagus-shaped woman with her unstyled hair, baggy dress and overlong worn-out coat laughed once more as if to show that she had completely regained her strength. Was it the effect of the Bourbon? Or the thought that she had found the solution to getting Spaulding back by believing that Anne-Sophie would help her?

She vanished as suddenly as she had appeared.

'Was it a dream, or should I say a nightmare?' asked Anne-Sophie, pulling herself together while signalling to the waitress for another round of drinks. Then, looking at the fifty-dollar bill on the table, she exclaimed, 'Someone is going to get a big tip tonight …'

'Actually, that was all quite funny,' I ventured.

Anne-Sophie frowned at me, but then started giggling.

'Yes, the whole thing is laughable, but what am I going to do now?'

'Ignore Spaulding at work from now on. Nothing needs to be discussed further. And don't worry, I have a feeling you won't have to do anything. You'll never see that woman again.'

'Good. Jessica, thank you, I trust your judgement as usual.' Anne-Sophie leaned over to hug me.

'No problem. She's really something, isn't she? No wonder Spaulding wants some time off from her.'

'Enough of all this foolishness! Dear friend, pass me the chocolates. I'm suddenly craving these sweet treats for the intense pleasure and comfort I need right now.'

I took the chocolates out of my bag and ceremoniously handed them over to her.

'Hmm, champagne and chocolates, at the top of my number-one city in the world, *qui dit mieux?*' I said, smiling.

Pierre Hurel was back at the piano by then, playing a popular piece of his, 'The Crush' – so appropriate, I thought, my eyes following the pretty new waitress as she moved from table to table.

A year has passed. I'm at the Zenith Bar waiting for Anne-Sophie, just like every Tuesday night. Tomorrow will be another Valentine's Day, and for the first time I'll have a real date. I'm pretty excited. I met Regan a year ago. She was the new waitress here at the Zenith Bar that I couldn't keep my eyes off on the night of the St Valentine's Day tragicomedy.

Funny how my prediction that Anne-Sophie would never see Mary-Whitney again was proved right.

A few weeks after that fateful evening, Spaulding went into work and announced that Mary-Whitney had had a big promotion, and the family was moving to Portland, Oregon, the following month. Such an opportunity couldn't be passed up.

It seemed that Spaulding didn't have any choice but to go along, since Mary-Whitney had always been the main breadwinner, and he was too weak to leave the comfortable life he led with his wife – even if he was constantly tempted by extramarital affairs.

The saddest thing for him was that he never had the opportunity to say goodbye to Anne-Sophie properly. She didn't go to the farewell party that the office organised for him. She simply couldn't make it. It was a Tuesday night, after all, and we were together having our weekly happy hour, and with champagne, *s'il vous plaît*!

Jessica's Favourite
Anne-Sophie Recipes

Gougères (Savoury Choux Buns)

A *gougère* is a choux pastry puff often served as an *amuse-bouche*. It's a speciality of Burgundy, where Anne-Sophie is from. The recipe makes 10–12 small *gougères* or one large one to serve 6 people.

Basic dough:
80g butter, cut into pieces, plus extra for greasing
pinch of salt
1 cup (120g) plain flour, plus extra for dusting
4 eggs
½ cup (60g) grated Emmental cheese (or other hard cheese)
ground black pepper

1. Preheat the oven to 180°C/350°F/Gas 4. Heat ¾ cup (200ml) water in a saucepan with the butter and salt. Once it has come to the boil, remove from the heat and add the flour all at once. Beat well with a wooden spoon until the flour is completely incorporated. Return the saucepan to a moderate heat and cook, stirring, until the dough is smooth, thick and glossy. Remove from the heat and add the eggs one at a time, beating well with each addition. Stir in the grated cheese (or your chosen flavouring from the list of variations, below) and two pinches of pepper.

2. Grease a baking sheet and lightly dust with flour. Using a tablespoon, place individual spoonfuls of the dough on the baking sheet, or spread into a large single round. Bake for 30 mins for the small pastries or 40 mins for a large one, until well risen, crisp and golden. Serve hot as an *amuse-bouche* or as a main dish with a green salad.

Jessica's Variations of Gougères

- *Ham:* Add 1 cup (120g) cooked or smoked ham, cut into tiny cubes and, if desired, 2 sautéed finely chopped spring onions, at the same time as the cheese.
- *Blue cheese (any kind):* Omit the grated cheese and instead add ½ cup (100g) crumbled blue cheese mixed with 2 tbsp cream.
- *Goat's cheese and aubergine:* Omit the grated cheese. Instead sauté one small finely chopped aubergine and 1 small finely chopped onion in olive oil until softened. Add to the dough with ½ cup (120g) crumbled fresh goat's cheese.
- *Clams:* Omit the grated cheese. Instead add 1 tin (184g) of clams, drained and chopped and mixed with 2 tbsp cream and a handful of chopped flat-leaf parsley.
- *Tapenade and sundried tomatoes:* Omit the grated cheese. Instead add ½ cup (100g) tapenade, ½ cup (100g) chopped sundried tomatoes and 1 tsp dried *herbes de Provence* or dried oregano.

Anne-Sophie's Version of
Pain d'Épices (Gingerbread)

Pain d'épices is another speciality of Burgundy – of Dijon, to be exact. This recipe makes two loaves of approximately 800g each. Jessica likes to freeze one and eat the other straight away.

6 cups (700g) plain flour
1½ cups (340ml) honey
¾ cup (150g) sugar (caster, soft brown or half and half), plus 2 tbsp brown sugar for topping
½ cup (125g) ginger preserve
180g softened butter, plus extra for greasing and 2 tbsp for topping
2 eggs, at room temperature
½ cup (125ml) milk
2 tsp baking powder
2 tsp bicarbonate of soda
½ cup (100g) candied peel
2–3 tsp anise seeds
¼ cup (60ml) orange-flower water or milk
¼ tsp ground cinnamon

1. Preheat the oven to 190°C/375°F/Gas 5. In a large bowl, beat together the flour, honey, sugar, ginger preserve, butter, eggs, milk, baking powder and bicarbonate of soda. Add the remaining ingredients and mix well.

2. Grease and line two 9 x 5 in (23 x 12.5cm) loaf tins. Divide the mixture between the tins and bake for 30 mins. Spread 1 tbsp butter and 1 tbsp brown sugar over each cake, then return to the oven for 15 mins. Use a skewer to test that the loaves are cooked through. Turn off the oven but leave the cakes in for 5 mins, then remove from the oven and cool in the tins before turning out. *The pain d'épices* will keep for 10 days in an airtight tin, or can be frozen.

Did You Say '*Fromage*'?

'A dinner without cheese is like a
beautiful woman without an eye.'
Jean Anthelme Brillat-Savarin, 1755–1826,
French lawyer, politician,
epicure and gastronome

Another weeknight like any other. Paul had just come home from work. Adam was preparing some delight in the kitchen while listening to Paris Combo, the group they were into at the moment. Even Pastis, the cat, seemed to be enjoying the jazzy music, as he lay with his usual poise on his beloved red sofa in the little kitchen alcove, facing the entrance. He didn't take much notice of the newcomer.

'Hi, Paul. How are you?' Adam asked, cheerfully as usual.

No answer.

'How was your day?'

Still no answer.

'Come on, Paul, what's up?'

'Oh, don't ask.'

'All right. Hey, I'm cooking that special cheese dish for dinner.'

Paul looked at Adam vacantly.

'Come on, make a bit of an effort!'

'Yeah, sure ...' mumbled Paul. He gave a big sigh and mooched off to his room.

Well, you don't seem very enthusiastic at all, Adam thought, a little apprehensively. But he decided to say nothing just then. Let Paul have his shower, then drink a beer in front of the TV while he watched the news and petted Pastis – should the cat feel inclined to leave his sofa and go and sit with his master in the media room. Paul ought to be a bit more relaxed after that.

Hoping Paul would soon be in a better mood, Adam returned to preparing dinner while sipping his preferred aperitif: a glass of pastis from Marseilles. Hearing his phone, he donned his hands-free headset so he could talk to Rita, Paul's mother. She needed some advice about a recipe she was following for Spanish garlic soup.

Rita had been taking cookery classes for more than three years, and had entered wholeheartedly into the joy of it. Handling the food, holding the ingredients to her nose, and observing the chemistry of their combination – all had been complete revelations to her.

'It's like magic! And it brings me so close to Mother Nature!' she would say.

She was now trying to make cooking a mandatory course, starting from ninth grade, in every high school in New England because she believed that everyone should have the same wonderful experience as her. Besides, people would be healthier. More than twenty schools in the region were already seriously considering her proposal. She was also supporting the schools' cooks in their efforts to continue serving healthy lunches to students, often having to argue with parents who didn't care very much about their children's eating habits as long as they ate things they liked and therefore didn't complain, which on the whole meant fries and pizzas.

Paul liked to make fun of his mother's new interest. 'You could say she has a lot on her plate!' he laughed, but he knew that she was right to try to give young teenagers some insight into cooking, as some of their parents were a lost cause on that front. He just wished Rita had thought of it earlier; he would have been much better fed when he was growing up.

Rita asked Adam if she could talk to her son, but he told her how morose Paul was that evening and suggested she ring back later to find out what was wrong.

'He'll tell me about it over dinner,' Adam assured her. 'Food and wine usually help him relax and be more talkative.'

'I hope it's nothing too serious,' Rita said anxiously.

'I shouldn't think so. Otherwise, he would have called me from work.'

'Right, I'll call later then. Back to my garlic soup. It smells so good ...!'

When Rita had hung up, Adam announced that the pasta would shortly be *al dente*. Paul turned off the TV and came to sit down at the bistro table in the kitchen near the Victorian stained-glass window. Mechanically he lit the scented candle on the table. The boys thought candles not only made the place seem cosier, but they were also therapeutic, and got rid of cooking smells. Paris Combo still playing. Pastis hadn't moved from the red sofa. He probably didn't want to deal with Paul's bad mood.

As a condition of their being flatmates, Adam, the owner of the apartment, had laid down one of the essential household rules: no watching television during meals! And no TV in the kitchen or dining room – only in the media room and in Paul's own room.

Adam thought that the ugly-looking appliance would clash horribly with the graceful antique furniture he cherished and polished so much. At first, Paul, a self-confessed television addict, hadn't been too happy about not having a TV in the rooms where he ate his meals. However, when Adam was away he still enjoyed TV dinners in the media room.

Paul's addiction was not his fault. He'd grown up watching TV most of the time. The set had been his constant companion, his pal, always there for him at home, while his mother had always been out.

But as long as Adam did the cooking – and he was undeniably talented – Paul was reconciled to eating without watching moving pictures on a screen. Besides, with Adam's adage, 'Eat well, eat together', dinner was the time when the two of them could share good food and wine, chat about their day, complain about their significant others, and put the world to rights.

But that evening, even the cheerful atmosphere of the kitchen, with its French bistro decor and lively music, couldn't put Paul in a better mood. It was clear from his expression that he wasn't happy.

Problems at work? Adam wondered.

He hoped his flatmate would cheer up when he had a full plate of pasta and some nicely chilled Pinot Grigio in front of him.

'As I said, Paul, I cooked your favourite cheese dish …'

But when Paul finally realised what was on his plate, he moaned as if in pain and pushed the plate away.

'What? I thought you loved it!' exclaimed Adam.

'I do, I do …'

Paul downed a full glass of wine, far too quickly for Adam's liking, and sighed loudly.

Adam waited. He knew that, with a bit of patience, he'd get an explanation.

'Well, today Lily-Fromage, as you call her, sent me a long email to inform me that she's met another guy.'

'An email? Couldn't she have met you in person, or at least called you if she didn't want to see you again?'

'I know …'

Adam regarded Lily-Fromage as a loser. He'd never liked her.

In a prompt but tactful gesture, he removed the plate of pasta alla cottage cheese from the little round table. Discreetly, he gave some to Pastis, who had just roused himself, finally getting what he had been waiting for. The cat loved nothing better than the combination of pasta and cheese. And that evening there was also smoked salmon and vodka in it. Yummy!

Adam then quickly produced olives, slices of *saucisson*, and rosemary crackers and put them in front of Paul.

Better to have a little something with the wine, he decided wisely.

Paul, still looking miserable, poured himself another glass but didn't drink it. His mind was wandering somewhere beyond the stained-glass window, both his hands clasping the full glass; outside, the branches of the trees, covered with a thin layer of snow, shimmered in the glow of the gaslights. He picked up an olive and a cracker.

'I'm sorry to hear about her depressing email,' Adam said, wanting to know more, forgetting that he had been quite hungry a few minutes before. 'It's pretty sudden, isn't it? Didn't you just go out with her two nights ago to that eco-friendly restaurant Some Like It Soy?'

'I know, and she was fine, I think. Though, actually, she didn't want us to go to her place afterwards, which was unusual.' Paul frowned and, still staring into the darkness outside the multicoloured window, mumbled, 'I have to admit that the food was terrible at Some Like It Soy. Its texture was as bland as its flavour. The worst of it was the alcohol-free wine we had to order because of Lily-Fromage since there wasn't any root beer at the restaurant.'

He turned to Adam, who nodded in sympathy. He agreed that alcohol-free wine was an offence.

Wine has to have some alcohol in it, otherwise it isn't wine. Let the hypocrites enjoy their sour-tasting grape juice! It would be like cooking French fries in boiling water!

Pastis had finished gulping down the pasta with delight and jumped on to Paul's lap, expecting some attention now that he'd had his meal. But Paul slowly sipped his glass of Pinot Grigio and continued talking without paying any attention to the cat.

'Listen to this. She met this terrific guy – so she says

– a month ago at a Cheese Is Good for You workshop in Vermont.'

Adam recalled Lily-Fromage talking about it when the three of them were at a neighbour's party. He could never find anything to say to her except when she talked about cheese. Like Adam, she loved any kind of cheese (as long as it wasn't processed) – perfectly ripened, with strong flavours, like unctuous and pungent Époisses from Burgundy, creamy Stilton from England, runny Vacherin from Switzerland, or tangy Pecorino Romano from Italy – not at all like the insipid processed cheese that resembled yellow or orange chunks of plastic typically found everywhere in this part of the world. But even if Lily-Fromage's palate was attuned to the best cheeses in the world – and the stronger the better – she would eat them only with water crackers accompanied by sweet, syrupy root beer.

She would repeatedly say, 'Mmm … cheese is good, real good.'

'Real*ly* good!' Adam would correct her, but she'd never listen.

Lily-Fromage had an even more bizarre obsession with cottage cheese. She rarely had a meal without it, absolutely adoring the fresh sweet-and-sour taste of the little white curds. Her theory was that women, as well as men, didn't consume sufficient amounts of calcium. Cottage cheese was the solution since it could be prepared in a variety of ways and used in almost any savoury or sweet dish.

But Lily-Fromage wasn't disposed to try sophisticated recipes. Cooking with cheese had to be very quick and easy for her on the occasions when cheese wasn't a meal on its own, served with a little salad, the usual crackers, fresh or dried fruit ...

Paul's tone of voice was still rather depressed. Pastis jumped off his master's lap, realising that he was not going to be petted by him tonight. He leapt on to Adam's instead.

'I guess she wanted to make sure that *Mr Cheese* was going to be the one before dumping me. But she wrote that she really liked me. I don't understand women.'

Why do you think I gave up on them? Adam was tempted to say. But he kept this thought to himself.

Paul cleared his throat, hesitating. 'Um, she'll definitely miss my cooking! She said that at least ten times in her email!'

'I'm not surprised!'

If only she knew the truth, Adam thought with a smile.

Soon after Adam and Paul had become flatmates three years earlier, they'd made a deal after a long discussion they'd had one evening about love and relationships. They'd always been truly open with one another, probably because they were good friends and not a couple.

Paul firmly believed that, nowadays, in order to seduce a woman, you had to be a good cook. His mother had told him this long ago, but he'd been truly convinced since reading *Attract your Significant-Other-to-Be in 20 Lessons of Stylish Cuisine*. Needless to say, the book had been a great commercial success with men of all ages. But, even so, it hadn't really helped Paul. He was just not into cooking at all and had no real talent for it. He didn't have a clue how to prepare anything, having been raised on processed frozen meals, peanut butter and jelly, or bologna sandwiches.

Adam, always optimistic, wanted to believe that Paul would develop an interest in cooking one day. Certainly living with Adam had been a real education for Paul. He'd discovered many foods from different cultures, as well as sophisticated dishes that he'd only vaguely heard of before. All this thanks to Adam, an amazing cordon bleu cook, able to adapt and improve almost any recipe, and who dined with so many friends from different cultural backgrounds.

Adam, having lost interest in women, regarded them as simply too complicated and too hard to satisfy. He lived quite happily, having found a balance between his long-term secret relationship with a married man from Boston high society and his straight flatmate, Paul, who had become his best friend. Cooking remained his greatest passion, however.

When Paul had asked Adam if he would cook a nice dinner for a new date he wanted to impress, Adam had found the idea amusing and accepted right away.

What would his reward be? If the woman was seduced, the two friends would go to Quebec City for a weekend and Paul would treat Adam to dinner in some fine restaurants; a new one each time for another culinary discovery. This was now an established arrangement between the two friends. Adam loved Quebec City; for him, the beautiful Canadian city was the place to find unpretentious, authentic French gourmet food at its best.

When Paul had a woman over for dinner, he and Adam had an agreement that Adam would go out. Most of the time, Adam went to Rita's place, as she lived close by. Paul could then pretend that he was the one doing the cooking. Adam simply prepared everything in advance, and all Paul had to do was heat it up. The second reason for Adam not being there was that Paul feared that his dates might fall for Adam, who was quite good-looking and very fit.

'You can't blame the women,' Rita had told Paul. 'He is so gorgeous, like most gay men are. It's not only their physical appearance, it's the whole package: taking good care of themselves, and their fine manners.'

Rita had actually had a bit of a crush on Adam when she'd first met him. Too bad he wasn't attracted to women any longer.

Rita was convinced that her son could learn so much from Adam. She still blessed the day she'd found the ad Adam had placed on the bulletin board at a fancy supermarket in the neighbourhood, seeking a flatmate. And she loved it that her son was becoming a little more sophisticated. Rita was aware she hadn't been able to give Paul the best education, being a single working mother with two children. Since getting to know Adam, she tended to speak quite highly of gay men. In addition to being cultured and good-looking, she maintained, they usually had money. And why was that? Because they didn't have to spend all their income on little brats, needing to satisfy their budding consumerist appetites! At times Paul even wondered if Rita would have preferred him, her own son, to be gay.

It was true that Rita had always dated men who were a little effeminate. She hated the macho male chauvinist type

71

and thought hairy chests and big muscles were repulsive.

Paul was still talking about Lily-Fromage's upsetting email.

'... And she assured me that if she hadn't met this new guy, she would have stayed with me.'

Since the first meal Adam had cooked for Paul's seduction of Lily-Fromage – needless to say, every dish was made with cheese, from appetiser to dessert, with the obligatory chilled bottle of root beer instead of wine for her – he'd regularly used cottage cheese, just to please Paul who, oddly, had taken to it as well. That was why Adam had decided to cook this evening's pasta with cottage cheese and smoked salmon.

'The guy even has a farm and makes his own cottage cheese. She said it's the best she's ever tasted in her entire life! She seems completely smitten by him. And she also says that he's a kind of spiritual guide for her. She had the nerve to accuse me of never really being into cheese; that I was only pretending to like it to please her.'

How could Paul ever triumph over Mr Cheese Guru, who makes his own cottage cheese? Adam wondered, trying to suppress a grin.

The situation was ridiculous and rather comical, Adam thought. He had never been quite sure why Paul had fallen for that cheese-obsessed idiot in the first place. *Ah, l'amour* and its opaque mysteries.

'And listen to this: the two of them have decided that they're going to work on a cookbook of cottage cheese recipes.'

'She won't get mine,' Adam said light-heartedly.

Not that he really cared if someone stole his recipes; on the contrary, he would have taken it as a compliment. But Lily-Fromage? He didn't think she should have any recipes from his kitchen after what she'd done to Paul.

'Funny you should say that because she asked me in her email if I could help her a little.'

'She's got some nerve, hasn't she?' Adam mumbled. 'Tell her that if she wants your recipes, they're actually mine.'

'Oh, *I* know they're yours.'

'She'll have to reconstruct them from memory.'

'Her memory is not her strongest feature …'

What was her best feature, actually? She didn't even speak English properly, Adam thought.

It suddenly dawned on him that he and Paul should get out of the house tonight, and he woke Pastis from the digestive nap he was taking on his lap.

'Let's go out! How about a big, juicy steak and crispy French fries?'

'Yeah, great idea! And no cheese for a while …'

They left the house, braving the cold and looking forward to the delicious meal they'd soon be eating. All the talk of food had made them hungrier than they realised.

Meanwhile, Pastis was back on the cosy red sofa in the little alcove, dozing off and quite content not to be human, since it seemed to be so complicated.

Six weeks went by. Spring was definitely in the air. It was another night like any other at Adam and Paul's. Paul was just coming in from work. Adam was preparing something delicious in the kitchen while listening to the latest Paris

73

Combo CD, which he'd bought when he and Paul had gone to see the band playing at the Somerville Theater a few weeks before. He was humming the tune, though he knew the lyrics by heart. Pastis, who also appeared to be enjoying the music, watched him, perched on one of the black bistro chairs.

'Mmm. That smells yummy!'

Adam knew then that Paul was in a good mood. When he commented on the food or asked about the evening's menu right after walking through the door, it was a sure sign that he was happy.

Good, Adam thought. It's been a while!

And even better tonight! After a quick shower, Paul came back to the kitchen, walking lightly and whistling along to Paris Combo tunefully instead of going into the media room and switching on the TV. Even Pastis seemed to share his master's sunny mood. Paul uncorked the bottle of red wine he'd just bought at the corner store, to give it a few minutes to breathe and come to room temperature.

'Jeez, a Madiran 1989!' Adam exclaimed. 'You must have some special news.'

'Yes, I have, but it's also because you said you were going to make an *entrecôte au bleu* for dinner.'

Adam hadn't cooked with cheese for weeks, not since Paul had suffered his email dumping by Lily-Fromage, because he'd been afraid it would be too upsetting for Paul. But he'd decided to do so tonight because Rita had given him a beautiful wedge of Roquefort. She'd wanted to know if Paul was getting over his breakup; could her son ever eat cheese again?

74

Adam was pleased because he'd been starting to miss having cheese for dinner.

'Like a glass of pastis first?'

'Yep!'

Like his friend, Paul loved the aromatic drink from the South of France.

He sat down and watched Adam as he made dinner. In turn, Adam noticed Paul was smiling cheerfully as he sipped his aperitif, ate cured black olives and petted Pastis, who now purred contentedly on his knees.

'Today I met this incredible woman …'

Adam smiled and rolled his eyes, waiting for the details.

'Actually, she started working at my company two weeks ago. We were never officially introduced, but she had caught my attention, and today I went over and said hello.'

If Paul had met her at the office, maybe there was a decent chance that they had something in common. He worked for a firm that dealt in international luxury products. The employees seemed to be chosen first and foremost for the way they presented themselves. So, since Paul listened closely to Adam's advice, he usually looked suitably stylish when he went off to work every day. This was the first time that he'd met someone there he liked, however. Until now he'd been intimidated by most of his female colleagues. What a change after the sloppy root-beer-drinking Lily-Fromage.

Paul described the new woman.

'… And guess what!' he continued. 'Who is the lucky guy who gets to work on a project with her?'

They raised their glasses.

'We went to lunch together to discuss the project. Instead of talking about that, though, we spent two hours chatting about all kinds of things.'

'You took her to Le Petit Champlain, I suppose?'

Adam thought that Paul was fortunate because every time he had an important business lunch, he got to go to Le Petit Champlain.

It was an excellent authentic Quebecois restaurant. The chef was passionate about his style of cooking, and even emerged to talk to customers about what he was preparing before they ordered. The rest of the time he was in the kitchen making sure everything ran smoothly so that his customers would be happy. Once in a while he returned after dessert to thank them and ask how they'd enjoyed their meals. He was not like so many so-called chefs: interested only in making money or becoming stars, too busy with business to spend much time in the kitchen, opening restaurants all over the place, where they never showed up, or playing the part of celebrity chef on TV, cooking to techno music with their top-of-the-range equipment.

'While we were having dessert we started talking seriously about fine food and wine.'

'That's a good start!'

'Her name is Audrey-Nicole.'

'Part French?'

'She may have some French family, you're right, with the Nicole part. I'll ask her.'

'Be careful, it might be a mistake to date another woman with French blood. Remember Justine's bad temper! I liked her a lot, though.'

They both remembered when Paul had dated Justine, a French au pair, who had been stressed out most of the time, in addition to being moody. She would laugh loudly and sincerely, then a minute later be in such a rage that it was frightening to witness, or she would cry as if all the evil of the world had fallen on to her shoulders. And she smoked like a chimney! But she was a very good cook. Adam didn't have to do a thing. And he'd learnt a lot from her. Paul had broken up with her when he'd realised that Justine was spending more time having fun in the kitchen with Adam than she was with him.

'Well, Audrey-Nicole seems to be a real gourmet. But, she doesn't like to cook because she thinks men are better at it than women.'

So, she's not a real gourmet. Real gourmets enjoy preparing food as well as eating it, Adam thought. And here we go again. Another twenty-first-century feminist, convinced that men should replace women in the kitchen. Men and women should enjoy the pleasures of the kitchen together, side by side!

In a way, though, Adam couldn't blame today's women for having no desire to cook since, over the centuries, so many had been treated as slaves in the kitchen, having to feed entire families with hardly any thanks or recognition. Where was the enjoyment when you had to prepare meals, day in day out, for a husband and children, and sometimes even for siblings or elderly parents, who often didn't care at all what they were eating and simply wolfed down their food like animals?

Well, Adam decided, contemplating the tender steak on his fork, the ideal mother-housekeeper from the 1950s, with a spotless apron around her waist, has disappeared. Now nobody wants to cook. That's sexual equality, for better or for worse. It explains why our society eats so poorly: no one wants to be in the kitchen.

Pastis was happy stretched across Paul's lap; the two friends exchanged smiles as they listened to his purring.

'I suppose I'll have to cook a gourmet dinner soon,' Adam said, with an amused look. 'I'll enjoy it a lot more than making something with cottage cheese or, even worse, soybeans.'

They both laughed at the memory of Melissa, who was a fanatical vegan, always asking and worrying about every ingredient in every dish when she wasn't eating at home. Paul had quickly tired of her.

Being in the mood – the *entrecôte au bleu* and the Madiran helping things along – the two friends went through the list of Paul's other ex-girlfriends that Adam had had to cook for. Apart from Justine, Paul had never dated a woman long enough for her to discover that he hadn't been the one doing the cooking.

Feeling that another trip to Quebec was on the cards, Adam announced with a wry smile, 'By the way, I just read this week in the food pages of the *New York Times* that a new Breton-Normand restaurant has opened in Rue Saint-Jean.'

'It's good to know,' Paul replied. 'Don't worry, our deal hasn't changed. You'll have your weekend in Quebec and, of course, I'll be there to share it.'

'Glad to hear it!'

They shook hands, laughing.

Every time Paul revealed that he'd just met the woman of his dreams, Adam was amused because he enjoyed the challenge of creating a new menu.

First of all he needed to know a little more about this Audrey-Nicole. What should he cook for the first dinner date? Was Audrey-Nicole allergic to any foods or spices? Did she have a favourite dish? How many courses should he prepare? What kind of aperitifs and wine did she like? Where and how should the table be set? Would they eat in the kitchen or in the more formal dining room …?

Paul, of course, couldn't answer most of these questions yet, but he promised that he would find out soon.

'Won't you have to look smart all the time with this Audrey-Nicole? Isn't she a little too polished for you? I dread to think what you'd be wearing to work if I wasn't here to raise your standards,' Adam laughed.

'I don't know really. I've only seen her in the office up to now. But I'm prepared to make even more of an effort for her, if necessary.'

Paul seemed to have met a real gem from the way he was talking about Audrey-Nicole. But then he always did his best to please the women he dated – even pretending to enjoy dishes made mostly of tofu or cheese, for example. He was like a chameleon trying to adapt to every new situation.

'And the best thing of all is that Rita will be happy,' said Paul. 'Because in addition to being beautiful and stylish, Audrey-Nicole doesn't want to have any kids.'

'You've talked about kids already?'

'Well, it's just that there was a couple with a child having a tantrum at the next table. It became so bad that they got up and left the restaurant. On the way out the woman stopped at our table and asked whether we had children. We said no, we didn't. She then said that if we ever decided to have any we should think twice about it! That's when Audrey-Nicole told me that being a mother wasn't in her plans.'

'Yes, kids who take the best years of your life, as your mother would say.'

They both laughed again.

So this Audrey-Nicole doesn't cook and doesn't want kids, Adam thought. Well, I'm starting to picture her: ultra career-oriented, very high maintenance, eating in very expensive restaurants. Fussy, fussy! Certainly the opposite of a cheap date, that's for sure. But I'd better keep all that to myself; she may turn out to be just the woman Paul has been looking for, after all.

And there was every chance that Rita would be thrilled with Audrey-Nicole, in spite of the fact that she didn't cook. Paul was her last hope because, according to Rita, her other son was living a very dull and uninteresting life: he'd got married too early, to his high-school sweetheart, lived in a gigantic, tasteless box of a house in the suburbs, with an ugly above-ground swimming pool, already had four kids, plus an enormous dog, two cats, four TVs, three cars, including a gas-guzzling SUV, and so on – a life that might be materially satisfying, but was culturally and spiritually empty.

Rita maintained she had enough grandchildren. They drove her crazy when she visited them, with all their computer games and electronic gadgets as well as their cell phones. These seemed to be the only hobbies and interests they had. They never listened to her, especially when she tried to interest them in cooking. It was all rather disappointing.

Rita believed that Paul's life was richer than his brother's, and certainly more entertaining and relaxing. He had a fun job with a bit of travelling between New York and Europe, a cool flatmate, who had become his best friend, good food, amusing pals from nearly every socio-cultural-sexual background, and lots to do in the city. Basically everything she'd never had access to until her children became responsible adults and could take care of themselves.

After a little time for reflection, Adam declared, 'All right, I have a few ideas already.'

'I knew you would! Thank you so much, buddy. I'll try to find the right time to invite her over. I think she really likes me.'

'Sure, sure she does! Who wouldn't?'

They shook hands on their new deal, Paul thinking about Audrey-Nicole being the new love of his life, Adam picturing the new Breton-Normand restaurant in Old Quebec. He could hardly wait to go there.

'Where's the book *Attract your Significant-Other-to-Be in 20 Lessons of Stylish Cuisine*?' asked Paul.

'Why? I thought you weren't interested in learning how to cook?'

'I know, I wasn't, but it's bizarre: I've suddenly got the feeling that I *do* want to learn …'

Of course, if things work out, Adam was thinking, it

might be the only way for the two of them to be fed at home, since Audrey-Nicole doesn't cook.

'Wow, this new conquest must be really different. I've never seen you this smitten by a woman – and you've been interested in quite a few since I've known you. I gave the book to Rita the last time she came. She wanted to check something in it.'

Paul called his mother right away.

'Rita? Hi, it's Paul. How are you?'

'Fine! I'm making fresh pasta. But it's maddening! I'm glad you've called because I need a break from all these little pieces of dough sitting drying all over the kitchen.' She sighed heavily.

'Do you think I can stop by, then?'

'Sure! And you can have dinner with me.'

'I already had dinner, Rita. It's nearly nine o'clock.'

'Is it really? Making this pasta has taken longer than I expected ... I'll give you some to take back home.'

'Good, I'll be there in a few minutes. I've got things to tell you, and I need to collect a book that Adam lent you.'

With a joyful spring in his step, Paul closed the apartment door behind him, and the sound of his whistling a Paris Combo number faded, leaving Adam smiling happily and Pastis gazing out inquisitively from his beloved red sofa. Neither had ever seen Paul quite so jubilant before. Happiness was very much in the air.

Adam's Cheese Recipes

Pasta alla Cottage Cheese

Four variations.
Each serves 4.

In a bowl, gently mix together your chosen combination of ingredients from the variations below:

- 1 cup (150g) cottage cheese – 1 cup (150g) diced fresh tomato flesh – ½ cup (60g) chopped pitted black olives – 1 crushed garlic clove – 1 tbsp dried *herbes de Provence* – 1 tbsp balsamic vinegar – 2 tbsp olive oil. Leave to marinate at room temperature for an hour.

- 1 cup (150g) cottage cheese – 1 cup (100g) chopped smoked salmon – 2 finely chopped spring onions – 1 tbsp chopped fresh dill – 1 tbsp lemon juice – 2 tbsp vodka

- 1 cup (150g) cottage cheese – 1 cup (100g) chopped cooked or smoked ham – ½ cup (75g) diced cooked carrots – 2 finely chopped spring onions – 2 tbsp chopped flat-leaf parsley

- 1 cup (150g) cottage cheese – 1 cup (100g) tomato salsa from a jar – 1 yellow pepper, diced and cooked – 1 tbsp extra-virgin olive oil (optional) – 2 tbsp chopped fresh coriander

Season the cottage cheese mixture, to taste, with sea salt and ground black pepper. Cook 400g of dried pasta according to packet instructions, until *al dente*. Drain the pasta and stir in your chosen cottage cheese mixture. Serve hot, or allow to cool and serve as a pasta salad.

Entrecôte au Bleu
(Rib-Eye Steak with
Blue Cheese Sauce)

Serves 2

1 tbsp butter
1 large rib-eye steak (450g) or 2 medium-size ones
  (225g each)
sea salt and ground black pepper
2 spring onions, chopped
2 tbsp port
½ cup (100g) crumbled blue cheese (such as Roquefort,
  Stilton or Danish)
2 tbsp sour cream or crème fraîche (optional)

1. Heat the butter in a frying pan. Season the steak and cook in the butter until done to your liking (about 2–4 mins each side for a 225g steak). Set the meat aside, covered, to rest.

2. Return the pan to the heat and sauté the spring onions in the meat juices for 2–3 mins. Add the port, cheese and cream, if using, and heat gently until the cheese is completely melted and the sauce is bubbling. Season to taste. Pour the sauce over the steak on serving plates and serve with potatoes and a green salad.

Smart Food Shopping

'The gentle art of gastronomy is a friendly one. It hurdles the language barrier, makes friends among civilised people, and warms the heart.'
Samuel Chamberlain, 1829–1908,
American soldier, painter and writer

At last, I finally had a little break. A quick glance through the window at the park and I decided to go outside. It was a lovely day, and, to my mind, spring is just the best time of year. The sight of the fresh blossom on the trees would put me in a better mood, I knew, and the dazzling colours of the tulips were enough to raise anyone's spirits.

A little icon at the top right of my computer screen told me that I had an IMPORTANT email message. I noticed it was from Mariette and so I opened it straight away.

Hello Claudia
I've met a terrific man! I'm hoping it could lead to something serious because of where we met. Can't be wrong this time! When you know the whole story, it'll get you thinking. You may even want to give it a try yourself. Can we meet today around 6 p.m. at Fontaine and I'll tell all?
Mariette

I replied right away. I'm always happy to meet up with Mariette.

Mariette, I'll be there. I can't wait to hear your news!
C.

Then I emailed my friend Kelly to tell her I wouldn't be able to see her after all. She'd understand, knowing that I always put my grandmother before everyone. I decided to give Mariette the banana bread I'd made for Kelly. I knew she'd be pleased.

A few minutes later I was sitting smoking on a sunny bench among gorgeous red and yellow tulips, and gazing at the beauty of the park in bloom.

Some passers-by scowled at me as if I were committing a crime with my cigarette. I wanted to tell them that my health was my business and no concern of theirs. And I dug the ash into my pot plants to help keep the parasites away.

I'd resolved to stop smoking only if one guy – the right one – told me to do so. So I could be puffing away for a while yet …

Aaah … I took another deep, comforting drag. It was so pleasant to be able to relax for a moment, away from that fake red-haired witch at the office.

I thought about Mariette, who'd just turned sixty-three and had met a terrific man.

Well, actually she'd met a few of them since Grandpa died ten years before. Mariette was having much more fun in her sixties than I was at twenty-five. She actually met men! If I had to wait until I was sixty-something to meet the guy who was going to make me quit smoking, I feared I might well die of lung cancer first!

I wondered if it was because Mariette had a lot of free time that she had so many dates. Working people just thought about their careers and making more and more money. If you didn't work with nice guys – and I didn't – where would you meet them? I disliked encounters in bars because I never knew if the men were sober or drunk. And the internet? No, I wasn't *that* desperate.

Unfortunately I'd become a bit of a workaholic, though not by choice: if I wanted to keep my job I had no alternative. And if I wanted to eat, and sleep under a sound roof every night, I'd got to work crazy hours and put up with my ghastly boss. I could have looked for another job, of course, but even the thought of it made me feel tired, and anyway, it might turn out not to be any better. At least I worked downtown, near the pretty Boston public garden.

On the other hand, why was I worrying about meeting somebody? I was only in my mid-twenties. My mum and Mariette had got married pretty young, and I wasn't sure they'd made the right choices.

I preferred to take care of myself and spend some quality moments with my family and friends in what little free time I had. That thought made me realise it was time to get back to the office.

I kept my cigarette butt to throw it in the first trash can I passed. I smoked, but I didn't litter.

In fact, the park looked much cleaner now that the city had introduced so many green bags for garbage and pink ones for paper recycling. They were everywhere, and the anti-terrorist cops were able to see right away what was in them since they were transparent and not too big. And they got replaced frequently. Very clever!

The city also looked much nicer since the mayor had decided that it had to be cleaned every two days. You saw more and more street sweepers around. At least my taxes were being well spent, and the cleaning initiative created jobs too.

On that positive note I went back to the office.

The rest of the afternoon passed so slowly that I had trouble staying awake. Fortunately, my fierce boss was there to snarl at me to make sure I did.

Six o'clock, finally! I couldn't wait to see Mariette. I flew out of the office, even though I hadn't quite finished my filing.

Fontaine's inviting terrace was open on that warm April night. I loved the ancient fountain with its cherubs, at the centre of the terrace, surrounded by tables. It added a little old-world charm.

Mariette waved when she saw me. She looked stunning as usual. But what was with this new outfit? Long, black flouncy skirt, a red matching top with baggy sleeves, and big hoops in her ears ...

But she didn't give me time to ask about her clothes.

'Hey, girl, you look tired. I bet you're working too hard,' she said as she kissed me.

She was always so energetic, and I always looked so weary.

'Thanks for reminding me of that.' I frowned.

'When you think that so many machines have been invented to help us avoid unpleasant tasks, and allow us to work less … Yet it seems that everyone just works harder and harder.'

'Mariette, I'm stuck in the system. Like most folks around here. And you know I can't move to a country like Germany, where I'd have six weeks' vacation a year. Please spare me all this.'

'And you're not a teacher with four months' annual vacation. You should have been a teacher. I've told you that so many times …'

'I can't cope with kids. They are rotten, spoilt brats nowadays.'

'Except the ones you'll bring into this world one day.'

'Sure.' We both laughed mirthlessly.

'Not all of them are brats, though there certainly are plenty that could drive you nuts. I'm glad I retired. It was hard at the end. TV and the internet were more important to them than anything I could say. And since they had no discipline at home, how could I ever hope to civilise them? And—'

I was eager to change the subject; I'd heard enough about this one over the years. Besides, I wanted to know about the new guy she'd met. But first we needed to order our beers. Roasted fat-free, salt-free soybeans were brought to us.

Yum yum … I took a good handful.

'Extremely well-mannered,' Mariette said suddenly, talking about our waiter after he'd taken our order.

And extremely good-looking, but he's obviously …

I sighed, thinking it a pity that handsome, gallant men were so often gay.

'So what about the new guy?' I asked, looking away from the gorgeous waiter.

'His name is Juan José. He's—'

'Juan José?'

This hinted at exoticism and might explain Mariette's Spanish look. I told her I'd noticed.

'Yes, how do you like it?' she asked, standing up and pirouetting.

'Fabulous!' I told her, a little jealous of my grandmother's style. She always looked amazing.

I wouldn't have been surprised if she'd started taking flamenco or tango lessons.

'Let me guess: he's a retired Latino dancer or a singer.'

'I wouldn't have minded that at all!' Mariette exclaimed, a twinkle in her eye. 'Actually, he told me that he's a good dancer.'

Of course!

'He's from Spain!'

'So, a flamenco dancer, after all!'

'No, he's not. Stop thinking in such clichés, Claudia! Although I'm seriously considering taking flamenco classes.'

So who's thinking in clichés now, then?

'And I've been listening to some great Spanish music. I'll make a few tapes for you.'

I'd kept an old tape recorder, which stood in my kitchenette, just so I could listen to the tapes Mariette compiled for me. She hadn't yet made the transition to CDs – much less MP3s. I had to admit, though, it was usually good music, which I enjoyed listening to while I was cooking.

Our beers arrived and we had a toast in honour of Juan José. I sighed deeply as I gazed again at the waiter as he moved away.

'So, if you didn't meet him at a dancing class …?'

'We met at the supermarket!'

I was so taken aback that I almost choked on my beer. It took me a few seconds before I could reply.

'Um, let me guess … at one of the trendy supermarkets near your house, in the international food aisle, where the Spanish olives are,' I teased her.

I suddenly realised that was all I knew about Spanish food.

'Not at all!' she laughed.

'Wow! I can't imagine myself flirting with the guys I see at my supermarket. Most of them look just like the food they buy: potato chips, Cheez Whiz, Wonder Bread, peanut butter, grape jelly, Cool Whip, sugary sodas – phoney, tasteless and boring.'

'Yuck!' we exclaimed in unison.

'And,' I went on, 'these guys would be amazed if they saw what I have in my cart.'

'Let me guess …' Mariette frowned in concentration. '… Lettuce, spinach, white fish, turkey breast, extra sharp Cheddar cheese, plain yogurt, extra virgin olive oil, wholewheat bread, muesli, nuts and seeds, blueberries, red wine and sparkling water, most of it organic.'

'Don't forget the carrots, the bell peppers and the apples,' I added, giggling.

Mariette was exactly right. She knew me so well, especially my fascination with all the beautiful colours of fruit and veggies. But, then, wasn't she the one who had told me how to eat well?

'Yes, indeed. Good girl, I'm proud of you. You keep to a good healthy diet in spite of the fact that you still smoke.'

I was keen to move on swiftly.

'And I drink a glass of red wine with dinner ...'

'Since it's one of the best antioxidants after pomegranate juice,' Mariette confirmed.

'At least, if there's something I'm good at it's buying the right food.'

'Yes, that's healthy ... but not that exciting! Don't you think?'

'But you're the one who ...' I stopped, confused.

Mariette didn't say anything.

In my mind I pictured my food cart.

'Yes, not that exciting, admittedly, but the choice of healthy food is rather limited where I shop.' I didn't know what else to say.

'But it's also good for you not to think solely about your health when you eat.'

'But, Mariette, you are the one who taught me about eating basically no fat, little meat, more grains, and lots of fruit and veggies.'

'I've changed a bit.'

'This is down to Juan José?'

I couldn't believe it. She'd only just met him and already

she was abandoning her own strict rules about nutrition.

'I'm learning not to feel guilty if, once in a while, I have a dish with a good splash of olive oil, or if I eat some fatty cold cuts, or drink a very rich hot chocolate with *churros* …'

'*Churros?* What's that?'

And she told me about the sausage-shaped fritters that were dipped in heavenly thick, syrupy hot chocolate. They sounded divine.

'Before I met Juan José, I was paying too much attention to what was "good" for me. I had the impression that I was becoming a little orthorexic, or to put it another way, a health-food junkie.'

'Ortho— what?'

'Orthorexic. *Orthos* means "correct" in Greek, and *orexis*, "appetite". It's when someone spends most of their time trying to avoid additives, preservatives, food colouring, salt, sugar, any kind of fat … eats, not to be fed, but to be in good health or to be cured. Food becomes, in the end, not only a medicine but also the cause of ailments.'

I recognised the former teacher here.

'I don't think you were like that. You ate loads of different things. You paid attention to what was on your plate, that's all.'

'I was becoming a little too obsessed with eating only healthy food. I was avoiding cheese, for example, and I wouldn't eat beef any more, only turkey and lamb.'

Were turkey and lamb the healthiest meats? I thought I remembered reading that somewhere, actually. I had to admit that I hadn't noticed any of these changes in

Mariette's diet. But now that I thought about it, the last few times we'd been together she'd usually had fish, turkey or lamb. And there were no more delicious cheeses like Saint-André or Stilton in her fridge. She had also lost some weight.

'And all of this because of Magnolia. She's a real orthorexic,' Mariette added.

Oh, yes, Magnolia! She was one of Mariette's best friends, an ageless, skeletal New Ager, an artist, who for years had constantly painted the moon in every colour one could imagine. She had certainly had time for it since she'd never had to work for a living. Good for her, because it seemed that no one was interested in buying any of her celestial art. I'd never cared much for her, and had always thought she was a bad influence on Mariette.

'So you'll gain some weight if you add more olive oil. Be careful not to put on more than you should,' I added, just to tease her.

Mariette shrugged to show that she didn't really care. 'Juan José is here now to save me from my close brush with orthorexia.'

She returned to her story of their first encounter.

'The supermarket where I met Juan José is upscale compared to the ones you're used to. The men who go there really care about what they eat. Believe it or not, some of them dress nicely even when they're just shopping for groceries.'

'Wow, I've got to see that!'

You ate well and you dressed well – those first impressions mattered to Mariette.

94

As if to confirm this thought, she said, 'And you know I believe in the adage "Tell me what you eat and I'll tell you who you are."'

The gorgeous waiter came up and asked if everything was OK.

'Sure,' I lied.

Of course not! Don't you see the effect you're having on me? Why are guys like you – beautiful, elegant, well-dressed, well-mannered – so often gay? What a waste for us women!

There were an increasing number of gay people in the city, thanks to the legalisation of same-sex marriage, and I had the impression that they were everywhere. Certainly they seemed to be the only kind of men I fell for at that time – which was, of course, a total non-starter.

'Nice guys who really care about what they eat and what they wear around here? They prefer men! Especially in your neighbourhood,' I said.

'Not all of them. Not Juan José, for sure. I can tell you …'

She smiled at me mischievously.

She'd never change. I was sure she had already shared some intimacies with this Juan José. She always said that she couldn't wait for ever to see if a relationship was going anywhere or not. So she moved it on quickly when she met a new man. If the romance worked out, fine; if not, as she said, 'There are so many beaux out there.'

We giggled like teenagers.

'So which supermarket did you go to?'

She told me that she'd wanted to try the new one specialising in healthy and sophisticated southern

European food. Fit Gourmet, it was called. I remembered then that I'd read in the paper about its opening. But there was no Fit Gourmet in my neighbourhood. My nearest supermarket should have been called Fat Guzzler, since hardly any fit or slender people shopped there. Most of the food was processed, full of preservatives, and didn't look appetising at all. However, I managed to find a few nice products in the tiny organic food section. Thank heavens they even had one. But the store was convenient as it was very close to my apartment. Once in a while, during my lunch hour, I'd buy produce from the farmers who came every week to the market in Copley Square, even if the prices were too high.

'You could come to Fit Gourmet, you know.'

Oh, sure, then I would have to take the Blue Line subway, then change to the Orange or the Green Line to North Station, and finally take the commuter train to your neighbourhood – just for grocery shopping.

Mariette guessed what I was thinking.

'You could come about twice a month, that's all. It will be worth the trip! And you can spend some time with me afterwards.'

Neither Mariette nor I owned a car since we both lived near a subway or train station. When I visited her, usually once a month, I stayed over for the weekend. She didn't live that far from the city, but the journey took a while on public transportation.

We usually met up downtown, near my office. We liked to have a drink, or eat at a little local restaurant.

Mariette's neighbourhood was the new place to be,

frequented mainly by young professionals or happy retirees – most of them gay. Admittedly it was a great area: stunning renovated Victorian houses, nice restaurants, art galleries, parks, cycle paths – though it was a bit too pricey for me.

'Shopping at Fit Gourmet must be rather expensive,' I said with a pout.

'Eat less of the good stuff, and money-wise it's the same as eating too much bad stuff.'

She had a point there, and she knew that I knew it, and that I tried my best.

'But there's the other good reason for going there: you could meet someone. So, twice a month seems pretty reasonable, doesn't it?'

I did a quick calculation.

'It gives me twenty-four possibilities a year to meet the right man … not bad. Far more than I have at the moment. Maybe I have a chance then.'

Mariette told me that she'd met Juan José at one of the Spanish Week stalls filled with a delightful assortment of *charcutería*. Of course, she had to explain to me what *charcutería* was. She'd seen him trying a piece of Serrano ham, so she'd known right away that he wasn't a 'dull, sissy vegetarian', as she labelled people who didn't eat meat.

'People need protein, and not only from legumes,' she always maintained.

'I just thought he was really good-looking, and I liked what he was wearing. He was giving the salesperson specific instructions about what he wanted to buy. Of course, in these kinds of stores, the salespeople are qualified and know something about what they're selling. I observed Juan José discreetly for a while. He was saying how much the food reminded him of his native Madrid, and that the *jamón* looked divine!'

I sat in silence, riveted by these details.

My grandmother hurried on. 'After that, he went to the fruit and vegetable display. I can still picture him smelling the cantaloupes to find the right one. He also bought fresh figs. I was still following him when I realised he didn't have a cell phone.'

Mariette hated cell phones. She thought there was nothing more stupid than someone talking on a cell phone in the street. She believed that people like that had problems with face-to-face communication. She wasn't at all interested in the sordid details of their lives, loudly broadcast to everyone in streets or stores, on trains or buses. Before the invention of cell phones, people had their phone conversations at home, so why didn't they do it any longer? Was it because they were bored to death with their dreary daily routine and wanted the world to believe they had exciting lives just because they could make phone calls in public places?

Another reason Mariette had met so many men might be because she seemed to inhabit a world where real human contact and time given to simple things were more important than cell phones or other superficial gadgets like MP3 players, which tend to isolate people from one another.

Let's face it: someone like Mariette would be very rare

in the younger generation. The last guy that I'd dated had been unable to stop touching his tiny cell phone to check for text messages, and had constantly taken pictures of me with it. It had driven me insane. I'd broken up with him after two weeks. That had been nearly a year previously.

'No cell phone! So that's another good point for Juan José, isn't it?'

'Yes. I'd been following him for a while and he never took one out of his pocket, but it also occurred to me that that might be a sign that he was single, because he didn't have to call his significant other to ask whether he should choose 2 per cent or 5 per cent fat sour cream, or whether he should buy carb-free or low-fat ice cream!'

Right! What could I say? She'd obviously been thinking about this guy the whole time. It was good to hear of someone who'd actually met a man in a normal everyday situation, one that didn't involve technology or speed-dating. I couldn't wait to tell Kelly.

'He was so charming, just shopping for his groceries! Dark hair—'

'How old is he?' I couldn't resist asking when she mentioned 'dark hair'.

'Only a few years younger ...'

'Younger than you?' I shouted louder than I intended. *I can't believe it!*

'Don't get excited! So what?'

'How old?' I asked again.

'Fifty-seven. And age isn't important when true love is involved.'

True love already? Fine.

'Fifty-seven. So he's dyeing his hair, isn't he?'

'He may be. So what? I do it myself, and so do you, don't you?'

Right! Ever since I'd decided to become a brunette, thinking I would get more respect from men. Well, so far it hadn't worked very well.

'Sexy, smart, witty …' Mariette continued.

The list of Juan José's attributes was starting to get a bit much.

'But aren't Spanish men supposed to be so macho?' I asked, pouting again.

'Stop being so hung up on stereotypes, Claudia.'

Mariette went on to tell me that, to attract Juan José's attention, she'd casually asked him for his advice about the best *charcutería* to buy when both of them had been 'coincidentally' standing at the Spanish Week counter.

'He was so thrilled to see someone who was interested in Spanish food!' she said triumphantly, and she repeated what Juan José had told her.

'"*Sí, por supuesto*, it's about time that some importance was given to the cuisine of my country. Too much Mexican, Chinese and Italian cooking around here, don't you think?"

'Of course I had to agree but I confessed right away that I needed to learn so much, being completely ignorant about Spanish food. He said that he would be delighted to teach me. His eyes and the tone of his voice were very inviting!'

Right! Sure. Why not?

Her story made me a bit envious. It would never happen

to me. By then I was dying for a cigarette to calm myself down a little, but I couldn't smoke in Mariette's presence.

'His Spanish accent is really adorable and funny. He's been here for a long time but he still can't pronounce certain sounds. I have to laugh most of the time, but he doesn't seem to care. He makes fun of me when I try to say a few Spanish words.'

'Because you're learning Spanish, of course …'

'Sure, what do you think? It's important that I understand his language. He is teaching me Spanish through songs. I love it! I'll make a tape for you. Besides, I may go to Spain soon. You could come with us, you know …'

I grimaced and refused to reply.

'Oh, sorry, Claudia. I'm so excited about the idea that I forgot about your fear of flying. You know, you could take a boat, but since you only have two weeks' vacation a year that might be kind of difficult,' my grandmother giggled.

'That's not funny at all, Mariette!'

She resumed the tale of her encounter at Fit Gourmet.

I could picture Mariette at the Spanish Week display, rolling her eyes and using her silkiest voice to attract Juan José. People always noticed her good looks, even at her age, and her generous personality.

Taking care of herself and having a good time had always been very important to her. She was actually the only fun person in my entire family. And the only one I knew I could always rely on.

Having told me all her latest news, she summoned the gorgeous waiter over and asked him to bring us more roasted fat-free, salt-free soybeans. She then returned to

101

the subject that she firmly believed was so important for my future.

'Claudia, when do you think would be the best day for you to go to Fit Gourmet?'

Having no idea, I just looked at her and shrugged.

'I've thought about it. I'd say, for your age range, Saturday morning is best.'

'Because ...?'

'Because it's when the single men—'

'More or less charming ...'

'They are all more charming than less in my neighbourhood ...'

'If they're not gay.'

'Come on, Claudia, it's time you gave up this obsession with gay men. They'll never give you what you want as a straight woman!'

'You're right. But I can't help it.' I glanced again at our delicious waiter, who seemed to be flirting excessively with a male customer.

'On Saturday morning, after a long week at work and a crazy Friday night, these charming bachelors finally realise that they have nothing left in the fridge when they want to have a late-morning breakfast.'

Mariette imitated perfectly the expression of a guy who had just woken up opening his fridge and finding to his disappointment that there was hardly enough milk left in the carton for his cereal. I burst out laughing.

'So these men take their courage in their hands, get into their cars or, even better, take their little shopping carts and walk to Fit Gourmet.'

'Um, well, um …' I mumbled, not sure about Mariette's new theory. Or the shopping carts.

'But never before eleven thirty. And you know why? Because since they've been out the night before, they need to recover a little by sleeping late. When they finally wake up they realise that they're really hungry.'

'They could go out to eat,' I suggested.

'Some do, but in my neighbourhood most like to put food in their fridges, and some even like to cook. These are the young men you should look for, not the ones who always eat out and order takeout pizza or Chinese food. I picture you more with someone who considers his kitchen to be an important place in the house, the centre of marvellous culinary creations, and not just a room with a fridge containing milk and beer.'

'I didn't know straight guys like that even existed!'

'In my neighbourhood they do …'

'OK! So, you're telling me that I should go to your local Fit Gourmet on Saturday morning at eleven thirty to meet The Man I may marry?'

'You got it, Claudia. But, remember, you don't have to marry him. At least don't tell him that right away. It may scare him off.'

Right!

That reminded me of Kelly's theory: if you want to get rid of a man, tell him you want to marry him in a beautiful, expensive white dress, and have three children! It's the best way to get him out of your life completely.

Actually, at that point, I would simply have liked to find a companion with whom I could share my life and thoughts without even considering marriage or kids.

More roasted fat-free, salt-free soybeans were put on our little table. I smiled as gracefully as I could at the gorgeous waiter. He smiled back. It didn't hurt, and since I knew he'd never be interested in me, it wasn't like I'd have to follow it up at all.

Mariette proposed another toast with our half-empty pint glasses of beer: to the man I'd meet at Fit Gourmet.

When she had something in mind, she didn't give up.

'Now, about your look when you go to the supermarket …'

She'd thought of everything.

'Yes, what should I wear? Do I need to look relaxed and casual, chic or sporty? Make-up or no make-up? Hair neatly done or a ponytail? I don't even know what the trendy way of wearing your hair is right now.'

Because I didn't care.

'Well, don't worry about your hair. You need to look neat and informal, *bon chic bon genre*, as the French say. You know how to do it most of the time.'

'As long as you don't look like a tramp, showing your belly and too much cleavage!' we exclaimed together, both laughing loudly. We thought that that fashion didn't show anyone to her best advantage, even if she had a beautiful figure.

We set a date for me to go to Fit Gourmet: next Saturday, the sooner the better.

Mariette took a glossy flyer for Fit Gourmet from her purse and looked it over.

'Next week is Italian Week,' she announced with a smile.

'Italian ... That sounds good. But I'd rather meet an American,' I said firmly, remembering the Neapolitan guy Kelly had dated, who had found her too liberated.

'You can meet an American who likes foreign food.'

Sure. Why not? My grandmother had an answer for everything.

Mariette had to leave then because Juan José was meeting her at her house that evening for dinner.

'I made my famous tomato pie,' she said, looking at me with bright eyes. 'I'll just have to reheat it. And Juan José is bringing his famous *tortilla española de patatas* and some *boquerónes.*'

Seeing my astonished look, she quickly explained what a *tortilla* was in Spanish cuisine, as well as *boquerónes* – anchovies preserved in vinegar and garlic. Until then, to me, tortillas were large, flat Mexican pancakes, and I had never heard of *boquerónes* before.

The *tortilla española de patatas* sounded rather yummy, though I wasn't sure about the anchovies. But I loved Mariette's tomato pie. Each time I put it on my table straight from the oven, it was like having the sun from the South of France right there in my kitchen. Usually I opened a bottle of French rosé to drink with it, just as they would do in southern France. Not that I'd ever been there, but Mariette had told me about it after she went there.

Before Mariette was into Spain she'd been fascinated by France, especially its capital and the South. Not surprisingly, she was the one who had introduced me to French culture.

I gave Mariette the banana bread I'd originally made for Kelly.

'Thanks, Claudia. I adore your banana bread. It will be the perfect dessert for tonight.'

And, taking a bottle out of her bag, she exclaimed gaily, 'I bought this great Rioja for you. Enjoy! *Hasta luego, querida!*' Then she kissed me goodbye.

Mariette didn't even give me time to thank her. 'Ziaf are singing later – why don't you stay and have dinner here?' she called over her shoulder as she left.

Definitely! I loved Ziaf – a local group that sang Edith Piaf's repertoire. I'd seen them a few times.

I looked at the menu. Suddenly I craved a huge juicy hamburger with lots of fries and onion rings, another beer, and a brownie sundae: a real unhealthy American meal. It was as if I wanted to take a little revenge on Mariette for her happiness and her obsession with Spanish food and men.

I called the dishy waiter over to tell him that I'd decided what I wanted to eat.

Staring at him as he walked to the kitchen with my order took me back to the little secret summer escape Kelly and I liked to organise whenever the two of us were tired of the macho male rudeness we constantly seemed to attract. Real men were supposed to be rough, otherwise they were sissies, right? And if they didn't show a little toughness, then they were scared of us women.

For our summer escape Kelly and I took the fast boat at noon to Cape Cod. As soon as we arrived at Provincetown, we sat at a table on the terrace of a great restaurant we knew on Commercial Street. We then spent the whole afternoon eating different hors-d'oeuvres, sipping Cosmopolitans,

106

and watching and grading the beautiful gay men passing by.

It was quite silly and extremely shallow but we had a hell of a good time. It was also an invigorating way to spend the day before the boat took us back to our real lives in Boston. We'd been doing this every summer for the last few years.

Ziaf had begun their set and a line in French caught my attention. Slightly tipsy from the beer and intoxicated by my chocolatey dessert, I agreed with the singer that, no, life wasn't that sad, after all.

After I'd finished my scrumptious high-calorie meal I said goodbye to the gorgeous waiter who, without any doubt, had become my platonic sweetheart for the foreseeable future.

'Hope to see you soon,' he said, with his striking smile.

'Definitely!'

And sooner than you may think, actually!

I decided I'd have to bring Kelly with me next time I came here.

However, Mariette was right: I'd been a little too much into gay men lately. Not good!

On the subway home, most of the people looked worn-out, sloppy, heavy and ugly, especially compared with the slim and elegant waiter. But then it was a Thursday evening and the end of the week was approaching. I didn't feel that great myself, having lost the habit of eating such a heavy dinner.

Mariette's scenario for meeting eligible men was drifting back into my mind. I didn't know if I really liked it but I decided to give it a try. After all, I'd got nothing to lose.

Later on, as soon as I'd collapsed into bed, hoping for a good night's sleep, the phone rang.

I didn't want to answer it, but when I heard Kelly leaving a message, I jumped up to catch her.

After an hour of girly chatting, Kelly had convinced me that I needed to go along with Mariette's scheme. Kelly thought the idea was fantastic and wanted to accompany me to Fit Gourmet the following Saturday morning. I knew that Mariette wouldn't mind, since she was very fond of Kelly.

I hung up, feeling absolutely ready to go to an overpriced gourmet food supermarket at the far edge of the suburbs, just to hunt for a man. Mariette's plan suddenly seemed cunning and attractive, much better than meeting someone online or at a speed-dating event, which was what Kelly had just been telling me about.

But even if the two of us found our Mr Rights, we would still have our yearly secret summer escape to Provincetown. We'd sworn to it, after all.

Three Recipes for Mariette and Juan José's Romantic
Dinner *à deux*

Juan José's Tortilla Española de Patatas

4 tbsp extra-virgin olive oil
1 medium Spanish onion, chopped
3 good-sized potatoes, such as Maris Piper, peeled and
  cut into ½ in (1cm) cubes
generous pinch salt
5 eggs, at room temperature

1. Heat 3 tbsp of the oil in a 25cm non-stick frying pan and
gently fry the onion for 5 mins. Add the potatoes and mix.
Sauté over a low heat for 30–40 mins, until the mixture is
tender and just beginning to colour. Season with salt.

2. Beat the eggs in a large bowl. Stir in the onion and
potato mixture and crush roughly with a fork. Add a little
more salt.

3. Return the pan to the heat, add the remaining 1 tbsp
oil and pour in the mixture. Cook over a moderate heat,
pressing down with a spatula from time to time, for about
15 mins, or until the egg is mostly set. Put a plate on top
of the pan and turn out the tortilla. Slide it back into the
frying pan and cook for a few mins more (alternatively,
finish under the grill). When the tortilla is lightly browned
on both sides, transfer to a plate and allow to cool. Cut into
slices and serve slightly warm or at room temperature.

Mariette's Tomato Pie

For the pastry:
1 cup (120g) self-raising flour, plus extra for dusting
1 cup (100g) oat flakes
½ tsp salt
1 tbsp dried *herbes de Provence* or dried thyme
120g butter, cut into pieces, plus extra for greasing

For the filling:
6 large ripe tomatoes, sliced, sprinkled with ½ tsp salt
  and left to marinate for 30 mins
1–2 tbsp Dijon mustard
¾ cup (80g) grated hard cheese
sea salt and ground black pepper
fresh *herbes de Provence* or fresh thyme, to taste
handful black olives

1. In a bowl, mix together the flour, oat flakes, salt and dried herbs, then rub in the butter until the mixture resembles fine breadcrumbs. Add teaspoons of cold water until the mixture comes together to form a soft dough. Leave to rest, covered, at room temperature for at least 30 mins.

2. Preheat the oven to 190°C/375°F/Gas 5. Grease and lightly flour a 9½ in (24cm) pie dish. Roll out the pastry on a floured surface and use to line the dish, then prick all over with a fork. Cover with a sheet of greaseproof paper and fill with baking beans. Bake blind for 15 mins, then remove the paper and beans.

3. Drain the tomatoes of their water. Spread the mustard over the pastry base, sprinkle with grated cheese and arrange the sliced tomatoes on top. Season with salt and pepper and scatter over the fresh herbs and black olives. Bake for 40 mins, until golden and bubbling. Serve hot with a green salad.

Claudia's Banana Bread

120g softened butter, plus extra for greasing
⅓ cup (60g) caster sugar
½ cup (100g) soft brown sugar
2 eggs, at room temperature
pinch of salt
½ cup (100g) plain yogurt
1½ tsp baking powder
1 tsp bicarbonate of soda
3 very ripe bananas, mashed with a fork
1 cup (120g) plain flour
1 cup (100g) oat flakes
2 tbsp cocoa
1 cup (80g) desiccated coconut
½ cup (80g) raisins
½ cup (50g) chocolate chips (any colour)
3 tbsp rum
½ tsp each ground cinnamon and anise seeds

1. Preheat the oven to 180°C/350°F/Gas 4. In a large bowl, cream together the butter and both sugars until

smooth and fluffy. Beat in the eggs, one at a time, with the salt.

2. Place the yogurt in a small bowl and stir in the baking powder and bicarbonate of soda. Pour into the egg mixture, add the mashed bananas and stir together gently. Fold in all the remaining ingredients.

3. Grease and line a 9 x 5 in (23 x 12.5cm) loaf tin. Transfer the mixture to the tin and bake for 40 mins. Test with a skewer that the cake is cooked right through. Leave to rest in the turned-off oven for 5 mins, then take out and cool in the tin before turning out. The banana bread will keep in an airtight tin for a week, or can be frozen.

A Delicious Destination

*'The discovery of a new dish does more for
the happiness of the human race
than the discovery of a star.'*
Jean Anthelme Brillat-Savarin, 1755–1826,
French lawyer, politician, epicure and gastronome

Thomas was back from his holiday in Turkey. Heidi saw him arrive through the large window that separated her office from the reception area. She was thrilled to see her closest colleague again after almost two weeks.

He'd been in her thoughts a great deal of that time. Now they waved to each other, both smiling broadly.

Every other day, Heidi had received emailed photos and messages from Thomas, telling her about the wonderful places he was visiting, showing her the fabulous sights and recounting what he'd been eating while he was in Istanbul.

Istanbul … the very name made Heidi dream, evoking for her the perfect exotic and mysterious destination.

Her holiday – only two weeks a year – was spent entirely with her mother and the twins in rural Ohio. Not that she didn't try to get along with her mother, for the sake of the children, but with that being her only break from her monotonous routine, it wasn't ideal. It was all she could afford, however.

At least with Thomas she could dream of more adventurous escapes. He knew so much about the world and visited a new country twice a year – in May and October. Heidi hoped to be able to go with him one day …

Thomas seemed very content. His holidays were obviously doing him a power of good. He never got much of a tan, although he'd been to a lot of hot, sunny places, but, as he told Heidi, he usually stayed in the shade because he was afraid of getting sunburnt and developing skin cancer.

Istanbul – Heidi sighed longingly – the Blue Mosque, Hagia Sophia, the Topkapi Palace and the vibrant bazaars. Thomas's hotel had had a nice roof terrace where he'd spent much of the time admiring the panoramic view of the Bosphorus, sipping Doluca wine or raki.

Thanks to his emails, Heidi had easily been able to imagine him visiting the different places, taking a break on his hotel terrace, dining on *imam bayildi, borek, sis kebap, dolma*, with baklava for dessert, as if she were there with him. She could almost smell the dishes, he described them so well.

She'd enjoyed reliving Thomas's trip in her mind. The photos that he'd downloaded on the tiny laptop he always took with him were so very picturesque, the colours so vibrant and the views so inviting. His attached comments and anecdotes were fun to read: a real travel journal.

Heidi would rather have received postcards with actual stamps on them, but while he was away Thomas preferred to communicate only via the internet. As he said, postcards took so long that they would often arrive after he was back at his desk. For him, that would certainly ruin the charm and immediacy of his day-to-day travelogue.

Heidi anticipated that Thomas would invite her and the twins, Nick and Tania, for dinner – maybe even as soon as the following Saturday. He'd want to cook them some of the specialities he'd discovered during his Turkish trip, and he'd conjure up the atmosphere of Istanbul with local music, decorating the dining room with a few artefacts and souvenirs he'd brought back, as if he were a magician. And then, having experienced the taste of Istanbul, they'd all sit and be transported right there by his computer slide show. Such a treat!

Heidi thought that Thomas was amazing. When he went to a restaurant he could work out what all the ingredients were in a particular dish and then re-create it at home. A proper food connoisseur, everyone called him.

'A connoisseur? Do you think so?' he'd reply modestly. 'You know, I just enjoy good authentic, simple food in a place that has atmosphere, and try to cook the same thing in my kitchen, that's all.'

One day Heidi had asked Thomas if he would teach her to cook. He'd agreed right away. Since then, he'd shown her how to prepare a whole range of the delightful recipes he'd brought back from his holidays.

These cookery lessons took place once a month at Thomas's comfortable home. He still lived with his mother, Mrs Reynolds, a lovely woman, who clearly enjoyed spending time with Nick and Tania, while the twins saw her as a distinguished and fun great-auntie.

Thomas was very special to Heidi. She was secretly in

love with him but believed that his kindness towards her was no more than friendship. Their monthly gatherings at his home, a few lunches *en tête-à-tête* – her favourite moments with him – chatting at work, and the email travelogue were all Thomas wanted to share with her, she decided.

Heidi even tried to read the same books as Thomas. He had a taste for classic fiction and that took her back to the world of literature she'd enjoyed so much when she was younger. Comparing notes with Thomas about novels they'd both read was another source of intense enjoyment to Heidi.

Thomas always had a compliment for her. But she wondered if he was only trying to cheer her up, knowing her life wasn't always easy.

Heidi bore in mind what her mother had told her countless times: 'Let's face it, my girl, this Thomas Reynolds, who seems to lead a peaceful, intellectual life – how ready would he be to share that life with a woman like you, divorced with two kids? And aren't you a little too young for him? Or maybe he's a little old for you.'

Well, I don't care about his age, since we enjoy each other's company. Let's see how things go, was Heidi's silent answer to her mother's acerbic comments. But the seeds of doubt that anything could ever come of their friendship were planted none the less.

'Heidi, so nice to see you,' Thomas hailed her warmly as he entered her office, stretching out his hand to take hers. They kissed each other twice on the cheek.

'Likewise,' she replied. Her face felt rosier all of a sudden.

'It's easier to come back to work with your smile around. It's the best welcome back there is, you know. Hey, I like this hairband. Nice colour. It goes so well with your eyes.'

'Thanks, Thomas. I'm very happy to see you too. The agency isn't the same without you.'

'Do you want to go out for lunch?'

'That would be great,' Heidi answered quickly, pleased that the invitation was offered, as she'd expected. She hadn't even packed a lunch this morning.

'There's no genuine Turkish food around here,' Thomas said with a wink, 'but Mounir's will be Middle Eastern enough.'

'Wonderful. And I like their little outdoor area so much!'

Having been away for ten days, Thomas was swamped with work, but even so, he was determined to find time to have lunch with Heidi.

When Thomas was on holiday he didn't want to know anything about the agency. He preferred to forget all about the clients, their files and their demands and, instead, immerse himself in a completely different atmosphere, far away from his daily office routine.

The only person he stayed in touch with at work was Heidi. He'd started sending her emails about his holiday two years ago when she'd timidly asked him to send her a postcard from Portugal. He'd made her promise then that she wouldn't mention anything about work in her replies.

Thomas wasn't too concerned about the huge amount of work he had to do that morning. Instead he was wondering how to explain to Heidi what he had to tell her when they went to lunch. He just couldn't lie to her any longer. She needed to know the truth, especially now he sensed their friendship was taking a different path, that his feelings for her could, in fact, be more than just friendship. He wondered if Heidi would have a relationship with a man like him, whose passions were cuisines of the world, reading and museums: a little boring for a young woman like her, and for her two spirited children. By the time he took Heidi to Mounir's he was feeling decidedly nervous.

'I really love these falafels,' Heidi gushed, after taking a sip of her glass of ayran.

Looking straight at Thomas, happily tucking into his stuffed aubergines, she went on enthusiastically, 'So far I've done nothing but gossip about work. Tell me more about your trip!'

Thomas set down his knife and fork and reached for his briefcase, from which he produced two nicely wrapped parcels. 'Here's a little gift for you first.'

Heidi was overjoyed when she unwrapped them. One was a jar of rose jam, with the recipe attached to it. The other one comprised two smaller bottles in a pretty pink box: one of rose perfume, and one of rose oil, plus a card inviting Heidi, Nick and Tania to dinner the following Saturday.

'Oh, thank you, Thomas. They're lovely!'

Heidi would have liked to kiss Thomas but she didn't dare. Instead she smelt the perfume and was transported by its exotic fragrance. Then suddenly she blushed at the sight of the crimson rose design on the bottle: the flower of passionate love! And it was the first time Thomas had brought her something that was not edible or drinkable. She felt a little confused, but, at the same time, hopeful.

Thomas was delighted by Heidi's reaction. *She's always so easy to please, and always positive.*

'I really liked the food flavoured with rose when I was there. I'll make a dessert with rose syrup on Saturday.'

'I'm sure I'll love all the Turkish food you'll prepare for us, and so will the twins. They send their love, by the way. Look what they made for you.'

She handed Thomas two drawings depicting him on holiday: one showed him in profile, with the Blue Mosque in the background; the second had him sipping mint tea from a tiny cup outside the Topkapi Palace.

'They were wondering why you're never in the photos you email me. I told them it's because you travel by yourself, and that you don't want anyone to use your expensive digital camera. That's why they wanted to draw pictures with you in them.'

Thomas was touched and told Heidi that he was eager to see her children again. He shared his mother's affection for Nick and Tania. Mrs Reynolds was always complimenting Heidi on how well she had raised them, often adding how unusual it was to see such well-behaved children. Thomas had explained to his mother that Heidi did her best to take care of her twins, spending all the time she wasn't at work with them.

'I'll give you and the kids the rest of the gifts on Saturday,' he said.

'You spoil us.' Heidi blushed. 'So, go on, tell me about

your trip. I enjoyed your lovely photos, and reading your emails. But I have so many questions to ask you ...'

Thomas didn't answer immediately. He cleared his throat.

He seems very hesitant today, Heidi thought. Is there anything wrong?

'Hmm. Well, before I say any more about Istanbul, Heidi, there's something I ought to tell you ...'

Oh my! Heidi bit her lip, convinced he'd figured out she had a crush on him. She'd been doing her best to hide it, but, even so, he'd caught on, and he didn't like it.

He's understood my feelings, but how? Is it because I blush so easily? Heidi wondered. Who would like me anyhow? I'm really very ordinary physically as well as mediocre intellectually, a divorced mother with two kids.

Her ex-husband had always told her she wasn't worth much, and her mother had always been pessimistic about Heidi's ability to attract a decent man. Thomas was the only man who had ever been kind to her.

Chasing away these thoughts, Heidi gathered her courage to accept what Thomas was about to declare: that he cared about her only as a friend.

'It's hard for me to say this, because you may not want to see me any more,' he said gravely. He looked at her, a worried expression on his kind face.

'Please, go ahead!' Heidi implored, unable to bear the anticipation any longer. 'I've had bad news in my life before, more than a few times, and anything you have to say cannot possibly be as awful as all that.'

Thomas knew how hard things had been for Heidi:

pregnant at eighteen, the inevitable shotgun wedding, the abusive husband, the divorce, life as a working single mother who never had enough money, the death of her beloved father, the bad relationship with her mother ...

'I've never set foot in Turkey. Or Vietnam, or Morocco, or Portugal ...'

'Oh?' Heidi replied calmly, wondering what Thomas meant. And then she thought: Is that all?

For a moment she felt a bit puzzled by his declaration but, after a few seconds, she realised that Turkey, Vietnam, Morocco and Portugal were the countries that Thomas had said he'd visited on his twice-yearly trips.

'So that's it? That's what you have to tell me?'

Thomas looked up, surprised. He had expected a stronger reaction.

How could Heidi explain that she was actually relieved at not having to face what she dreaded hearing?

'Well, I expect you have your reasons for fabricating these trips,' she finally conceded after a brief silence. 'I mean, you must have some motive for travelling to these places in your imagination like that.'

Wow, she really is open-minded! Thomas thought. But he still gazed at her with astonishment, wondering why she didn't think him strange or bizarre. Maybe she was simply a big-hearted and kind person? He could never have been that broad-minded if someone had admitted lying to him for as long as they had known each other.

'And what about the food: the *pho*, the tagines and the *bacalao* dishes you made? You're so good at describing the aromas and ... *façons de faire*, as you would say, from exotic places as if you really had been there.' Heidi's tone was euphoric.

'Heidi, you know that world cuisine is my first passion in life,' he replied a bit defensively.

'It's becoming more and more my own passion, thanks to you.' Heidi smiled. She couldn't really be mad at him. He had brought so much to her life.

She looked so kind and trusting that Thomas had no choice but to continue to explain. He owed her that much, after all.

'Every May and October, instead of actually travelling abroad, I just take the bus to New York for ten days or a couple of weeks.'

Heidi, who had never even been to New York City, was more than eager to listen to Thomas's story.

'I stay at my brother Jack's place, in the East Village. Jack goes away to Germany for work at the same time twice a year. So he lets me use his place, a nice one-bedroom apartment on a quiet street, which is really a treat in Manhattan.'

'Don't tell me that, like me, you've never been outside the States?' Heidi asked. 'You've also talked about Paris like you really went there, but … oh, it's so confusing.'

'I'm sorry. You'll understand when you know everything.'

Thomas stopped to eat a little of his kebab, then continued with his confession.

'I used to travel for real.'

'So you really went to Paris, didn't you?' Heidi asked, her eyes shining.

'Yes, and several times.'

'What happened, then?'

Thomas explained that after a few trips abroad he became more and more irritated: longer and longer queues at the airport, overbooked planes, delays, babies bawling in the seat next to him, execrable food and bad movies, lost luggage ...

'Since I'm not an adventurous traveller, and I only speak English, I used to travel with organised tours. But I couldn't afford the kind of trips that would allow me the authentic experiences you could have if money were no object.'

Even as he said it, Thomas knew this last statement sounded a little absurd, and he paused to think it over.

'Actually I'm not at all convinced that money brings you authenticity ... A certain flair, maybe, but not the real atmosphere of ordinary, everyday life. And I think I'd rather not travel anywhere than spend time only in places that offer merely artificial, prefabricated luxury, and which are the same everywhere you go.'

'That's a good point,' Heidi agreed.

'Luxury for me is a simple lodging with a bit of authentic charm and a beautiful view, being able to meet and talk with locals, and tasting real dishes from *le terroir*,' Thomas added, still pleasantly surprised at the extent to which Heidi appeared to share his opinions on the subject.

'Yes, *la cuisine du terroir* – you told me all about it. I wish we were more into it in America. I wonder if your kind of luxury does exist anywhere any more.'

With a big sigh Thomas admitted, 'It doesn't much, or it's hard to find.'

'And too many outsiders spoil the authenticity of a place.'

'Exactly! And the funny thing is that locals don't always appreciate what they have since it's simply part of their daily routine.'

Thomas went on to complain about where he had been taken during his last all-inclusive trips abroad.

'Besides the barely adequate quality of the food, the run-of-the-mill hotels were also noisy, and there was far too much time devoted to shopping! And there are the same chain stores and restaurants everywhere in the world now, whether you're in St Petersburg or Bangkok! People wear the same kind of clothes, walk about looking stupid with their mouths open all the time, talking endlessly on their cell phones. The same insipid Hollywood movies play in all the theatres; you hear the same boring pop music everywhere …'

'But the unique sights, the monuments that still make a place so special – what about those?' Heidi asked.

'Of course, most of them are beautiful, but travelling with a group was becoming less and less bearable for me. I also noticed that many of my travel companions rarely appreciated their new surroundings, and would talk about how much better America was as they constantly snapped pictures of everything they saw instead of listening to the guide and really trying to see and understand the sights right in front of them. I usually had the feeling that I was just part of a group of vulgar tourists.'

Thomas stopped and looked up, realising he probably sounded too resentful.

'I didn't think travelling could be so terrible,' Heidi remarked.

'Most people must be a lot more relaxed than I am, otherwise nobody would travel at all. Any little incident bothered me in the extreme.'

'Come on, Thomas. What about the real atmosphere of a place, a feeling that you can't bring back with you?' Heidi tried.

'Real atmospheres are disappearing, as I was saying earlier.'

'Hmm …' Heidi didn't sound convinced. 'But what about Paris? You went there, and several times, didn't you?' She was beginning to get desperate. 'At least that's what you said …'

Her eyes suddenly grew brighter. Paris was her absolute dream, the one and only place abroad she really wanted to visit. She started fantasising aloud.

'*La plus belle ville du monde*, as my French teacher used to say: the cafés, the Eiffel Tower, the Seine, Montmartre and its artistic soul …'

'Yes, Montmartre,' Thomas interjected. 'Oh, I can certainly tell you a lot about Montmartre because I stayed in that neighbourhood the few times I went to Paris.'

'So, you see!'

'In fact, there was this adorable little café I really fell in love with. Café du Coin, it used to be called.'

'Used to be?'

'Yes, *used to be*. When I saw that my little Café du Coin had been replaced by a coffee shop chain, I cried.'

'I don't blame you. They are absolutely everywhere.

It's dreadful!' Heidi replied. She no longer went in them since she'd become friends with Thomas.

The two of them looked at each other, as if aware of the spectre of globalisation sitting with them at their small table in this tiny local Middle Eastern restaurant.

Heidi, regaining hope, broke the silence, declaring confidently, 'If I were to visit Paris I'd definitely go to a real café. Please don't tell me that they've *all* been replaced by insipid coffee shop chains!'

'Of course not. Fortunately Paris still has lots of authentic cafés. The closing of the Café du Coin was a real shock, though. I used to sit on its terrace every night. The owner, whose name was Josette, was a highly respected woman. She would talk to me sometimes; with her smattering of English and the few French words I knew, we were able to understand each other well enough. She was my image of a real authentic *Parisienne*, with her throaty voice and non-stop banter. There was a group of older men who lived in the neighbourhood who came in every evening to have a drink at the bar and chat with her. I used to watch them enviously. I couldn't understand what they were saying, but I wanted to believe that they had known her for ever and were all secretly a little in love with her.'

Like you? Heidi wondered, but she said nothing.

'It was a place where everyone knew everyone else,' Thomas continued. 'These people knew perfectly well where they belonged, and were an integral part of the neighbourhood. Every time I went to Paris, I would ask my travel agent to make sure he put me in a group staying in Montmartre so I could be near the Café du Coin. I didn't care much for the silly activities they'd organise in the evening at places like the Moulin Rouge, with half-naked women wearing feathers dancing on stage – well, if you call it dancing. Instead I would spend the evening sipping some Beaujolais, eating the best *croque-monsieur* you can imagine, while listening to CDs of singers from the past, which Josette would play, and listening to other customers talking.'

'I really love *croque-monsieur*,' said Heidi. 'I know that they're not that fancy, but they're just delicious.'

Thomas made a mental note of this.

'I would watch the non-stop "live" show the café and the street offered me,' he told her. 'The Café du Coin was basically the reason I went to Paris four more times.'

'Four more times!' Heidi exclaimed, thinking that Thomas went back there more for Josette than anything else.

'But on my last trip I found that the Café du Coin had disappeared. I immediately started to see only the negative changes: more fast-food restaurants and souvenir stores filled with tasteless, useless gadgets *made in China*. The Paris that I was so fond of seemed to be fading away.'

'That's sad.' Heidi's tone was understanding. 'I wonder what happened to Josette.'

'I suspect she was forced to close because the rent was too high. That must have broken her heart. However, she was a hard worker; she'll make it, I'm sure. So, after all that I decided not to visit "exotic" countries any longer. It was just too depressing. It may sound silly, but that's how I feel deep down.'

What could Heidi say? Should she be angry with Thomas for lying to her, or should she feel sorry for him since he sounded so bitter and disappointed?

'I know now why you never wanted to send postcards with real stamps on them,' she said finally, going back to Thomas's imaginary travels.

'Without the internet, I couldn't have "lied" to you like that. I couldn't have sent you pictures that I found on the Web.'

'They were beautiful,' she sighed. 'And even if you didn't take them, they still helped me to dream.'

Disappointment, indulgence, forgiveness? Thomas didn't know how to interpret what Heidi had just said. She wasn't looking at him any more. She was staring out at the street. She had a contemplative attitude that he wasn't sure he understood.

A couple of minutes passed in silence.

'Hey, what about the gifts?' Heidi exclaimed suddenly.

'You can find anything in New York, and I made most of them myself,' Thomas told her, smiling wryly.

Heidi remembered that the labels on the food gifts he had given her always looked hand-made. Thomas had told her that he did the wrapping himself back home to make sure the pretty paper wouldn't be spoilt on the journey home. She'd believed him. Still, she expected more explanations.

'OK. And what about the little stories you always told me? Did you invent those too?'

'I read a lot about the places I supposedly visit, go to special art exhibitions, and see movies and documentaries while I'm in New York. It's my way of discovering a new country and its culture.'

'Hmm … and I suppose that for the "exotic" food it was easy to find ethnic restaurants in Manhattan?'

Thomas nodded.

'The evocative flavours you told me about seemed so real to me. You certainly know how to describe them.'

'Well, you know that everybody at the agency is aware of my passion for cookery and that's the only thing I seem to get any respect for. So I'd never dare lie about that. I really have tasted all the dishes I told you about.'

Right, Heidi said to herself.

People at work didn't particularly appreciate Thomas because he was too much of a loner for them. Nobody paid him much attention. It made Heidi feel special being the only one of his colleagues he really got on with. However, when it came to his recipes and restaurant addresses, Thomas was willing to share, and then everyone at the agency listened to him. That was basically the only interaction any of them had with him.

'So what's your secret? TV cooking shows, recipe books, gourmet magazines, cooking classes?'

Just then the waiter approached their table.

'Would you like some dessert and coffee?'

Thomas and Heidi looked at him with surprise, having completely forgotten they weren't alone.

'May we have some baklava and two coffees, please? Heidi, is that OK with you?'

'Sure,' she answered, not even looking at the waiter, whose arrival had just broken their spell of intimacy.

The waiter went away, and Thomas continued with his confession.

'Well, when I got back from my last trip to Paris, Jack invited me to stay with him for the weekend after I told him about my latest travel frustrations. New York is a city I'd never really liked. I always thought it was too big and too dirty. Jack wanted to show me that it was one of the most magnificent and exciting cities in the world, and since I love ethnic food and restaurants he decided to take me to places you can only find there.'

The dessert and coffee arrived. The baklava looked scrumptious, little diamonds dripping with honey and sprinkled with the soft green of pistachios; the coffee thick, black and comforting.

'So the two of us went to different French places for lunch, dinner, or sometimes only for a drink. They all seemed pretty authentic to me – even if imported – true to the nostalgic image that I had of Paris. I could even hear Edith Piaf's songs.'

'So atmosphere can be exported, then?'

'Only a semblance of it, perhaps, but it's good enough for me.'

'I suppose it's a re-creation of what has sometimes been lost from the country,' Heidi pointed out.

'You're right! That's exactly it: a re-creation of what people left behind in order to keep it alive and share it with others in their new lives. It will never be exactly like it was, but it's still to be treasured.'

Thomas was a little happier now. He smiled, liking what Heidi had just led him to say.

She went on, 'New York is so big and is home to so many people from all over the world. That's what gives it such a variety of atmospheres.'

'I had so much fun there with Jack that I almost felt I *was* in Paris – well, the Paris that I remembered, or as I wanted it to be.'

They finished their baklava and sipped their coffee slowly.

'When Jack saw how much I enjoyed myself on our "French tour" in New York, he suggested that instead of spending money on disappointing trips I should just come and stay at his place while he was away in Germany. I could take care of his plants, and I'd discover a new country through the diverse neighbourhoods, restaurants, shops and cultural events in New York. What I needed for a vacation, he said, was some change from my routine, wherever I went. It seemed pretty good to me.'

'The idea is simply awesome! I love it!' Heidi said enthusiastically.

'Well, that's pretty much the whole story,' Thomas finished with a big sigh of relief.

'I think it's very interesting,' she replied. 'You see, I really do understand what made you invent your imaginary trips. Under the circumstances, I might have done the same thing.'

Heidi's eyes were bright. She was proud to have Thomas as a friend. She honestly wasn't angry with him because his made-up stories hadn't really been lies after all. Thomas had simply been having a good time by visiting a foreign country in a different way, as well as sharing his 'travelling' with a friend. There was nothing wrong with that, Heidi reasoned. She honestly thought it a great idea.

'Well, I guess you'll have to tell me about your "trip" to Istanbul another time, since I have to go back to the office,' she said, checking her watch.

'I told Dave that you probably wouldn't be back till later, since we have to discuss the McKenna file.'

Thomas looked at Heidi very seriously then. 'Promise me you'll keep our secret?'

'Of course I will! It's so much fun, and telling anyone else would spoil the whole thing! Besides, it will make our friendship even stronger, I believe, and maybe—'

Heidi bit her lip and reddened, realising that she'd said too much.

'Maybe …?'

But Thomas didn't insist further. After this significant conversation they both knew that their relationship was likely to take a different path from then on. While they prepared to work on the McKenna file, they wondered which country would be the next to be explored in New York – and they very much hoped they would be there together.

Thomas's Feast for Heidi and the Twins

Thomas's Imam Bayildi

The Turkish name for this cold aubergine and tomato salad
literally means 'swooning imam'.

Serves 6

3 onions, sliced thinly
3 large tomatoes, sliced thinly
6 garlic cloves, sliced thinly
1 tsp granulated sugar
1 tsp salt
5 tbsp extra-virgin olive oil
2 aubergines, sliced into ¼ in (0.5cm) rounds
ground black pepper
handful of flat-leaf parsley, roughly chopped
Greek-style yogurt, to serve (optional)

1. In a bowl, mix the onions, tomatoes and garlic with the
sugar and salt. Leave to marinate at room temperature for
at least 30 mins.

2. Brush the base of a wide, deep, lidded pan with a little
oil. Arrange half the aubergine slices in a layer over the
base, followed by half the tomato mixture, then repeat to
make another layer of each. Whisk 3 tbsp water into the
remaining olive oil and pour over the layered vegetables.
Cover and simmer for 30 mins, pressing the mixture down
with a spatula from time to time, until the aubergine is

very tender. If there is still a lot of liquid, uncover and cook over a high heat for 5 mins more. Season, sprinkle over the parsley and leave to cool. Serve chilled or at room temperature, with a little Greek yogurt, if you like.

Josette's Croque-Monsieur

These toasted ham, cheese and tomato sandwiches evoke a happy sense of nostalgia in Thomas.

For every croque-monsieur :
2 slices white or brown bread
2–4 thin slices cooked or smoked ham
2 slices Cheddar, Emmental or firm mozzarella cheese, plus 2 tbsp of the same cheese, grated
1 tsp Dijon mustard
4 slices tomato
2–3 pinches of dried *herbes de Provence* or dried oregano
sea salt and ground black pepper

Preheat the oven to 200°C/400°F/Gas 6. Lay one slice of bread on a baking sheet and top with the ham and sliced cheese. Cover with the other slice of bread. Spread the top of the sandwich with the Dijon mustard and sprinkle with the grated cheese. Arrange the tomato slices neatly over the cheese and sprinkle with the herbs. Season with salt and pepper. Bake for 15–20 mins, until golden and bubbling. Serve hot with a green salad.

Thomas's Rose Cake

Thomas now makes this lovable dessert in a
heart-shaped tin for Heidi.

3 large eggs, at room temperature, separated
pinch of salt
softened butter, same weight as the eggs, plus extra for
  greasing
plain flour, half the weight of the eggs
fine semolina, half the weight of the eggs
caster sugar, same weight as the eggs
1 tsp baking powder
2 tbsp rosewater

For the syrup:
¼ cup (60ml) rosewater
½ cup (100g) caster sugar
2 cardamom pods, seeds only (optional)

For the icing:
5 tbsp icing sugar
4 drops red food colouring (optional)

To serve (optional):
fresh or sugar roses, strawberries and whipping cream

1. Preheat the oven to 180°C/350°F/Gas 4. In a large
bowl, whisk the egg whites with the salt and ½ tbsp water
until they form soft peaks. Set aside. In a separate large

bowl, whisk the egg yolks with the butter until smooth and creamy. Add the remaining cake ingredients and mix well, then fold in the egg whites

2. Grease and line an 8 in (20cm) round / 7 in (18cm) square / 9½ x 10½ in (24 x 26cm) heart-shaped tin. Transfer the mixture to the tin and bake for 30–40 mins. Test with a skewer that the cake is cooked through. Leave to rest in the turned-off oven for 5 mins, then remove from the oven and cool in the tin for 5 mins before turning out on to a wire rack.

3. To make the syrup, place all the ingredients in a small saucepan with 3 tbsp water and simmer for 5 mins. Strain out the cardamom, if using. While the cake is still warm, prick all over with a fine skewer and slowly pour the warm syrup over it, reserving 2 tbsp for the icing.

4. To make the icing, mix the icing sugar with the reserved rose syrup and red food colouring, if using. Chill for 10 mins. When the cake has cooled completely, spread over the icing, then refrigerate for at least 1 hour before serving. Decorate with fresh or sugar roses, if desired. Excellent served with strawberries and whipped cream.

Thomas's Rose Jam

Makes about two 8 oz (250g) jars of this delicate treat.

150g unsprayed fragrant red or pink rose petals
1 cup (200g) granulated sugar
1 cup (200g) jam sugar (with added pectin)
juice of 1 lime or lemon

1. Carefully wipe the petals, cut off the white area at the bottom and discard. Place the petals in a non-metallic bowl and sprinkle with the granulated sugar. Cover with cling film and leave overnight.

2. Next day, place the jam sugar and lime or lemon juice in a large saucepan with 3 cups (750ml) water. Heat gently, without stirring, until the sugar dissolves. Stir in the sugared rose petals and simmer gently for 15 mins, until softened. Bring to the boil and boil hard for 20 mins, until thick. The jam will not set completely, but remain loose textured. Pour the hot jam into clean, sterilised jars, seal with waxed discs and cover tightly. Label when the jars are completely cold.

Freedom Fries and Idiot Cheese

'Take time in your preparation of coffee and God will be with you and bless you and your table. Where coffee is served there is grace and splendour and friendship and happiness.'
Sheikh Ansari Djezeri Hanball Abd-al-Kadir,
sixteenth-century Middle Eastern philosopher

'What'd you like?' asked the girl behind the counter sharply.

She had purple hair, a pierced eyebrow, nose and lips.

'Er, I'm not sure. You know, it's the first time I've ever been in here …'

'You've got to decide because there's a line, as you can see.'

I shuffled to the end of the line without a word, my eyes still fixed on the extensive list of drinks. Many of the names – especially for the coffee and tea – were unknown to me. I had no idea what to choose.

Usually I drank my coffee either at home, at work – where there was a high-spec espresso machine – or at Due Amici, the café across the street from my apartment. When I went there I always asked for an espresso because I loved real full-flavoured Italian-style coffee.

I hadn't been to a place like this for years. Actually, not

since I'd moved back from Lyons, six years earlier. After experiencing French cafés I'd acquired a taste for drinking my coffee in a china or ceramic cup, either sitting at a table outside, or inside at the bar. In France I'd chatted with a friend, a neighbour, or another regular customer, or just looked at the people around me, who had sometimes been as attractive as the place itself.

Why should I stand in line for a cup of coffee? I asked myself. I'd rather sit down at a table and be served by a waiter. And I didn't need to drink a pint of tasteless brownish liquid just to get my daily fix of caffeine.

Just then I felt like having a small cup of real coffee, giving off a real coffee aroma that I could both smell and taste. I suspected I wasn't in the right place for that, though.

It would be my turn again soon. I heard the man in front of me saying, 'Smooth light-blended crème vanilla bean Frappuccino!'

What in the world is that?

The purple-haired, fully pierced girl, who might have been pretty without all her strange accoutrements, was still behind the counter looking fed-up. She asked the man, 'Big, bigger or massive?'

'Give me a massive. I've got miles to drive tonight,' he said, beaming. He evidently couldn't wait to have his 'fuel' in hand.

I looked back up at the drinks list; I still hadn't made my choice. I stared bewildered at the man, now holding a large white polystyrene cup containing his enormous Frappi-something drink, exiting the place with an even bigger smile on his face.

My turn once again.

'Know what you want yet?' snapped the girl behind the counter in the same bitter tone she'd used earlier. I was beginning to find her rather scary now, especially with all her piercings. If she didn't like working here, it was hardly my fault, was it?

'Do you have plain coffee, er, espresso?'

'Of course!' Then she leaned towards me and muttered, 'What do you think the machines behind me are here for?' She rolled her eyes as if I were a real moron.

I didn't want to start an argument over her remark, which I thought was uncalled for, so I just told her that I'd opted for an espresso.

She reeled off the list as a matter of course: 'American, Colombian, Puerto Rican, Costa Rican, Italian, French, or decaffeinated, French vanilla-, raspberry-, hazelnut-flavoured, or …'

French vanilla-flavoured coffee? Yuck!

'Just a double espresso made only with real Colombian coffee, please.'

'Do you want it plain, with whole or fat-free milk, soy milk, real cream, half and half, non-dairy creamer, sugar, brown or white, or sweetener?'

All this for a simple cup of coffee? Since I wasn't sure how good the coffee would be, I asked for some milk in it. Safer that way.

'Whole real milk that came from a real cow and nothing else, please,' I said, trying to be funny.

But the girl just rolled her eyes again. She really seemed to think I was from another planet.

Well, sorry, but, as I said earlier, this is my first time here — and certainly my last.

I could see that there were some bright yellow and blue ceramic mugs on the shelves near the coffee machines. I wondered if they were merely for decoration.

I asked the girl to pour my coffee into one of the colourful mugs, if possible. She did so, but with obvious reluctance, practically grimacing. She was probably thinking about the fact that she'd have to wash the mug afterwards.

I paid quickly, sensing that the customers behind me in the line, as well as the purple-haired girl, wanted me as far away from them as possible.

If you are too slow when queuing up at a fast-food or coffee place, it's so easy to throw the whole mechanised system out of whack: order, pay, get your food or drink and get out. NEXT! Order, pay, get your food or drink and get out. NEXT!

I no longer went for lunch at the food court near my office because I was never fast enough. I was constantly annoyed by the impatience of the customers, and by the disparaging glances of those who seemed completely satisfied with this dehumanised process. Instead, I simply took my own lunch to work. It was healthier, anyhow.

Taking my mug of coffee, I went to find a seat, my gaze sweeping over the eclectic mix of customers. I wondered who these people were and why they came to such a place. The decor had no charm; it was identical to all the other coffee shops in the chain. The music was a wishy-washy mix of jazzy electronic melodies, uninteresting and not meant to be listened to. Wherever you were – in Detroit,

San Francisco or Miami – identical drinks would be served in the same huge polystyrene cups, the same industrial sugary pastries would be eaten, all in the same dull, impersonal atmosphere. It plain depressed me.

I also noticed that almost all the customers were by themselves. I'd always thought that going to a coffee shop was a way to meet and talk to other people. At least in my neighbourhood that's what most people did. But we didn't call them coffee shops, we called them cafés. Possibly the name indicated the distinction.

Apart from a group of three women who seemed to be deep in conversation, having what looked to me like cappuccinos, most of the others sat at single tables with their laptops, or sometimes with cell phones in their hands. Were they students? Businessmen or -women? Writers? Was I surrounded by the latest generation of today's trendy communicators, unable physically to face other human beings but constantly broadcasting the mundane facts of their lives via machines? Workaholics who couldn't stop to relax for even a minute, and who took their computers and cell phones with them wherever they went?

I sat down near the huge bay window through which I could watch the passers-by out in the street. At least the real world outside would make my wait more entertaining.

Glancing at my watch, I saw that Jon was late, as usual. He was always late because he insisted on driving everywhere, even if he did live close to a subway stop, and even though the price of gas had gone up drastically. It was only when Jon was behind the wheel of his car that he felt strong and confident. That was why he tried to spend as much time as he could in his black Mercury. He practically lived in the thing.

I knew that parking at the Square on a Friday night was a real hassle, and that he'd struggle to find a spot.

Jon had chosen the coffee shop where we were meeting that evening because they served a drink that he liked, and it was near an excellent liquor store that he could shop at afterwards, just as he did every Friday night.

I would have preferred the wine bar next door because they had a nice patio. It was a beautiful late-spring evening. I really felt that I'd like to be outside with a glass of Merlot.

Jon preferred indoor air-conditioned spaces, even if it was a perfect seventy-five degrees outside. As he'd sounded miserable on the phone that morning, I hadn't argued and had let him decide where we'd meet. Besides, I could walk to the city's best movie theatre from there. Earlier I'd noticed that they were showing *The Party*, in my opinion one of the best comedies of all time.

My cell phone rang.

'Hey, Luc, I'm still looking for a place to park,' Jon drawled in his usual indolent tone.

'No problem.'

What else could I say?

I sipped my coffee. Actually it was better than I'd thought it would be. It just needed to be served somewhere with more authentic rituals.

Jon had been seeing Magalie for a few months by then. I'd had the opportunity to meet her with him sometimes and I'd enjoyed her company. She was very attractive, and I had to admit that I felt envious of Jon. I wished I had met someone like Magalie, but I hadn't been very lucky with women. It seemed that I wasn't ambitious enough for them.

I wondered what Jon wanted to tell me. He maintained that I was the only guy he knew that he could talk to and discuss anything with face to face rather than feeling obliged to sit at a bar counter staring at a football or baseball game on TV. Most of his friends said that at his age it was unusual to see two men chatting at the same table, unless they were related or gay. And the sharing of a bottle of wine – bad heterosexual etiquette according to a silly *New York Times* style article, if you didn't want people to think that you were gay. Since he'd turned thirty, Jon had been finding it increasingly difficult to cultivate friendships with men he could really talk to.

I'd known Jon since pre-school. Our parents still lived on the street where we'd both grown up. Jon was like family: I hadn't chosen him but he'd always been around when I'd gone through difficult times. The two of us were very different, but we accepted each other the way we were. We tried to meet about once a month. He usually came to my place and I'd cook him a hearty dinner, or we'd meet in a little Italian restaurant somewhere, or an Irish pub, either in his neighbourhood or where our parents lived.

But just then, sitting waiting in that coffee shop, I felt like an outsider because I had absolutely nothing to do. I had no one to talk to, I was not staring at my cell phone or tapping a text message; I had no book, no notebook, much less a laptop. So I just leaned back and looked out the window, sipping my coffee.

I loved to watch the goings-on in the street, which was exactly what I'd done when I'd lived in Lyons for a few months before jumping into the real world of work. I had to admit that in France I'd spent more time in cafés than I had in class, where I was supposed to be improving my French. Life in the streets had been more appealing and instructive to me than learning the rules of the subjunctive or memorising endless lists of vocabulary! I'd enjoyed having my *café crème* with croissants so much every morning that I'd ended up having to change my schedule because I was always late for my first class.

The traffic was still fairly intense at that hour. I could picture Jon trying to find a parking spot, patiently passing through the same streets again and again, listening, as usual, to Lionel Richie or Celine Dion.

I found it hard to believe Jon was going out with a woman like Magalie. For a start, he always looked so sloppy. He didn't care how he dressed at all. He was the type of guy who would wear white sneakers with a navy pinstripe suit! And it wasn't lack of money. He just had no taste in clothes. His hair was always dishevelled, and he didn't even shave regularly.

And secondly, Magalie was French! Jon, being simple-minded at times, believed that France should change its political stance regarding the war in Iraq. He basically never wanted to hear anything about that country: he no longer drank French wine – not that he was a wine drinker, anyhow – and he would inanely use the word 'freedom' instead of 'French' to describe fries. When I considered it, associating freedom with France was a great compliment because 'freedom' was a beautiful word, if used in its proper sense. I'd heard that somewhere in France, in answer to the Americans who wanted to banish French from their vocabulary, American cream cheese had been named 'idiot cheese'. A bit less flattering to the States!

Jon's attraction to Magalie had quickly erased any resentment he felt towards the French once they'd begun dating.

I'd seen her three times since my ex-wife's house-warming party at various get-togethers to which she, Jon and I had been invited. I'd really enjoyed chatting with her while Jon was busy talking with someone else. We'd mostly talked about politics and film, subjects I had never even considered discussing with Jon, the two of us having completely opposite opinions.

Magalie had revealed to me how she'd fallen for his dazzling green eyes – it was true that Jon, being half African-American, half European-American, had striking good looks, especially his eyes – and also how happy Jon made her. She appreciated his carefree attitude, the fact that he never complained and never argued, even when they didn't agree. Needless to say, he had never dared say anything bad about the French in front of her.

Magalie was right. Jon's laid-back attitude and his lack of worry and concern could be refreshing. If he complained about something, it meant that he was really cheesed off, but that didn't happen very often.

Magalie had come to live in Boston for her job. She and Jon had met at a yoga class. Magalie had been in her Zen period, as she put it. She'd needed to find a way to be less stressed out as she was often overworked, and yoga had seemed ideal.

I hadn't heard from either of them for more than a couple of weeks, as I'd been away on business.

I finally saw Jon stroll into the coffee shop at a leisurely pace, even though he was quite late. Why should he bother to hurry? He walked towards me, a big bag of French fries in his hand.

'Hey, buddy. How are you?' I greeted him with a big smile.

'Um, could be better, Luc. Want some *freedom* fries?' he offered.

I held out my hand to decline: French fries with latte, yuck!

'And what about you?' he asked with his mouth full.

'The usual: work, work and more work.'

'Yeah? Hey, let me get a frozen chai latte frappé.'

'No coffee with milk to go with your fries, as usual?'

'No, I'm a little hot. I'd rather have a cold drink. Do you want anything else?' Jon asked, looking at my nearly empty mug.

'No, I'm all set. Thanks.'

What on earth was a frozen chai latte frappé? Chai sounded Asian to me, latte Italian, and frappé French. And why did it have to be frozen? I'd have to ask Jon. Why create such weird drinks? The last one I'd seen advertised in the subway was a beer with some added caffeine, guarana and ginseng! Was I unadventurous, or just growing old and bitter, or was the world changing too much for my taste? Were people no longer able to appreciate simple, authentic tastes?

Jon returned from the counter with his huge frozen chai latte frappé, still munching on his French fries. His drink looked like pale caffé latte, with a huge dollop of whipped cream at the top. It was in a light-blue transparent plastic container that resembled a goldfish bowl, with a flashy multicoloured straw poking out the top.

Jon didn't give me a chance to ask about his drink.

'Magalie and me, jeez, it's over, man!' he said quickly. He took a big sip of his frozen chai concotion.

I wasn't that surprised. The two of them were so different.

'She dumped you, didn't she?'

Immediately I regretted what I'd said. But it seemed the only obvious explanation.

'No. *I* dumped her!'

'Oh! What happened? You were so proud to have her as your girlfriend.'

Even if she was French, I thought but didn't say.

'Actually, we had nothing in common.'

Right … They most definitely had nothing in common from the beginning.

'You should feel relieved, Jon. You're the one who took the initiative to break up, after all.'

'She didn't seem that sad when I told her. That's a little hurtful, you know,' he said, taking another gulp of his frozen chai latte frappé.

'This is delicious,' he added, forgetting Magalie for a moment. 'Want to try some?'

'No, thanks.'

Jon went on placidly, 'She's complicated, let me tell

148

you. I wonder if it's because she's French.'

I looked straight at him but said nothing.

'It's the first time I've dated someone who isn't American, now I come to think of it.' With a sigh, he continued, 'She was so stylish! Not that I care much about that, but I could feel other guys envying me when I was with her. I liked that feeling.'

I would have thought someone like Magalie would have encouraged him to pay more attention to his appearance, or got him to think about his personal style. But no.

'We were so different,' he repeated. 'Everything she liked – except yoga – I didn't.'

'But you can't really build a relationship on yoga alone.'

'And I also admired her being the queen of leftovers …'

'What?'

'Yes, I've got to confess that I really enjoyed watching her transform leftover food the way she did. She'd come home and do amazing stuff with whatever she could find in the fridge. I've never met anyone who could do that before.'

'A talented artist …'

'She was always saying that, for her, cooking had to be a challenge: either using whatever food happened to be available, or leftovers.'

Especially a challenge in our country, where leftovers usually go straight into the garbage.

'Well, you know that my palate isn't really used to non-American-style food.'

Right.

'At the beginning, everything was going so well …'

149

No kidding! Exactly like almost 98 per cent of relationships. The initial discovery of the other person is so thrilling!

'... but after a while we needed to move on, you know.'

My ex-wife had only been interested in stamp collecting. I'd found her hobby interesting too at first, but after a while, to my mind, it had become incredibly boring. I hadn't realised how obsessed she was: she would spend all her free time at home with those little scraps of paper spread out in front of her on the dining-room table; in the end I'd really despised them!

'You learn so much from them,' she'd declare fervently, without even lifting her eyes from her stamp albums to look at me.

I'd leave her to her passion, and go out and sit in the Due Amici café with my neighbour Gino, with whom I'd practise my Italian – my mother's first language. Gino was always there because he didn't get along with his daughter's Goth boyfriend, who had moved in with the family. He couldn't do anything about the situation since his wife found the teenager darkly profound and thrilling.

Jon was now listing all the things that had gradually pushed Magalie and him apart.

'She loves to spend hours just sitting at a table, eating and talking ...'

I suspected that if I were to ask people in the coffee shop about the last time they'd spent more than an hour eating a good meal, I would hear, 'It was so long ago I can't even remember' or, 'Do you think I have the time for that?' or most likely, 'What do you mean?'

'She loves wine. I drink mostly beer, sometimes vodka.'

'The French I met in Lyons all drank wine, and spent a lot of time really enjoying what they cooked and ate. It's an important part of their culture.'

'But you know I've never been crazy about the French.'

'I know.'

'Besides their politics, they eat weird stuff like snails, and tripe. Too *awfully offal* for me. Eating guts! Yuck!'

I shrugged and said nothing while he laughed at his supposedly clever play on words.

'I was still very attracted to her even when I found out she was French.'

At first sight Magalie had looked to me either French or Italian. But that might have been less noticeable in yoga class, where she and Jon met, since everyone would have been wearing pretty much the same clothes.

'You'd be surprised! I even tried some rabbit she cooked once. It wasn't so bad, but I'll never tell Ma.'

Your 'ma' would never eat a bunny, that's for sure.

'Her cake *salé* was delicious!' I said, remembering the potluck dinner party where I'd met Magalie for the second time. 'It was so unusual. I should have asked her for the recipe.'

'And then she started making comments about my favourite snack …'

'Freedom fries and café latte …' I'd always found the combination hugely unappetising.

'Comments about my beer-drinking while we were eating cheese …'

Beer with cheese! Oh, please!

'She would only eat her cheese if it was left out of the fridge for at least a couple of hours. Some of it was actually runny and it stank! I could barely stand to taste any of it!'

'The French like it that way: perfectly ripe and at room temperature.'

'But I don't like smelly cheese.'

'You simply don't like cheese, then.'

'Whatever, I don't care.'

Looking in cheese-shop windows had been a great source of pleasure for me when I was in Lyons. I'd wanted to try every type of cheese. I must have tried almost a hundred different kinds – not too bad in four months.

'Every weekend she would write up the whole week's menus and tape them to the fridge door, because she would cook all the time for her and her roommates. You can't imagine how long she would spend faffing around in the kitchen. I've never seen a woman behave like that before. I can still picture her in her little apron … Wow, she was pretty, though!'

He sighed and sipped his frozen chai latte frappé.

'But our conversations got more antagonistic every day. After we'd said all we could about yoga and our past lives, there just wasn't much else I could talk about with her. Then she started talking all the time about her country, and the rest of Europe, which she described as great, and sometimes she criticised America. I realised that she was getting on my nerves with all her annoying opinions, as well as her strange food habits.'

'She may have been homesick. Didn't you ever think of that? It's not always easy to live in a foreign country.'

But how could Jon understand this? He'd never even been out of the States.

'Why doesn't she go back to her great country, then?'

'I'd like to meet a woman like her, who would share my passion for cooking, who would appreciate real coffee, fine wine …'

'In a way, the two of you would have been a better match. She's always said good things about you, you know.'

I looked at Jon, quite surprised that he'd told me that.

Staring at my empty mug, he suddenly burst out laughing. 'Do you know that you're the only one here who's having his coffee in a ceramic mug?'

'Yes, so?'

'When Magalie and I went out for coffee, we always had to find a place where we could sit down, where she could have her coffee in a real cup. She could never drink standing up and from a paper cup.'

'I don't blame her.'

'She could be so annoying. What difference does it make, anyhow? Coffee is coffee.'

I didn't think so. I tried to explain.

'Taking time to drink coffee turns it into more of a ritual: smelling it, sipping it slowly to savour it – it's so much more than putting caffeine into your system like gas in a car.'

Jon stared at me with an expression that reminded me of the purple-haired girl earlier.

'Like I have time for ritual when I drink coffee. Just like Magalie, you can be a real snob sometimes!'

I shrugged. That was the sad story of our lives. We didn't take time for the essential, simple things in life!

Everywhere I went, people drank what passed for coffee from hideous giant plastic containers as they drove their cars, or sat on buses or on the subway, and even while they were walking down the street holding their cell phones to their ears!

'You'd rather get up later in the morning, buy your coffee at the corner store and drink it in your car,' I said.

'Yes, I would,' Jon admitted. 'So? Everyone does it, don't they?'

With a sigh he repeated, 'Magalie and I – we were just too different.'

I tried to cheer him up. 'You'll get over it, and you'll meet someone who's more like you. A good American girl who loves big juicy burgers and beer, has French fries and coffee with milk while watching TV, and who likes to drink chai latte frappé in a huge plastic cup while she rides in your big Mercury listening to Lionel Richie or Celine Dion!'

'So what? There's nothing wrong with that, is there? Lionel Richie and Celine Dion are a lot better than the cheesy Italian songs they play at Due Amici. That's all too much Eurotrash for me.'

I laughed, remembering how much Jon had disliked the little café the first time he went there because the service had been too slow, the coffee too strong and served in a tiny cup, with no French fries available, and the beer had only come in small bottles. On top of all that, the Italian pop music had pushed him over the edge!

I suddenly remembered something I'd wanted to ask Jon for a long time.

'How did you ever get involved in a yoga class in the first place?'

'For Christmas, my boss bought all his employees a gift certificate for yoga classes to help us deal with stress.'

I personally thought that less work, more vacation, and more time spent relaxing in cafés would be better at relieving stress. Though, actually, Jon was seldom stressed out. He was custom-made to be the perfect American workaholic, since he had no passions outside work except watching sports on TV and driving his big black car – two activities that were perfectly compatible with workaholism, that perfectly respectable addiction in today's society.

'But you're *not* stressed most of the time.'

'I know, I know, but all the guys I work with went. So I figured I should go as well.'

His cell phone rang, the tone immediately recognisable as 'The Star-Spangled Banner'. Jon was such a flag-waver.

'Hello …?'

After listening for a few minutes Jon said, 'Let me get some booze and I'll be right there.'

He put the phone back in his shirt pocket. 'I've got to go.'

'Cherry, again?'

Jon nodded.

Cherry, the favourite cousin, always called Jon whenever she got dumped by a boyfriend. It happened pretty much every two months. Each time, she got drunk and wanted to kill the bastard who had broken her heart, and then herself. But before she did anything really silly she always phoned Jon, who rushed in to save her from her distress.

'Don't get too deep in despair with Cherry!'

'I think I'll get a bottle of vodka and get smashed myself. Care to join us?'

No, thanks! Spending an evening with Cherry, watching her get more and more drunk and hearing her drone on about her failed life was not my idea of a good night in.

'No, thank you. I think I'll go to the movies next door. They're showing *The Party*.'

'Never heard of it. You always have such weird taste in movies anyhow.'

We left the coffee shop and Jon sauntered away towards the liquor store. I walked to the movie theatre, happy to breathe some fresh air and promising myself I'd never go into that place again. Even if the evening air seemed a little polluted by the traffic, it was still better than the enclosed over-cooled, over-conditioned air of the coffee shop.

Well, Magalie, what would you think of The Party?

Jon's offhand comment that she would be a good match for me kept going round and round in my head.

I knew where she worked. Maybe someday I could go to the food court in her office building, pretending I was there to meet a client or a friend, and just bump into her.

What would Jon think? Maybe nothing would come of it, in which case he'd never even know. And if something did happen, I'd find a way to tell him.

* * *

Two weeks had passed since I'd met Jon at that awful coffee shop and I was just back at the office after a quick business trip to Toronto.

I checked my emails.

> Hey buddy, I've attached Magalie's cake salé recipe. I called her because I'd left a few yoga DVDs that belong to Cherry at her house, and Cherry absolutely wanted them back since she's met a guy who's really into yoga. I told Magalie you still remember the cake. I'm getting over her. I'm staying at my parents' for a few days. Ma is recovering from surgery. Nothing serious.
> Jon

Two days later, I was ready to meet Magalie. Seeing her savoury cake recipe in Jon's email had given me the courage and inspiration. I decided to try to meet her 'by chance' at lunchtime the following day.

'Magalie?'

'Lucas! What a lovely surprise! What are you doing here?'

'I had a meeting in the building and decided to grab something to eat before going back to my office. Hey, thanks for the recipe you emailed to Jon for me.'

She smiled.

'I enjoyed our talks,' I went on tentatively, trying to build a conversation.

'Me as well!' Then she added, 'Of course you know that Jon and I broke up?'

'Yes, I do. I'm sorry!'

What a lame liar I was.

'Oh, it's better this way,' she said, looking at her watch. 'Please excuse me, but actually I have to meet a client for lunch.'

'Why don't we have a drink one of these days?' I suggested with sudden boldness.

'I'd like that. Here's my card. Give me a call or email me.'

'I've never been here before,' Magalie said as we stepped into Due Amici. 'It's got a distinctive atmosphere. I like it.'

We ordered *cafés crème*, some limoncello and *sfogliatelle*. Due Amici was famous for these delicate flaky pastries from Naples.

'And they're playing Italian pop songs!' she suddenly said rather loudly, in an excited voice.

I was humming along to the famous song in the background.

'*Parli italiano?*' she asked.

I hadn't known she spoke Italian as well. Something else we had in common.

Inevitably, we started talking about her and Jon.

'We were not compatible. I was too French for him, and he was too American for me, as he put it, if that means anything to you.'

'Yes, *les différences culturelles*, but they don't always have to be a problem, do they?'

'Of course not. In any country there are people who stick to what they know, thinking that they live in the best place in the world, and others who are more open-minded because they've lived in other countries.'

I nodded.

Magalie continued, 'That's why it didn't work out with Jon. I liked his carefree attitude at first, but then I realised that he was not open to anything beyond his own little world. It made me more and more defensive about my own country. There's nothing wrong with the fact that Jon doesn't appreciate any culture other than his own. That's just the way he is. I'm sure he'll meet someone more like himself.'

Then she announced, 'I'm having an *apéritif dînatoire* goodbye party in two weeks! I would like you to come over, Lucas, so save the date.'

'A goodbye party?' I was taken aback.

'Yes. And I'll make some cakes. I know it's very sudden. I was offered a tempting position in Milan, and I said yes right away. Boston is a beautiful and interesting city, but I feel closer to the Italian way of life. People here work too much, and, besides, I think the *aperitivi* in Milan are fantastic!'

So do I! Our eyes met. There was a reason we were here together at the Due Amici café: a prelude to Italy.

'My company has an office in Milan …'

I looked into Magalie's eyes again and I knew I wasn't mistaken. All the time she had been with Jon I'd been trying to ignore the feeling, but I knew at that moment that there was no resisting love. Suddenly it was clear what I had to do. The following morning I'd ask for a transfer to the Milan office.

Nothing more needed to be said. Laughing, we raised our glasses of limoncello in a silent but heartfelt toast to our future.

Magalie's Cake Salé
(Savoury Cake)

Makes one large loaf to serve 6 as a main course or
10 as an appetiser.

For the dough:
1½ cups (175g) plain flour
3 eggs, at room temperature
pinch of salt
½ tsp baking powder

1. Put the flour into a large bowl and beat in the eggs, one
at a time. Add the salt and baking powder, stirring gently
until well blended.

2. Fold into the dough, according to your mood/taste/
what you can find in your kitchen, any of the following
combinations, seasoned with sea salt and ground black
pepper to taste:

• ½ cup (115g) crumbled feta or goat's cheese – 1 cubed
medium-size aubergine sautéed in olive oil – ½ cup (80g)
chopped sundried tomatoes – ½ cup (60g) chopped pitted
black olives – 4–5 finely chopped fresh basil leaves

• 1 red and 1 yellow pepper, finely chopped and sautéed
in olive oil – 150g tinned tuna, drained and flaked – 120g
tinned sardines, drained and flaked – 4 chopped salted
anchovy fillets – 1 tbsp chopped capers – ½ cup (60g)
chopped pitted black olives – ½ tsp dried *herbes de Provence*

• 400g tinned salmon, drained and flaked, or 400g fresh cooked salmon, or 250g smoked salmon, diced (or half fresh and half smoked salmon) – 2 spring onions, 2 leeks and 2 carrots, all finely chopped and sautéed in butter until tender – ½ cup (125ml) sweet white wine or vermouth

• 1 cup (120g) diced cooked or smoked ham – ½ cup (60g) chopped pitted green olives – ½ cup (125ml) dry white wine or vermouth – ½ cup (60g) grated Cheddar cheese

• 1 cup (120g) chopped back bacon and 1 large onion, finely chopped, sautéed together in olive oil – ½ cup (100g) crumbled blue cheese – ½ cup (50g) chopped walnuts

• 1 cup (100g) drained tinned sweetcorn or cooked diced fresh baby corn – 1 red pepper, finely chopped and sautéed in olive oil – 1 cup (120g) diced cooked chorizo – ½ cup (60g) grated Cheddar cheese – ½ tsp chilli powder

• 1 large chopped onion, 1 cup (120g) diced pork sausage and ½ cup (60g) chopped back bacon, all sautéed together in olive oil – 1 cup (200g) drained sauerkraut from a jar – 1 tbsp Dijon mustard – 1 tsp cumin seeds

• ½ cup (120g) green pesto – ½ cup (80g) chopped sundried tomatoes – ½ cup (60g) chopped pitted black olives

3. Preheat the oven to 180°C/350°F/Gas 4. Grease and line a 9 x 5 in (23 x 12.5cm) loaf tin and transfer the mixture to the tin. Bake for 40 mins, until golden. Test with a skewer that the loaf is cooked right through. Serve warm or cold with a green salad.

July

Breakfast for Two

'The way to a man's heart is through his stomach.'
Fanny Fern, 1811–1872,
American writer

'... *Er, er, allô* ...?' I could hear a big masculine yawn.

'*Allô, Paris? Salut, Pierre*, it's Brune!'

'Who else would it be so early! I'm shattered, you know.' Another yawn ...

'I've something to tell you.'

No reply.

'Something quite mouthwatering.'

'*Mais bien sûr* ... otherwise you'd have emailed or texted me.'

We both knew how easily electronic messages could be misinterpreted and then we'd have to pick up the phone anyway to clear things up.

'And I wanted to hear the sound of your sweet voice.'

'*Bonjour*, apple of my eye.' Pierre was obviously waking up now.

'*Bonjour*, honey-bun. Wait until you hear the exciting news! *Une nouvelle chance* for you, Pierre. Food for thought.'

'*Pourquoi pas?* 'Another big yawn ... 'Hold on, I need a

reviver! Let me have a glass of my *eau miraculeuse*, as you call it. I think I need it.'

Smiling to myself, I waited patiently until he'd returned from his kitchenette. Pierre and his entire family believed that if you took two teaspoons of organic cider vinegar with two teaspoons of organic honey in a glass of water twice daily, it would keep you in good health. Much had been written about the benefits of this drink, if taken regularly, and I knew Pierre prepared a jar of this miracle water at the beginning of every week.

'Brune, did you get the webcam, like you said you were going to? I want to be able to see how delicious you look right now, *en direct*. Are you wearing something hot?'

We liked to amuse ourselves using foodie expressions since both of us were rather obsessed with all things culinary.

'"No" is the answer to both your questions.'

'OK, *j'écoute*. But let me assure you that your delectable face is etched into my mind anyway. So what's cooking?'

I knew that Pierre always liked to hear from me, whether online or on the phone, even if it was a bit early on a Sunday morning. Just then I had terribly important news to impart. It might even change his life – and it was about time something did.

'Hey, the sunrise is amazing this morning! Not such bad timing, after all. Let me open the window.'

Once again he put down the phone, and I could hear him fiddling with the catch. I pictured him with the pastel light of a new day on his face, looking out at the unique panorama of Parisian roofs. I imagined a peach-coloured sky to add to the beauty, even accordion music playing …

'I'm back and all ears. Go ahead, spill the beans!' Pierre's voice cut short my romantic reverie about an idyllic Parisian early morning. And, actually, my view from our roof deck of the star-lit Boston skyline was certainly nearly as stunning.

'Pierre, have you made your decision yet regarding the job in New York?'

'No, not yet.'

'How much more time do you need to chew it over?'

'I don't know …'

'You can't keep them waiting for ever. You remind me of a fallen soufflé every time you need to decide anything.'

'Well, I don't know anybody there.'

'I'm in Boston …'

'True. And it's not that far away, like you said. I'm sure we could have dinner together, just as we used to do.'

'This could be a great opportunity, you know. Something new. The spice of life is what makes it seem worth living.'

'It could also be a recipe for disaster.'

Good one. Now I had the feeling that he was going to talk about his age.

'I'm forty-two, you remember.'

I knew he wouldn't disappoint me.

'I've ripened into full manhood.'

'You're not a wizened old fruit yet!'

'And starting over …'

As if he had ever started in the first place.

Next chapter, there's so much to savour in Paris.

'I like my life here and—'

165

'Yep, chasing twenty-something tomatoes or being a couch potato, vegetating in front of your TV set!'

Pierre sighed loudly. 'Stop using that silly term "tomatoes" ...'

'Is "tarts" a better label?'

'It's not my fault if young women are fond of mature men like me.'

Right. Pierre, mature?

'In a way, I don't blame you ... Paris is so beautiful!' I conceded.

And I missed it sometimes, but I didn't want to talk about my occasional homesickness, at least not right then. I wanted to get back to the original purpose of my phone call.

The view of the Boston skyline at night was captivating. A slight breeze freshened the air. I was sitting sipping cranberry juice next to my little round mosaic table on the roof deck.

'You know, Pierre, I really think you need a change, for a couple of years at any rate. You should get away from the insipid life you're leading right now.'

'Brune la Sage, can we have this rather serious conversation a little later? You're starting – once again – to drive me nuts. I went out last night. I ate and drank a little too much ...'

I realised I should be nicer. I'd woken him up so early on what should, after all, be a day of rest.

'Sorry, sweetie-pie.'

But I couldn't help thinking that Pierre deserved so much better than a life filled with partying, as if he were a college freshman. And why did he still behave that way? Simple: he'd once been badly hurt. That was it. *Voilà*, now he didn't trust women at all.

'Sorry,' I repeated.

'OK, so what are you cooking up now?'

'Well, I met a great woman earlier tonight …'

'Oh, please, after Brune la Sage, now it's Brune the matchmaker making another futile attempt. That takes the biscuit!'

It was true that I'd tried to fix him up several times, but none of my plans had come to fruition. However, I really thought the woman I'd just met would make a terrific match for Pierre.

'I can find women on my own, you know …'

'Pierre, I beg you, stop dating tomatoes that are too young for you. You need a full-grown person closer to your own age—'

'Like Olga, Melanie or Michele? I'll have none of your sauce any more!' Pierre interrupted.

At least he remembered all the women I'd introduced him to. But I hadn't finished yet.

'A full-grown woman, a good egg, capable of making commitments, like—'

Silence.

'Yes, like who? Like you, dear Brune? Am I right?'

I didn't say anything but we both knew perfectly well that the two of us could have been such a good match, if only …

If only!

'But, dear Brune, you're taken, and you don't want to

leave your appetising cowboy for me!'

'Jimmy doesn't look like a cowboy at all!' I hated it when Pierre called him that. 'But, yes, he's a real dish,' I added.

'If you could see the sweet light of Paris this morning …' Pierre whispered after a pause.

'I can see it,' I answered, closing my eyes. Tender thoughts of that wonderful city replaced the ones I was having of Jimmy. Once again I could hear accordion music, and now the poignant voice of a street singer.

Actually, it was Eva, Jimmy's mother, who'd helped me discover an idyllic Paris, a Paris from a vague and nebulous past, a Paris you could be nostalgic about when you lived away from it, a Paris with accordion music and the heartbreaking voice of a street singer, and full of delightful sensations that I never would have found without her.

It was thanks to Eva that I'd developed a love of old black-and-white French films, and listened with new-found yearning to singers like Edith Piaf or Lucienne Delyle.

How could I have learnt about these beautiful moving voices and poetic lyrics by myself? After all, I grew up in a dull suburban family for whom the best French singer ever was Johnny Halliday! Living in the suburbs didn't really allow me to explore the romantic Paris that I had been able to re-create in my mind only here in America, thousands of miles away from it.

I wish young people today would learn to appreciate the touching, realistic poetry of those old songs. Thanks to my American mother-in-law, I felt more French than I had ever been.

Another big masculine yawn.

I sighed loudly.

'I'm thirsty again. Hold on.'

I heard Pierre walking away from the phone into his kitchenette once more. I'd have to wait again because even though he liked new technology, continually purchasing the latest trendy gadgets, he still hadn't mastered pouring a drink while holding the phone. Well, I guess that was inspiring in its own way. It seemed to me that everyone was multi-tasking, especially behind the wheel of a car. I was always scared someone would crash into me while they were enjoying coffee and doughnuts and at the same time trying to follow the instructions of their GPS.

The splendour of the early Paris morning had faded from my mind. I was back facing the beauty of the twinkling Boston skyline.

I just couldn't put this conversation off. I was sure that what I was about to tell Pierre would help him decide to move closer to me. It would be great to see him more often. Pierre was like family to me. And having a 'relative' close by would help me get over my occasional homesickness … wouldn't it?

I was so excited – this Elsa was fantastic! I had to tell Pierre right away, even if Jimmy had told me to wait until the morning, and to email Pierre before I talked to him. Men are different: they *can* wait, whereas we women can't put things off for even a minute. Well, I certainly can't.

Jimmy was downstairs finishing cleaning the kitchen,

and I was up here trying to convince Pierre to change his life.

'Very revitalising, this *eau miraculeuse*,' Pierre said, with satisfaction. Even his voice sounded refreshed. 'All right, go ahead, I'm listening, my sweet friend. Did you say *une nouvelle vie* for me earlier?'

'Yes. I organised a nice dinner tonight on the roof deck for the Fourth of July celebration. I invited Morgane and Jeff. Elsa, one of Jeff's friends, came with them. We all watched the fireworks. It was awesome!'

'Oh, I remember Morgane: plump as a ripe grapefruit, and a great cook!' he exclaimed. 'But, sadly, also kidnapped by another cowboy.'

Ignoring his last remark, I told Pierre about Elsa. I'd basically spent my entire evening – besides playing hostess – noticing which dishes she liked the most, as I usually did with my guests. Their appreciation of my cooking was the reward for all my hard work.

'And listen! Surprise! I've just sent you some of the shots I took tonight with my digital camera. So you can see pictures of Elsa right now!'

'*D'accord!*'

'The two of you seem to have the same hobbies, which I find quite surprising!'

I then reminded him of what he liked to do – a lot, actually; he had many interests, besides running after women far too young for him. I finished each sentence with 'Elsa, as well'.

'Interesting. Is she single?'

'She told me she isn't dating anyone at the moment.'

'You asked her?'

'I had to, didn't I? You can be such a noodle sometimes.'

Pierre laughed.

'How old?'

'Thirty-something.'

Pierre didn't say anything for a few moments. Then: 'So what did you cook?'

The French are always so fascinated by *le menu*, aren't they? And Pierre loved to eat, even if he didn't know how to cook. He only sorted out his breakfast: he went to the bakery, bought a fresh baguette and a few buttery croissants, which he served with his mother's home-made jam and farm-fresh butter, then he switched the espresso machine on. Most of the time he ate in restaurants or bought takeouts, unless his mother dropped by with food she'd made, each carefully labelled and lovingly stacked in his fridge for him.

Here I was, trying to tell him that he might soon meet the woman he'd spend the rest of his life with, and all he wanted to know was what we'd eaten that evening.

'Since it was the Fourth of July we had red and blue food. Jimmy wanted a patriotic table.'

'Come on! I'm not swallowing that!'

I ignored his remark. You'd have to live in America to understand that kind of patriotism.

'We had a *ceviche rouge*.'

'Which is …?'

I explained.

'Sounds appetising! A good tasty start.'

I told him about the rest of the meal: grilled lobsters,

and blue crabs, crimson salad, home-made blue potato chips, blue cheese with cranberry red onion confit, and a *tarte rosette tricolore*.

'Mmm, the very names make my mouth water!'

Pierre could stomach the thought of a gourmet meal at barely seven in the morning even after a night of excessive food and drink.

'Hey, I've just got your email!' he exclaimed. 'I'm looking at your photos now. Yum, you still look very edible, Brune, you know! I love the peppery red little top you're wearing. The icing on the cake ...'

I ignored these last remarks, as well I might.

'What do you think of Elsa?' I asked, genuinely curious.

'She's all right. Seems a little skinny, no?'

'Well, she could do with putting on a few pounds. She's much better in the flesh. You know how photos don't always show you at your best.'

A silence followed. I supposed that Pierre was still looking at the pictures.

'*C'est pas vrai!*' he exclaimed.

'What?'

'I didn't know you'd become *that* patriotic: red and blue food – OK, but look at all the American flags. And you're all wearing red, white and blue outfits!'

On the Fourth of July Jimmy also liked to have cutlery and table linen in the colours of the American flag.

'Everybody here does it ...'

Well, sort of. But I wouldn't tell him that. It was true that Jimmy could be very American – as American as apple pie, he'd have said himself.

'Anyway, my sweet friend, your red and blue dishes look truly delicious!' Pierre repeated. 'Better than what I ate last night.' After another sip of his miracle water, he went on, 'And I'm supposed to be in the country where we eat better than anywhere in the world.'

Sure, after the Italians in Italy, or the Spanish in Spain, since everybody lives in the country with the best food! The Americans think the same thing about their food as well.

After he'd told me about an insipid dinner in a bland restaurant to celebrate the departure of a colleague, I went back to my dinner party.

'Anyway, Elsa not only likes to eat, but she is a specialist in fusion cuisine. A real star at what she does: *la crème de la crème!*'

'Fusion cuisine?'

'It's a very fashionable concept here: a mixture of traditional and contemporary styles of cooking using ingredients and techniques from all over the world.'

'Sounds a little too complicated for me.'

'I enjoy it myself when my friends and I try to add an exotic twist to our traditional dishes. You see, I haven't forgotten my old French recipes, but I like to experiment with new ingredients and flavours from other parts of the world. America has really taken fusion cuisine to its heart.'

'Should I try a *romantic petit déjeuner fusion* myself? You could give me some tips.'

'Don't tell me that you brought a tomato home last night?'

'No, I didn't. What I mean by a *romantic petit déjeuner fusion* would be me sitting on my tiny balcony with dishes from the market that I'd buy to please you. We have Vietnamese and Middle Eastern stalls at the market now, you know. I would have my breakfast gazing at an empty chair across the table, wishing you were there.'

OK, fine! Let's get back to Elsa.

'Elsa's just moved to Manhattan, where she works for an international gourmet magazine, as a fusion cuisine consultant. Jeff told me that she's an amazing cook herself. She seems to really know her onions. And her sumac.'

'This is starting to become interesting.'

'She thought a two-tone meal was a fantastic idea. She took some pictures and wants to write an article about tonight. Isn't it great?'

Pierre agreed.

'Elsa has worked in restaurant kitchens since she was seventeen. Now, she'd rather give culinary advice and write reviews of restaurants she eats at. I don't blame her. Eating in restaurants for a living – lucky her!'

'Yes, it sounds good.'

'She could probably take you along with her sometimes to try different places. It would be a great way for you to discover New York.'

'Really? If so, what a delicious opportunity!'

I could tell I'd piqued his interest if only for the sake of his stomach.

'This Elsa may be of interest after all! Brune, I know what good taste you have. I trust you about Elsa if she impressed you that much. But does she only go to these trendy new fusion cuisine places? The dishes there must be a little bit scary and expensive, aren't they?'

I agreed and admitted that the prices were indeed high. Chefs were not afraid to create over-elaborate dishes to attract a fancy clientele prepared to pay the price. Some customers didn't seem to care if they didn't understand a word of the menu, as long as they were eating in a restaurant that was all the rage. And it worked. Not for us, though. Jimmy and I, and our friends, preferred to invite one another for dinner at home and try to cook something scrumptious, or else to eat in unpretentious, authentic diners or ethnic restaurants, rather than spending twenty-eight dollars on a plate of pasta with a fancy strawberry hot pepper sauce.

'Listen, Pierre, Elsa doesn't know anyone in New York, and it would be great for the two of you to meet, if only as friends. She really could take you to some amazing places.'

'What a job, when you think of it,' we said in unison, picturing ourselves working hard sampling the best restaurants in the city.

Then Pierre had another thought. 'But a woman like that – smart, with a good career, who knows how to cook well when most women today don't want to cook at all any more – she sounds too good to be true, *and* a bit intimidating.'

'She's certainly very different from the twenty-something *tomatoes* that you're accustomed to. Whoops! Sorry, that just slipped out!'

'Sure, I believe you, apple of my eye.'

'Elsa happens to be the only person I know so far who lives in Manhattan. I'd like you to meet her. I know I've sprung this on you, but she's made such a good impression.

You'll have to decide about your job quite soon, won't you?'

'By the end of this week, I think.'

'I told her that you might be moving to New York. She seemed interested, especially after I showed her a picture of you.'

Every woman who met Pierre or saw his photo thought he was a real dish.

'Brune, you always speed ahead with everything. Your brain is working overtime.'

And Pierre's needed to work a bit harder! It wasn't his fault. He'd always had someone to spoon-feed him. But I kept that thought to myself.

'It would be good for you to move away from Paris for a while. It could boost your career, and …'

… and your love life would be more fulfilling if you stopped spending time in clubs that are more like meat markets.

I kept that to myself, too.

'… And this is not pie in the sky. You can make it if you decide to.'

'If this Elsa is that nice and still single, what's wrong with her?'

'Look at yourself.'

And at all the wonderful people I knew who said they couldn't meet anyone. Was it because they were all too fussy or was it the craziness of our modern world that made it so difficult to form lasting relationships?

I explained to Pierre that even if he left his beloved Paris the decision wouldn't be irreversible – he could still go back whenever he wanted. His job allowed him to be flexible and to move around. He didn't realise how lucky he was sometimes.

'I don't know, I just don't know …'

'I'm not asking you to give me an answer now, but chew it over for a bit.'

Well, I'd said what I had to say. Pierre needed to be left alone now to consider the situation. After all, if he didn't want to change his life – and in my opinion he should, since he was wasting it completely – there was nothing I could do about it. He'd always be one of my very special friends.

'OK, Brune, thanks a million. You are such a sweetheart! I promise that I'll think about everything you've said – and very seriously.'

'Whatever your decision is, Pierre, I wish you the best.'

'Thanks, my angel cake.'

After a pause, he asked, 'What's the name of the gourmet magazine Elsa works for? Maybe I'll find it at the international newsstand today.'

I told him the title.

'I can't go back to bed. This conversation's made me hungry, actually. I'll go down to the market when it opens in half an hour and bring back a little *petit déjeuner fusion* to eat up here …'

Looking at the empty chair where I should be sitting? I hoped he wouldn't put his laptop on the table with my picture on the screen.

'… reading Elsa's gourmet magazine, if I'm lucky enough to find it.'

I liked that better!

'But, of course, with your picture looking back at me from my computer, my breakfast will be even more delicious.'

All right.

After saying '*Au revoir*, honey-bun' and '*Au revoir*, sweetie-pie', we hung up. I had a positive feeling about what Pierre was going to say to his boss by the end of the week.

Could it be that, because I'd met Elsa, Pierre's life was going to change? Would it change my life as well? Would our relationship lose its flirtatious double entendres if he became involved with Elsa?

Back downstairs, I walked into the bathroom. I looked at myself in the big mirror above the basin – face to face with the Real Me. I could see a strange light in my eyes. The thought that had pleased me when I'd hung up was starting to scare me a little. What had I done? Had I been too impulsive? Once again, I was trying to set Pierre up with a woman.

In the eerie light of the bathroom I was beset with other questions: was it really because of Elsa that I wanted Pierre to move to New York, or did I want him closer to me? What was Pierre thinking about right now looking out over the Parisian roofs flooded with morning light? Did he also see this as an opportunity to be closer to me or was he genuinely interested in meeting Elsa?

I was suddenly very tired and confused. What a dog's breakfast this might turn out to be! Had I done the right thing? Oh, well, no point crying over spilt milk now.

I went to bed. Jimmy was sleeping peacefully next to me, as always. Life was so straightforward for him. How I envied him sometimes!

After half an hour of tossing and turning like a Caesar salad, I still couldn't sleep. I got up, went to the kitchen and poured myself a small glass of Chambord liqueur, plus another glass of cranberry juice and took up to the roof deck a little something to eat. There was a cool wind now, which was invigorating; I wanted to feel the taste of the night as much as I could while I slowly ate a piece of shellfish left over from the party.

I put my cell phone down on the other chair. Pierre's photo appeared on the tiny screen. I was looking at the sky in the direction of Europe. I wanted to call him back, but decided not to after all. Instead my imagination was building a long, tall bridge over the ocean with piles of delicious food on each side. A few huge faces were floating around the elongated bridge: Elsa with her pretty smile, eating a lot to gain some weight, Pierre and me with confused expressions, looking at each other ... Suddenly I realised that I really was in the soup!

Brune's Tricoloured Recipes for a Very Special
Fourth of July

Red Ceviche

Brune's piquant red salad is a feast for the eyes as well as the
palate. Use very fresh fish.
Serves 4–6.

100g each raw skinless tuna and salmon fillet, cut into
2cm cubes
8 scallops, with coral if possible, cut into 2cm cubes
juice of 3 limes and 1 lemon
16 cooked, peeled prawns
½ 400g tin red kidney beans, rinsed and drained
1 blood orange or red grapefruit, pared and segmented,
the segments cut into small pieces
1 small red onion, finely chopped
2 tbsp fresh pomegranate seeds

For the dressing:
juice of 1 lemon
2 tbsp extra-virgin olive oil
1 garlic clove, crushed
pinch of salt
1 tsp chopped fresh red basil

To serve:
16–20 radicchio leaves
whole red basil leaves and pink peppercorns

1. In a non-metallic bowl, gently combine all the seafood except the prawns. Pour over the juice of the limes and lemon. Cover with cling film and chill in the fridge for 4–6 hours. Add the prawns half an hour before serving.

2. When the seafood has rested, drain off the juice. Fold in the red kidney beans, blood orange or grapefruit segments, red onion and pomegranate seeds.

3. In a small bowl, whisk together the lemon juice, olive oil, crushed garlic, salt and chopped red basil. Pour the dressing over the fish salad. Divide the radicchio between four deep plates and arrange the ceviche on top. Garnish with red basil leaves and pink peppercorns.

Red and Blue Salad

This beautiful Italian-American potato salad serves 6.

For the salad:
800g blue salad potatoes, such as Salad Blue or Shetland Black, or ordinary salad potatoes
2 small red onions, finely chopped
½ cup (100g) crumbled blue cheese (any kind)
½ cup (80g) dried cranberries
6–8 slices Parma or Serrano ham, cut into fine strips
12 slices Italian salami, cut into fine strips
½ tsp paprika, to serve

For the dressing:
¾ cup (175ml) mayonnaise
2 tbsp Dijon mustard

½ tsp sundried tomato paste
2 tbsp red wine vinegar
2 tbsp oil

1. Boil the potatoes in their skins in salted water for 20 mins, or until tender. Allow to cool, then peel and cut them into 1 in (2.5cm) cubes. Place in a large salad bowl with all the other salad ingredients, except the paprika.

2. Make the dressing by shaking all the ingredients together in a jar with 2 tbsp water. Pour over the salad and toss carefully. Refrigerate for 1 hour. Sprinkle with the paprika before serving.

Cranberry and Red Onion Confit

This relish makes a delicious accompaniment
to blue cheese.

2 tbsp vegetable oil
2 red onions and 2 white onions, chopped
1 cup (160g) fresh or dried cranberries
2 eating apples, grated or finely chopped
½ cup (100g) sugar (caster or soft brown)
1 cup (250ml) red wine
2 tbsp red wine or cider vinegar
2 cloves
½ tsp cinnamon
sea salt and ground black pepper

Heat the oil in a large saucepan, add the onions and cook over a low heat, covered, for 15–20 mins, until softened but not browned. Gently stir in all the rest of the ingredients and bring to the boil. Cover and simmer gently for about an hour, stirring occasionally, until thick and jammy. Leave to cool and transfer to an airtight box. The confit keeps well in the fridge for 2–3 weeks and is best left to mellow for 24 hours before serving.

Tarte Rosette Tricolore

Brune's white chocolate and berry tart, as pretty
as it is delicious.

For the base:
150g shortbread biscuits
100g dark chocolate (min 70 per cent cocoa), broken
  into pieces
30g butter
½ cup (60g) ground almonds

For the filling:
350g white chocolate, finely chopped
1 cup (250ml) full-fat crème fraîche
100g each blueberries and raspberries
250g small strawberries

1. Place the shortbread biscuits in a plastic bag and crush with a rolling pin (or blitz in a food processor) to make fine crumbs. Pour into a large bowl.

2. Gently melt the dark chocolate with the butter in a bowl over a pan of simmering water. Pour the chocolate butter on to the biscuit crumbs. Add the ground almonds and mix well. Spread the crumbs over the base and sides of a shallow 9½in (24cm) pie dish, pressing evenly to form the tart base. Refrigerate for 30 mins until firm.

3. In a small saucepan, gently heat the white chocolate with the crème fraîche, stirring until smooth and well blended. Spread over the cooled crust. Leave to rest at room temperature until the filling begins to set. Decorate with decreasing circles of the fruits to form a rosette pattern. Refrigerate the tart for at least 6 hours before serving.

The American Dream

'Kissing don't last: cookery do!'
George Meredith, 1828–1909,
English novelist and poet

Matt was spending a few months in Montpellier, in the beautiful Languedoc region of southern France. He'd always dreamt of going abroad after his graduation. The deal was that his parents would pay all his expenses, so long as Matt came back afterwards to work at his father's company, near Los Angeles. There he would settle down to a comfortable life exactly like his parents had.

Matt had chosen Montpellier because Madame Cabanel, who'd taught him French at college, came from the city. He had so much admiration for this attractive, witty woman. She'd told him that to become a citizen of the world, you should live in at least one foreign country for a few months, an experience that would shape, define and strengthen even the dullest personality. She'd also passed on to Matt a real passion for France. If there was one country he simply had to discover before he started his career back home, it was France.

Matt was eager to visit all the places Madame Cabanel

had mentioned in her classes. During the week, he stayed in Montpellier and studied international business and European cinema. Then every weekend he drove his Citroën 2CV along the country roads to acquaint himself with this picturesque region. He wanted to discover places off the beaten track – '*la France profonde*', as he'd learnt to call it. He'd chosen to drive a 2CV in imitation of Madame Cabanel. She'd even had her little Citroën shipped over to California, a purple one. Matt's was anthracite grey, and he too was thinking about having it shipped home when he returned. His family and friends would probably make fun of him, since they all drove big, gas-guzzling American cars, but he didn't care. Actually, he thought, he'd probably buy a basic, reliable car to take him to and from work and keep the 2CV just for his own amusement.

He had a list of restaurants that Madame Cabanel had recommended. She'd also written a few comments about each place. That Sunday Matt decided to lunch at Chez Bastien, which she'd maintained was one of the most authentic in the region.

He enjoyed driving on the narrow roads, listening to an interesting French singer he'd just discovered, Benjamin Biolay. Although Matt didn't understand all the lyrics, he liked the music and the sounds of the words. He knew that the song he was listening to was about *le Rêve Américain* and his home town of Los Angeles, and this added an extra dimension to his enjoyment of the music.

The village that was home to the restaurant was lovely, with a jumble of old stone houses with faded terracotta roofs. In contrast, Chez Bastien, with its yellow façade and bright-blue shutters, stood conspicuously at the edge of the town's only square.

Matt parked his grey 2CV in front of a big house. Crimson geraniums bloomed at every window. He got out and started walking slowly towards Chez Bastien, taking his time to look around and enjoy the sweet, dusty aroma of the village. He crossed the square. A simple ancient fountain decorated with baskets of geraniums added some freshness to the hot air, and there was welcome shade from a stand of plane trees. The inevitable group of old men, a few sporting berets, most of them with cigarettes in the corners of their mouths – the sort of men you would find in any European village, generally sitting on a bench in the shade of the trees – were watching with interest as another group played a game of *pétanque* on one side of the square. A few farmers were selling their produce from stands set up under the trees: goat's cheese, honey, dried sausages, olives and olive oil, hand-made soaps …

Matt bought some olives, for which he'd acquired a real passion. He found the olives in this part of the world – soaked in their own oils, along with lemon juice, garlic and *herbes de Provence* – a luscious delight, much tastier than the ones back home.

He felt as if he'd discovered a little piece of heaven in this French village. His eyes were captivated by its beauty, his senses taking in the enticing smells of the food and the sun-warmed air. He had a feeling of being utterly alive such as he'd never experienced before. Madame Cabanel had been right: this place was very special. A good meal would add the final touch to this visit to paradise.

Matt approached the restaurant full of eager anticipation. He entered the elaborate wrought-iron gate over which a carved wooden sign announced brightly: 'Chez Bastien'. On the restaurant's terrace were four or five circular tables awaiting customers, set with blue and white gingham tablecloths and small vases of fresh lavender and yellow roses. Mauve wisteria and crimson roses climbed up a wooden fence and spread to the yellow stone wall of the restaurant.

There were enough trees to shade most of the tables from the harsh August sun.

On the other part of the terrace stood a few bistro *guéridon* tables, where some people who appeared to be regulars were having their aperitifs, chatting merrily while sipping glasses of muscat wine from the region or chilled cloudy-white pastis, the quintessential drink of the Midi, munching olives and squares of toasted bread thickly spread with home-made olive tapenade.

Matt looked at his watch: eleven fifty. It was too early for Sunday lunch. He certainly would not be served before noon. He decided to explore the village for a while longer, even though it was becoming quite hot, although the dry heat was bearable and a pleasant little breeze rustled the leaves of the plane trees.

He walked back past the old villagers sitting on their bench. '*Encore un étranger certainement,*' he imagined them saying to themselves. Their intense study of him made him feel even more conspicuous.

Matt didn't look French, in spite of doing his utmost to play the part of a young Frenchman, with his Lacoste polo shirt and 2CV. At least, these were some of the things that he believed to be essential if one wanted to pass for French.

A bit past noon, and after an enjoyable walk through the streets of the village, Matt returned to Chez Bastien and sat down at one of the small tables on the terrace. He bent his head to the tiny vase to smell the subtle perfume of the lavender and yellow roses.

'*Bonjour, Monsieur, vous prendrez un apéritif?*' asked a thin young man who had appeared from inside the restaurant. He was polite; not friendly, just professional.

'*Une Mauresque, s'il vous plaît.*'

The waiter went to get Matt's Mauresque, a drink made of pastis and orgeat – anise liqueur mixed with almond syrup and water – that had become his chosen aperitif lately, to accompany the seemingly endless varieties of olives that he continued to discover.

Matt considered it a victory when the French understood what he said, because his pronunciation was terrible. He was trying hard, but just couldn't seem to master it. He began carefully studying the menu, which was beautifully handwritten. The list of dishes was hardly extensive – meaning that every item must be fresh.

The menu declared that the *magret de canard à la sauge miellée* was the speciality at Chez Bastien.

Matt had treated himself to a long lunch every Sunday since he'd been in Languedoc, making this his third. Back home, the whole family used to sit down together for a barbecue on Sundays. It was the only meal that they were all able to share, as during the rest of the week everyone was so busy.

Suddenly a young woman came running into the restaurant. Matt, absorbed by his study of the menu and his pocket dictionary, and savouring his tapenade on toast, glanced up in time to see that she was quite beautiful.

The chef of Chez Bastien, a man with a jovial round face and curly salt-and-pepper hair, began a round of the tables, describing the day's specialities. Most of the customers evidently knew him well. Matt found the chef very friendly and he even understood everything his host said, though he spoke quickly and with a thick Midi accent.

'I was thinking of the *magret de canard à la sauge miellée* for my main course.'

The chef was visibly pleased. 'You couldn't make a better choice, Monsieur, one of my finest dishes. May I recommend my *cuvée réservée*, from the Coteaux du Languedoc – an excellent red wine from the region?'

'*Avec plaisir!*'

And the genial host proceeded to the next table, greeting the customers with his broad smile.

What a happy man, who really seems passionate about his work, thought Matt. He had never seen his father nearly as satisfied with his job, even though he made lots of money.

Matt appreciated chefs who took the time to speak to their customers about what they were cooking for them; he felt it created a real human connection. After all, he reasoned, restaurants should reflect the personality of the man or woman in the kitchen, and these chefs who worked so hard to produce authentic regional food truly deserved the recognition they received.

Matt returned to his study of the menu.

'*Bonjour, Monsieur. Vous avez choisi?*' asked an enchanting voice.

The waitress at Matt's table was the young woman who'd run past a few minutes before. She looked into his eyes and gave him a welcoming smile.

Matt was stunned. She was the most gorgeous woman he had ever seen! A natural beauty: wavy auburn hair, green almond-shaped eyes, a voluptuous body – from what he could see, at any rate. He gazed back at her, his mouth open as if he'd suddenly lost his wits.

The waitress seemed to be accustomed to the effect she had on men and she paid no attention to Matt's awe-struck expression. She repeated her question, and Matt detected her delightful accent *du Midi*.

'Have you chosen, Monsieur?'

Matt could only stammer a few words, so taken aback was he by the waitress's beauty, and he wondered whether he'd drunk his Mauresque a bit too quickly, or if the heat was getting to him.

'Please … er, give me … er, a few more minutes.'

'I'll come back. Take your time.'

She went to another table.

Looking back at the menu, Matt realised that the more he ordered, the longer he could stay and watch the waitress. She was now chatting with diners who seemed to know her, surely *des habitués*. They spoke to her in the familiar way that they had to the chef. Obviously the restaurant was a relaxed place where local people came to meet their family and friends in a convivial atmosphere and to enjoy the good food together.

By the time the waitress came back Matt was ready to order. When he looked at her, the number two sprang into his mind; he wanted to order two of everything: two appetisers, two main courses, two desserts, two glasses of wine! *Two* seemed to have been burnt into his brain.

Two, two, two … Never had he had the desire to be *two* like that with anyone before. He had a girlfriend back home, Courtney-Ann, from a good family, like his. She was waiting for him but suddenly he didn't really care any more. There was also a girl from Denmark, Agnete, whom he'd met at his European cinema class the day after arriving in France. He'd seen her once in a while, but she was too much of a typical Scandinavian feminist for his taste, nearly as annoying as so many American girls he'd known.

Matt, who considered himself something of a ladies' man, wondered if he'd change for ever after meeting this beautiful waitress from Chez Bastien. Perhaps she'd win his heart for good. Maybe *le coup de foudre* wasn't just a myth after all.

He lingered over his meal; he wanted to feast his eyes on the waitress for as long as he could. And what a meal it was, certainly one to be enjoyed at a leisurely pace. Every mouthful was a sensation, especially the *magret de canard à la sauge miellée*! And the full-bodied red wine tasted very pleasantly of blackcurrant.

Once again, Matt felt he was in heaven. And he savoured this glimpse of paradise even while knowing it wouldn't last, since he'd have to go back to Montpellier later that day, and, eventually, back to his real life in Los Angeles.

It took such a long time to enjoy his two appetisers, his two main courses, and his two desserts that, by the time he'd nearly finished, only he and one other couple remained at Chez Bastien. It was almost three o'clock.

The waitress approached his table.

'*Excusez-moi, Monsieur.* I have to leave, but the other waiter will take care of you. *Au revoir, Monsieur.* I hope you enjoyed your meal. And we hope to see you again!'

'*Au revoir, Mademoiselle. Et peut-être à bientôt!*' Matt managed to reply.

As the waitress was about to leave, Matt saw the chef, with his friendly round face, calling to her to bring back some fresh bread later on. He could hear that her name was ... what? *Paprika?* What a curious name, unless he'd misunderstood ...

Paprika left in the same carefree rush as she'd arrived. But she didn't realise that she was leaving behind a devastated Matt, who was afraid that he would never see her again. His second dessert, *yaourt glacé à l'olive et au miel*, seemed to have lost much of its flavour now that she'd gone.

As she cycled to her sister's house not far from the village, Paprika remembered how funny the young man sitting at the small table had been. He was rather charming, in a way. English, American? His accent was quite terrible. Thinking of him, she laughed out loud.

Another week had gone by at the university. Matt had not stopped thinking about Paprika for a moment. He'd decided to have Sunday lunch at Chez Bastien again. He'd even told Agnete that he didn't think they should see each other any more. She hadn't seemed to be bothered. He'd also thought about writing a letter back home to Courtney-Ann, ending their relationship.

Matt got in his 2CV and drove to the village. He felt like a knight ready to sally forth and win his lady. At Chez Bastien Paprika seemed pleased to see him and he was encouraged by her warm greeting.

'*Ah, bonjour, Monsieur. Vous revoilà!* I remember you,' she said with a big smile. 'You're the one who ate so much last week.'

He is quite attractive, she thought.

Matt reddened at the memory of all the food he'd eaten. Paprika, thinking that her remark might have embarrassed him, tried to make up for it.

'It shows how much you appreciate my father's cooking. You seem to be a connoisseur of good food and wine. Where are you from?'

'I'm American, from California.'

Paprika didn't appear impressed, unlike some European girls he'd met. She didn't say anything right away. She seemed to be momentarily lost in thought.

Actually, when she heard Matt was from California, she understood why he ate so much, since Americans tended to complain about how small the portions were in French restaurants. And her father was careful about not serving too much food, but just enough for French palates. That probably explained why this young man had ordered two of each course.

'Would you like an aperitif?' she asked suddenly. 'On

the house,' she added, smiling.

'In that case, a Mauresque, *s'il vous plaît*!'

'*Tout de suite.*'

But today, even if Matt wanted to eke out his lunch over several hours, he resolved to choose only one appetiser, one main course and one dessert from the menu, with one or two glasses of the wine he'd had last week from the Coteaux du Languedoc. He really had eaten too much last Sunday and he'd felt a bit sick afterwards.

He hoped that Paprika wouldn't leave before he'd finished his meal, as she had last week.

But by the time Matt was finally having coffee, she was still there, busy with the other tables.

He decided to offer her a drink. She accepted, asking the other waiter to cover for her for a few minutes. She sat down across from Matt so naturally, without any fuss, which really impressed him. '*Pas de chichi*,' Madame Cabanel would have said.

The beautiful waitress suggested that he taste the Muscat de Frontignan.

Matt loved this naturally sweet wine, with its rich gold colour, served chilled.

The two of them sat languorously under the shady trees that surrounded the restaurant tables, facing each other in perfect symmetry, chatting good-humouredly, she about her beloved village, he about California and America. They were both genuinely interested in each other's lives, especially Matt, who was enchanted by this gentle, civilised world and wanted to know more about Paprika and her life.

'I heard your father call you Paprika. I've never heard a name like that before.'

'Well, that's my name, all right, and there's a little story behind it. My mother is from Hungary. You may know that the best paprika comes from there. My father wanted to call me Patricia and my mother wanted to give me a Hungarian name. My grandmother said: "Call her Paprika, then." Of course, the name was not accepted at the town hall. My real first name is Patricia, but everyone calls me Paprika. And I'm lucky that my hair is naturally auburn, just like the spice,' she added, laughing.

'I like your name. It suits you,' Matt said. 'Your mother's origins also explain the goulash *à la languedocienne* on the menu. I'll have to taste it next week.'

When Matt left, he was feeling especially happy because Paprika had asked him to come to the *fête du village*, which started the following Friday night.

He vowed to be there for sure.

While driving back to Montpellier in his 2CV, he began dreaming. How proud his family would be if he brought a gorgeous Frenchwoman like Paprika back home with him!

A few weeks passed and Matt had become a real *habitué* of Chez Bastien. More than that, he was dating the most beautiful girl in the village.

Daddy Bastien – which was what Matt called Paprika's father – had opened his kitchen to '*l'Américaing*', as he called Matt. Matt was eager to learn how to combine the different magical ingredients used in this *cuisine du soleil*. It was all new to him, as he had been banned from the kitchen at home where most of the time his mother would simply reheat takeaway food, and neither of his parents would allow their children to help at the sacred Sunday barbecue.

Matt had been introduced to Mara, Paprika's mother, whom he found very entertaining, with her flamboyant personality and the charm of her strong Hungarian accent. She made him feel better about his own French pronunciation. Mara didn't work at the restaurant but ran a small beauty salon in a town nearby, though she came to Chez Bastien once in a while, each time sporting a new hairstyle or colour.

Paprika also had a sister, who lived on a farm three miles from the village. She was happily married and had three fun children. She and her husband grew olive trees, produced their own olive oil, and made the most exquisite goat's cheese wrapped in olive leaves – the best Matt had ever tasted.

Matt hadn't known that family life could be as happy as Paprika's, where they all really loved and respected one another; apart, that is, from on American TV shows like *Little House on the Prairie* or *The Brady Bunch*, which his kid sister used to be addicted to.

Was it because of the calm, healthy environment the Bastiens lived in? They seemed to be so far away from the craziness of the wider world, where you needed to prove every day that you were better than everyone else.

These people were not wealthy in the American middle-class sense that Matt understood as well-off, but they seemed to live so peacefully, to appreciate what they had, to spend time together, and they did so in harmony with the rhythm and ritual of the seasons. In their lives they knew what really mattered, Matt thought.

Matt's idyllic sojourn in the sun of Languedoc was due to end in a few weeks. Soon he'd have to go back home to his world, where a fast-paced, competitive working environment awaited him. This was what he knew best, and what motivated him. Neither he nor Paprika had ever talked about the day when Matt would have to return to California, as if, by not mentioning it, their time together might last for ever.

Eventually, though, Matt knew that he must speak to Paprika about leaving.

He took her to a nice restaurant in the town where Mara had her beauty salon.

They sat at a table and read the menu in silence, both wondering who would be the first to mention his departure.

'Well, Paprika, I think we need to talk,' said Matt in a cheerful tone, because he had an idea that had occurred to him only the second time he'd seen her – that she could come with him. He had even spoken to his family about it. They couldn't wait to meet her – 'She seems so wonderful!' – and they'd found her very attractive in the picture Matt had sent them. They'd never really liked Courtney-Ann anyhow. She talked too much.

Matt and his parents had everything settled: an ideal future. Paprika could live with them in Los Angeles, so long as Matt came home for good. She would be able to go back to France to visit her family whenever she wanted, and her family would be able to come and visit them in California. Matt would be the happiest man in the world. He loved his dad's business and knew that one day he would become company president. Everything had been carefully planned.

Paprika guessed what Matt wanted to say. She was aware that he had to leave in two weeks, and this upset her because she loved him very much.

'You know that I'm leaving in a couple of weeks?' said Matt.

'Um ... um ...' Paprika answered evasively, her eyes on the menu.

'Well, since I really want us to be together, I was wondering if you would like to come with me to California. The beaches near LA are spectacular! Everyone there will love you and my family will be thrilled to meet you.' He said all this quickly, but with a good deal of confidence.

'Um ... um ...' repeated Paprika.

'Do you understand me? I'm inviting you to come and share my life in California!'

'Of course I understand you. But why don't *you* stay here? Why should I be the one to follow you?'

Matt had not expected this reaction at all. Paprika knew that he had to go back home and start working for a living. He couldn't disappoint his parents.

'Don't you like it here?' she asked, her eyes sad.

'Of course, I love it here. But we've both always known that I was only going to be here for a little while.'

'I had hoped that you might want to stay.'

Matt didn't answer. He was somewhat stunned by the direction the conversation had taken.

'Everything seems to be so calculated in your life,' said Paprika, still sad but very calm.

'Come on, Paprika, you know that I've got a big career waiting for me over there.' Matt wanted to persuade her. 'That's the deal I made with my parents that enabled me to come to Languedoc in the first place.'

'Sure, I know. But what about my career?' she asked.

'What career?'

As soon as these words were out of his mouth, he regretted them.

'I know that I'm only a waitress …'

'That's not what I meant. You're not only a great waitress, you make the place work. But you could get a job at any restaurant you wanted to in LA.'

'And your wealthy friends would make fun of you because you were dating a waitress.'

Matt hadn't thought of this, and it was true that the way he'd presented Paprika to his parents might possibly have been a little exaggerated. They might well think that she was the manager of an exclusive luxury restaurant. That was pretty much what she was, of course, but on a far smaller scale than the ones his family were used to.

'My father will help you get your own restaurant.'

'Oh, right! Of course, here is a typical new chapter of the insatiable American dream! Matt, give me a break, will you?' She rolled her eyes.

'You could call it Chez Bastien.'

'Stop it!'

He was beginning to get desperate. 'Actually, you won't even need to work.'

Matt didn't know what else he could say to persuade Paprika to come with him.

'And of course, Matt, you don't know how to do anything besides manage your father's business.'

'That's basically true,' admitted Matt. He'd worked there on and off since he was sixteen. His dad's company was his real world, the one he knew best.

'What kind of work could I do here then?' he asked her.

'Work with Daddy Bastien in the kitchen.'

He'd enjoy that, and he'd also fallen in love with Languedoc and Paprika's world, but he'd never even considered staying here. His father was counting on him to work for the company. Again, he tried to explain.

Her response came quickly.

'My father is counting on me at Chez Bastien, and I'll take over later on when he retires. Pretty much like you and your dad's company.'

'But I thought you loved me.'

'I love you, yes, but I don't want to give up my life here. I live in a beautiful sunny country that I adore, I've a great family that I get along with, I enjoy good healthy food that is fresh and seasonal. I don't like to rush all the time like you crazy Americans, who just think about making money, and then more money, to add to your insipid, materialistic lifestyle!'

Matt was taken aback. Paprika had never spoken to him like that before, but he decided to have one last try.

'But you won't have to rush in California, and it's a place that also has a lot to offer, you know. The food is good there as well, and there's plenty of sunshine. We could have a big house with a swimming pool; you'll have your own car, anything you want.'

'You just don't get it! What I want is here!' she said firmly. Then she continued in a milder tone, 'Maybe I could have all that you want to give me, and thank you for offering it to me, but I'm not interested. What I want is here. What you want to give me is not for an unpretentious person like me who is content with the little things in life.'

'You just need some time to think it over.'

'Matt, actually, for the first time since I met you, I'm a little disappointed in you. You seem to have decided for the two of us. Listen, I'll never follow you, and I know you'll never stay here. I can picture your life over there, with your important business career – competing all the time in order to be the best and to make as much money as you can. What you call happiness in your world I call superficiality. You hardly take any holiday and you barely stop to eat properly or spend time with your family, who smile all the time but with whom you don't really communicate. You told me so yourself, didn't you?'

'People seem to be in just as much of a rush in French cities.'

'Maybe, but you will never take away their five weeks of holiday, or the ritual of enjoying good food and company. As for rushing all the time, you're right. I studied in Montpellier for a while but I couldn't stand it: too many people running around constantly, and so many cars! I'm not a city girl. The life I want is in my village, in the country. I rarely listen to the news and stay away from newspapers because I don't want my happiness spoilt by the ugliness of a world I want to avoid as much as I can.'

Matt suddenly realised that he hadn't minded being cut off from the world since he'd met Paprika.

'And as for my career – and since "career" is such an important word for people like you – I'm going to take over my father's restaurant, as I said earlier, and keep on living as long as I can in the peaceful atmosphere of this place. You know, some people would like my father to have a bigger restaurant, to expand his business, but what for? Why can't people appreciate what they have? Why do they always want more? Chez Bastien is special because its size allows it to be authentic. We want to serve the *terroir* of Languedoc to our customers. My father likes working in the kitchen and coming out to talk to his customers, as you know. Of course, that may not seem very ambitious to people like you, but ambition doesn't bring happiness most of the time. And money? We have enough money for what we want in life. Money can't give us time to share with family and friends.'

Matt paused to think, then said, 'You have a point, but I'm afraid that I can't live like that all the time.'

'Yes, you're realising now that you've been in a holiday mindset for a few months and now it has to come to an end. Actually, I hope you enjoyed it because you may not be able to take a break for a long time now.'

Matt knew she was right.

'I love you so much, Paprika,' he sighed. 'I thought that you loved me as well.'

'I love you very much, and maybe more than you realise. I think we have genuinely strong feelings for each other. However, neither of us is ready to follow the other, and if one of us does, it might spoil what we have.'

'I'll never meet anyone like you again.'

'You won't because you'll never be in this situation. I don't know if I'll meet anyone or not. I don't know if I'll have children or not. I'd like to, in a way, and I hope they'll appreciate the peaceful life I have to offer them, as my sister's children do. I hope they won't be spoilt by the ugliness of the world.'

She stopped, took a sip of her water, sighed loudly, and went on, 'But I still have a few years of freedom in front of me. If I had been unhappy with my life here in my little bubble, I might have followed you. But I'm just too happy here.'

They sat for a moment in silence. Matt didn't quite know what to say or do.

'Let's have a toast!' Paprika announced. 'To your successful, glamorous life, and to the continuation of my simple little existence!'

The cheerful clinking of the champagne flutes erased their sad thoughts of the future without each other. What Matt and Paprika both wanted was to make the most of the little time they had left together.

Matt's Beloved Recipes from Bastien's Kitchen

Tapenade Maison (Black Olive Spread)

Enjoy this punchy spread with crackers, fresh or
toasted baguette, or pasta.
Makes about 500g.

2 slices toasted white or brown bread
2 cups (250g) pitted black olives, rinsed and drained
4 tinned salted anchovies, rinsed and drained
½ cup (80g) capers, rinsed and drained
½ cup (80g) sundried tomatoes, drained
2 garlic cloves, chopped
3 tbsp pastis or grappa (optional)
1 tbsp dried *herbes de Provence*
3 tbsp extra-virgin olive oil
3 tbsp lemon juice

Place the toasted bread into a food processor and blitz
to make crumbs. Add all the remaining ingredients and
blend to a smooth paste. Transfer into jars or an airtight
container. The tapenade can be stored in the fridge for 2
weeks.

Magrets de Canard à la Sauge Miellée
(Duck Breasts with Honey and Sage Sauce)

Daddy Bastien's house speciality
serves 4.

4 duck breasts, skin on
5 fresh sage leaves, chopped
4 tbsp honey
sea salt and ground black pepper

In a dry frying pan, cook the duck breasts over a medium heat, skin-side down first, until medium rare to well done (about 8–10 mins skin-side, 2–4 mins other side). Set aside to rest, covered, on a warm plate. Return the pan to the heat and add the sage and honey to the duck fat. Heat gently, stirring, until the honey is melted and bubbling. Return the meat to the pan and heat for 1 minute. Season with salt and pepper, to taste. The *magrets de canard* are particularly good served with sautéed parsnips.

Goulash à la Languedocienne

This traditional stew from Hungary with a
Languedoc twist serves 4.

800g beef stewing steak or lamb, cut into 1 in (2cm) chunks
sea salt and ground black pepper

3 tbsp extra-virgin olive oil
1–2 tbsp paprika, plus extra to serve
4 onions, chopped
4 large tomatoes, roughly chopped
1 aubergine, cut in half lengthways, then sliced into
   slim wedges
1 cup (250ml) red wine from Languedoc
1 tbsp chopped fresh thyme leaves
1 cup (120g) black olives
2 tbsp crème fraîche or sour cream

1. Season the beef well with salt and pepper. Heat 2 tbsp olive oil in a large, lidded frying pan and sauté the beef until browned on all sides. Add the paprika, onions, tomatoes and aubergine and sauté for 4–5 mins, until beginning to soften. Add the wine and thyme and bring to the boil, then reduce the heat, cover and simmer gently for an hour, stirring occasionally.

2. When the stew is ready, add the black olives and heat for a couple more minutes. Season to taste and transfer to a serving dish. In a bowl, mix the crème fraîche or sour cream with the remaining 1 tbsp olive oil. Drizzle the mixture over the stew, sprinkle with paprika and serve immediately. The goulash *à la languedocienne* is very good served with pasta or boiled potatoes.

Yaourt Glacé à l'Huile d'Olive et au Miel
(Olive Oil and Honey Frozen Yogurt)

A very popular and refreshing way of finishing a good
meal at Chez Bastien. Serves 4.

3 tbsp good-quality runny honey
2 tbsp extra-virgin olive oil
juice of ½ lemon
500g thick Greek-style yogurt

In a bowl, slowly mix the honey with the olive oil until
well blended. Add the lemon juice and yogurt and stir
gently. Refrigerate for at least 2 hours, then transfer to an
ice-cream maker and churn according to the instructions.
Serve immediately or store in the freezer until required,
allowing the frozen yogurt to soften slightly in the fridge
before serving.

September

A Taste of Summer in Burgundy

> *'When from a long-distant past nothing subsists*
> *after the things are broken and scattered,*
> *the smell and taste of things remain.'*
> Marcel Proust, 1871–1922,
> French writer

'Antoine!' I cried, overjoyed to see him after so long.

'Julie, how many years has it been since you were back here?'

Time goes by so fast … too fast. I stood there, trying to remember.

'I'm not sure now … four, five?'

'Definitely too long,' muttered Antoine, glaring at me. 'You haven't changed a bit.'

I wouldn't tell him that I thought he looked older. Or maybe he was simply tired?

'Hello, Delphine.' Antoine kissed our friend who I was staying with and who had come with me to the farm.

All of a sudden none of us wanted to talk, even though there were so many things to be said. Here we were, silently thinking about our shared past. Our eyes took in the beautiful countryside, like a green patchwork that covered the hills and plateaux. Right in the middle lay the small village, with its Roman church, the faithful sentinel.

Antoine's imposing stone house stood proudly on a hill. A little breeze caressed our faces. The future would always be uncertain, but we knew our fondest memories would always be here.

I was ready to sit down, delighted and melancholy at the same time: two feelings that I always had when I came back to spend a holiday in the south of Burgundy, where I'd grown up. The big table on the terrace around which we were all gathered had been nicely set for the meal and I began to feel very hungry.

Suddenly strident screams broke the silence and shattered our tranquil thoughts. Two young boys wearing cowboy outfits came tearing out of the house. They seemed a little overexcited.

'Bang, bang! You're dead. I got you,' shouted one to the other, who pretended to be dead.

'Mathis and Bruno, can't you just behave for once?' Antoine said firmly. 'Come and meet Julie.'

Antoine's strict tone of voice surprised me – that was something I didn't remember.

'Hi, Julie!' the two boys chorused in unison.

After I'd kissed them, Mathis, who seemed to be the bolder one, began: 'Dad told us you live in Chicago ...'

'Do you see Indians there often?' asked Bruno.

'Not Indians, stupid: gangsters!'

'Bang, bang!'

I could see that the legends of the Wild West, as well as the Chicago of Al Capone's time, were still alive in the Old World, as I liked to call Europe. Of course, I guessed immediately why Antoine's kids were so interested in these mythical aspects of America.

Mathis was keen to know more. 'Is it true that—'

He didn't have time to finish his sentence. At that moment a woman appeared on the terrace and Antoine held up his hand to silence the excited boy.

'Hello, Gégé,' I said, getting up from my chair. 'I'm so happy to see you.'

If I thought that Antoine had got older, Gégé hadn't changed at all. She was also very welcoming but, unlike her husband, didn't seem to be stressed out. Her smile was warm and her voice was smooth. She was still chubby, like many women I'd met who lived in the countryside, but it suited her. Her cheeks were rosy, proof of a healthy life in vivifying air.

'Let's have an aperitif,' she said.

Within seconds, home-made pâtés, cured ham, dried sausages, and *pain de campagne* were brought out. Everything looked delicious. How long had it been since I'd eaten farm produce like this?

I was happy to see that Gégé continued the tradition of rural Burgundy hospitality. In Antoine's house I knew it couldn't be any other way.

The boys both wanted to sit beside me and had endless questions to ask about the Wild West and 'gangsterland' Chicago. But Antoine wanted them to sit on the other side of the table so that he could be near me himself.

'Later then?' implored Mathis.

'Sure,' I answered with a big smile.

But rather than sitting at the table, Mathis and Bruno

began to slope off back indoors.

'Where do you think you're going? Stay here, we're about to have dinner!' shouted Antoine.

'We don't really want any of that, and since we can't talk to Julie—'

'"Any of that" is what's for dinner tonight, boys. Besides—'

'Antoine,' Gégé interrupted smoothly, 'they wanted burgers tonight because, with Julie here, it's like an American evening for them.'

'*Les hamburgers micros: trop cool!*' the boys piped up.

Gégé's tone was so sweet that I'd have thought it would evaporate almost anyone's anger – but not Antoine's.

'Oh, yes, nowadays children dictate what they want to eat. I forgot!' he said sharply. 'And microwaved burgers as well! Bravo, Géraldine!'

I remembered then that Antoine tended to call his wife by her full name only when he was in a temper.

I could see that Gégé wasn't happy about Antoine's comment, but she didn't answer back. Looking at me, she simply said, 'It's rather hard to please everyone. And you know, Julie, I wasn't going to cook hamburgers for you! That would have been sacrilegious!'

Should Antoine have allowed Mathis and Bruno to sit near me? Would they have stayed longer at the table then? I didn't know enough about children to answer these questions, but I could see that they seemed to be like so many kids in America with bad eating habits. But here, in this part of the world, and on a farm where the food was so good, I was surprised that Gégé was microwaving

212

hamburgers for her children. Was it a way to pacify them, or was it really because it was a sort of American evening for them in my honour?

Once again, I contemplated the beautiful countryside around me, which would have been mine if I had stayed here instead of trying to find myself in the 'New World' – as I called America.

The little white dots scattered across the green fields, framed by hedgerows and trees were Charolais cattle, which matured slowly, at nature's pace. How long had it been since I'd sat on a terrace like this one and gazed at such a peaceful, bucolic scene?

Gégé asked me if I wanted a kir, and of course I accepted.

When our drinks were served, we proposed a toast: 'To us, back together again.'

The *petit vin blanc* that Antoine bought from a friend who had a few acres of vineyards nearby was unpretentious and full of flavour – completely to my taste. I often find American wines too overwrought; there's nothing better than a simple, earthy wine. It's the same with food: it's better to let its natural characteristics shine through rather than adding extra ones that might spoil its authenticity.

Gégé made her own crème de cassis. Added to the wine, it made the best kir I'd ever had, in part because I was drinking it here, in this convivial atmosphere, and in the very landscape in which everything we ate and drank had been produced.

I wanted to go back to the past, to when my parents were still alive. They, my brother and I used to eat at the big table in the garden just as we were doing that evening on Antoine's terrace. Wine was always on the table, even when we were children. I remembered Sunday lunches when we would put a tablespoon of red burgundy into our water to add some colour to it.

The kir was bringing back more memories, just as the famous madeleine had for Proust. But I didn't have time to write hundreds of pages about it. Besides, nothing needed to be written down; everything was etched into my memory.

Enough nostalgia for the past!

'How is your brother?' asked Antoine. 'I don't think he's ever been back here since your parents passed away.'

'No, he hasn't. He's fine, thank you. He still lives in Singapore. He comes to see me in Chicago once a year with his girlfriend. They have an adorable little girl.'

I started talking about my life in Chicago, which seemed almost surreal now, in this southern Burgundy countryside. Everyone listened as they drank their aperitifs. The hors d'oeuvres were as delicious as they looked.

Then Gégé brought out my favourite dish. Antoine had evidently remembered and told his wife about it. How thoughtful of him. *Fromage blanc à la crème et pommes de terre nouvelles en robe des champs.* Yummy!

There was also an exquisite green salad with boiled eggs and bacon. I was already feeling a little full after all the appetisers, but I couldn't resist.

By now, I was totally contented, and I wished I could stay for ever in the midst of this beautiful tableau, which I had a naïve tendency to idealise: a sumptuous meal composed of fresh and delectable foods, with the perfect family consisting of mother, father and two kids, in a pretty house, surrounded by lovely serene landscape.

This was what I would have had if only ...

I met Antoine's gaze and I guessed his thoughts were running along the same lines.

If things had been different we would have been living here together; or over there, in his own American dream. Antoine had always wanted to go to the American West but he'd never done so. I knew I represented his dream because I was the one who'd gone away. He'd never followed.

I might have achieved his ambition, but did his situation correspond to my image of a perfect family life?

Were we both disenchanted by the reality of our dreams or illusions: the American West being no more than a faded legend, and Antoine's perfect family life being not quite so perfect after all?

I could feel some tension between Antoine and his wife and kids. The boys not eating with us had been a disappointment for me.

I didn't really want to think about family dramas. I've never understood why people from the same family, bound by blood, just can't get along. They should stick together since the outside world often isn't easy to face.

I suppose it was because of these cheerless thoughts I had about families that I was still living by myself at thirty-four, believing that happiness didn't depend on having a family of my own.

I was once again staring at the landscape while my thoughts kept drifting back to a golden past. Meanwhile,

Delphine and Gégé were deep in conversation.

Suddenly I heard Antoine asking, 'Why aren't you moving back, Julie? You keep looking longingly at the landscape,' and his question broke the spell of my nostalgia.

'I'll never move back here, Antoine, and you know it.'

He sighed and got up to serve another round of drinks.

How could I ever come back here? I was too different now. And let's face it: had the place been that great, would I have left in the first place? When I'd been at high school I'd found everything boring because my brother was always talking about exotic countries, and it had made me long to see the world even though I'd had a boyfriend I'd been really, really attached to – Antoine. Antoine had wanted to go away, too, but he hadn't done anything to make it happen, preferring instead to travel vicariously through films, where everything had been exactly the way he'd wanted it to be, and where he had always been the hero.

I still didn't have a steady companion, but I did have an exciting life in Chicago. At least I believed so …

Once again, I didn't want to pursue the thought. I wanted to enjoy the company of the people I was with right then: Antoine and Delphine – my two dear childhood friends – and Gégé.

The *fromage blanc* was wonderful. I appreciated the produce of the *terroir* all the more each time I returned.

After the main course we took a break and started talking about people from the village and what had happened to them – still single, or married with kids or divorced, or dead, and so on.

We hadn't smiled much since the evening had begun. Too many memories, perhaps.

I needed the excitement of a big city. True, food-wise it wasn't as great in Chicago, nothing like as tasty as the food here, but I managed.

After my three friends wondered how I could survive without all this delicious food, I heard myself saying, 'Well, when you're open-minded, and if you cook yourself, you can live pretty much in any country and appreciate the local produce. You know, there is something that I really like back in the States: potlucks. I love the concept of every guest bringing a dish to a party. It's a good way to try all kinds of different foods, and they're all home-made. My friends and I agreed a strict rule at the outset that every dish had to be cooked from scratch.'

'That sounds interesting,' Antoine ventured. 'But when I'm invited to someone's home, I'm not supposed to cook, am I?'

'As if you ever do anything in the kitchen,' replied Gégé, her tone still disarmingly sweet. 'I think it's a good idea,' she added, probably reflecting that she could have cooked less for tonight, even if she had enjoyed it.

'Anyway, yours is the best pâté I've eaten for a long time,' I complimented her, 'and your *fromage* remains the most delicious of all the amazing things you make.'

Gégé made her own Charolais, a cheese that could be eaten fresh, slightly ripened, or hard, when it turned a pale bluish-grey. She stored the cheeses to dry them in small wooden cages, then stood them on racks to mature.

'Thanks,' Gégé answered. 'You see, when people are

217

too used to good things, they take them for granted.'

Antoine didn't say anything, but I sensed that the remark was aimed at him.

'You could export them to the US. You'd make a fortune.'

'And turn the pleasure of making hand-crafted cheese into a factory operation? No, thanks!' And she laughed for the first time that evening. 'Besides, American regulations concerning imported dairy products are ridiculous.'

Gégé and Antoine raised a few chickens, rabbits, goats and pigs besides their cattle. So they made all their own pâtés, ham and dried sausages, which represented a tremendous amount of work.

How long had we been sitting at the table? Night was beginning to fall. I wasn't sure I'd be able to get up from my chair very gracefully because I was a little tipsy, and I certainly felt full!

I was glad I was wearing a simple dress that wasn't too tight. I always brought this forgiving kind of clothing when I came to Burgundy, knowing that I'd eat a lot while I was away, as I was invited to the houses of so many old friends. Then I would go back to Chicago and start a serious diet to lose the three or four pounds I'd gained.

For dessert we had fresh red fruit from the garden: strawberries, gooseberries and raspberries served with crème fraîche from the farm. The taste of fruit and vegetables eaten in season was a revelation! How could I have forgotten it?

I loved the tart flavour of the berries as well as their ruby colour, which blended with the unctuous white crème fraîche: *un pur régal* for the eyes as well as the taste buds!

In Chicago, I ate strawberries or tomatoes all year round, but most of the time they were flavourless even if they looked perfect. I resolved to eat only seasonal local food from then on, and I promised myself I'd go to the pumpkin festival in Morton when I was back.

My aunt Denise had said the previous night that you could buy anything any time nowadays, even here in rural France. She'd taken as an example *foie gras*, which used to be reserved only for Christmas time, but was now available all year round. The possibility of having anything we want any time gives us more choice, of course, but it also means we lose some of the nice traditions linked to food, which were a way to celebrate both the food itself and the culture that went with it.

Gégé stood up. 'I'm sorry but I have to leave you,' she declared apologetically. 'I've got to go to a meeting of the town council. That's why we had an early dinner. I'm the mayor's assistant.'

'Of course, no problem,' Delphine and I said at the same time.

Gégé came over to me and we kissed each other.

'Julie, I'm so happy you came tonight. I hope to see you again before you go back to Chicago.' Then she murmured, 'Delphine has convinced me to come with her when she visits you. I'll leave the children with Antoine …'

'And then we can have a really nice girly time,' I replied, which provoked a duet of giggling.

Actually, I was rather surprised by Gégé's decision, but also overjoyed by it, and I told her so.

After Gégé had gone, Antoine looked at me in silence, though I could tell from his eyes what he was thinking.

I thought he was about to speak when we heard a cry from inside the house. He got up and quickly went to the kitchen, Delphine and I following in his wake. We were curious to see the next instalment in this family saga: how to react when your children are naughty.

The kids were running round the table, having an ice-cream fight. Their bowls were almost empty. Their Game Boys had been set aside, along with a couple of small empty Coca-Cola bottles.

Coca-Cola seemed to have replaced the wine-coloured water I used to have with my Sunday meal.

The TV was on, showing something that seemed a little too violent in my opinion.

What chaos! This scene didn't fit my idyllic picture of rural family life at all.

'Stop this!' shouted Antoine. 'You're going to clean up all this mess and then go to bed. No more ice cream for two weeks.'

'We don't care!' was the immediate response from Mathis.

'I don't want to go to bed now,' complained Bruno.

'After what you've done, it's definitely time for bed, and, besides, tomorrow you've got to get up early to go to school!' Antoine seized the Game Boys. 'Do as I say, or no more of these either.'

This seemed to have the desired effect and the boys started cleaning up right away.

Now I had the answer to the problem of what to do

when your children were naughty: confiscate their Game Boys. I don't like these gadgets; I believe they make children rather stupid.

Antoine turned the TV off, and after the boys had finished their cleaning up, he took them to their room. I waved good night to them.

'When are you coming back, Julie?' I heard Mathis asking sadly, but Antoine marched him away before I could answer.

Delphine and I went back to the terrace and sat in silence. After a while we started talking about her and Gégé's upcoming visit to Chicago.

'They'll leave us alone now because I told them that they wouldn't get their Game Boys back if they didn't go to sleep soon,' said Antoine bitterly when he returned, dumping the wretched things on the table. He sighed loudly. 'They both drive me nuts! They just don't appreciate what they've got here ...'

'Why is that?' I asked.

Antoine didn't answer. He was still irritated with his children.

'The evening started well. We were all happy to see you. They even wore their cowboy outfits for you, and—'

'I didn't spend much time with them,' I said apologetically.

'It's my fault; I wanted to talk to you in peace.'

Delphine and I both knew that Antoine was dying to spend time on his own with me, but I couldn't allow that because I knew he would only put into words what I'd read in his eyes earlier.

221

'And I'm not always that patient with them,' he confessed.

'Well, if I may say,' replied Delphine, 'like Jean-Denis and I, you and Gégé are both parents of the twenty-first century, working a lot – and more – on the farm, always ferrying the children around in the car, since children nowadays can't just enjoy being at home. They always need to be busy going to play some kind of sport when they are not playing on their computers or watching TV. Plus, Gégé's involvement with the town council takes time. The boys' friends at school also have parents who are very busy. It doesn't matter if they live in the countryside or not; they come home in the evening and their parents are too tired to spend time with them. Most children are just stuck in front of the TV, or left to play with their electronic games, and given whatever food they want to eat. On TV, they watch happy kids having happy pizza or burger meals from fast-food chains.'

'That's too much of a cliché! And not here in France, please!' I exclaimed.

'You're so naïve, Julie. Europe is changing. You don't have children; it's hard for you to understand what it's like,' Delphine replied.

'I know,' I said, acquiescing.

'Delphine is right,' sighed Antoine. 'Mathis and Bruno don't want to eat the healthy food from the farm. They say it's not cool; their friends at school eat processed junk food – even here in France, as you said. And then, because I'm tired I don't have time to be more strict, so I don't impose any rules for healthy eating on them. In fact, we hardly eat together.'

I was speechless. The idealised image of the family sitting round the dinner table talking about their day was fast disappearing from my mind.

'Things have changed here since you left. Lots of fast-food restaurants have opened and they're full most of the time.'

Delphine acknowledged what Antoine had said with a nod, looking at me with sad eyes.

'I didn't expect that at all,' I said quietly.

'And Gégé lets them do whatever they want, since she's the one who spends the most time with them,' added Antoine.

'That's easy to say,' Delphine replied quickly. 'Stop being so macho, Antoine! You pretend to be firm, but it seems to me that you leave far too much to Gégé. You are their father ...'

'But I work harder than she does.'

And I know you blame her because you married her on the rebound.

'Not so sure about that,' Delphine said. 'You know, I'm glad Jean-Denis isn't a dinosaur like you. I wouldn't have been able to stand it.'

Agreeing with her, I told Antoine how hard women worked nowadays, having to take care of the house *and* follow their own careers. Most men, even in the new millennium, didn't help around the house that much, after all, despite TV ads showing the occasional token man changing a nappy or cooking a meal, an apron tied round his waist.

'Do you take time with your kids at all?' I asked him next.

'It's not that easy. They sometimes follow me around the fields …'

'What do you do in the evening? You said that you don't even eat together.'

'We don't have the same schedule. Living on a farm is tough, you know. I eat later with Gégé, watching the news on TV.'

I could imagine how little conversation there would be. And how could anyone appreciate a meal with depressing images constantly on the screen?

'After the news, I usually put a movie on. I still love American Westerns and gangster films …'

'I wish we could have had an American Bourguignon evening with the boys. They were so happy to show me their cowboy outfits. Maybe we can do something at your house, Delphine, before I go. I'll cook American for everyone.'

'What a great idea!'

After we'd talked about how we were going to organise an American Bourguignon barbecue, Delphine went back to the issue of how things had changed.

'Life in the countryside isn't what it used to be, you know, even in our beloved Burgundy, Julie. It seems that local people eat less and less farm produce; they usually just sell it at the markets. The tourists who come from all over Europe love it.'

Could things have changed so much since I'd left fifteen years before? Did the changes seem so drastic because I didn't return very often? Tonight, I suspected, I'd seen a genuine picture of family life in the twenty-first century.

But were people so caught up in their daily lives that they failed to see the insidious changes eroding it little by little?

'My mother blames TV,' Delphine went on. 'She keeps reminding me that when she was growing up, she didn't have one. Sure, everyone was busy on the farm, but free time was spent together as a family, not living other people's lives through a TV screen. Maybe people back then were more naïve, but they were also more relaxed, and not constantly bombarded with images of violence and meanness on TV. Sometimes I worry that we're merely animals, avid for violence and destruction. Are we going back to a time when primal instincts were all that mattered?'

'There *are* people who can still appreciate the splendours the countryside has to offer,' I said, willing myself to be optimistic.

'The people who really appreciate it are the tourists Delphine mentioned earlier – mostly people from England, the Netherlands and Switzerland. They don't know how hard it is working in agriculture. Some of them buy the old farms that have been deserted because they can no longer be run profitably. The good thing is these people have the money to renovate the old properties tastefully, but none of this solves the problems of farming these days. The small farmer is finished anyhow, swallowed up by the big agricultural corporations,' explained Antoine.

It's not only in farming, actually. All the little fish in this world are being gobbled up by greedy bigger fish.

Delphine added, 'That's why my sister and her husband opened a rural guesthouse. When they saw how hard it was running my parents' farm, they decided to renovate it. They also sell home-made cheese and jam. There's not much money in it, but not so much stress either.'

'The countryside and its food seem to have become a tourist business, then,' I concluded.

'Yes, you could say that,' Delphine agreed. 'I'm afraid that the finest produce will soon only be available to an elite that can afford to pay for it.'

'This new trend is called *le tourisme rural*,' added Antoine. 'You know, Julie, tonight I felt a little upset because I didn't want to show you how things have changed here.'

Looking at the Game Boys on the table, Delphine said, 'When we were growing up, we didn't have all this technology that seem to control life nowadays – computers, TVs, DVDs, mobile phones and so on. Do you remember how much fun we had when we played outside, even if it was wintertime?'

'Mathis and Bruno play with their stupid Game Boys most of the time. I confess that we bought them for them. But we had to, otherwise they would have felt different from their friends at school,' Antoine explained quietly.

I thought sadly about my neighbourhood in Chicago, where I never saw any children playing outside.

'Yes, things have changed.'

The three of us sighed loudly, our eyes wandering the dark landscape of the night.

'But we have to live in the present and make the most of it,' Delphine said, determined to be positive. 'Antoine, bring us some of your vieux marc de Bourgogne. That will perk us up a bit!'

Antoine nodded and got up quickly to get his famous homemade brandy that warmed the heart and soul.

I knew how we would finish the evening now. A slight, sweet drunkenness would steer us on to happy subjects, silly jokes or old French songs. We'd end up believing that we could still relive the past – for one evening, anyway.

I'd then take my plane back to the New World, thinking that I was truly happy in Chicago, but still wondering if Antoine could have been the love of my life after all.

My parents had passed away, my brother lived in Singapore, and I was not that close to the rest of my relatives. Besides a need to honour my parents and enjoy the memories of my childhood, Antoine was the main reason I came back here. My good friend Delphine had come to see me in Chicago and was hoping to do so again soon.

I was not planning to return again for another four or five years. Regrettably I felt I'd done with Burgundy for a while: the cold reality of life there today meant that it was difficult for me to recapture my idyllic childhood, even for a short time.

Julie's Choice of Recipes from Gégé's Culinary Repertoire

Terrine Maison (Cold Meatloaf)
Serves 6.

500g chicken livers, cleaned and sliced
½ cup (125ml) port
500g sausagemeat
200g black pudding, diced
2 shallots, finely chopped
1 egg, at room temperature, beaten
1 tsp each finely chopped fresh thyme and sage
½ tsp each sea salt, ground black pepper and grated
  nutmeg
1 tbsp duck fat, goose fat or lard
12 rashers unsmoked streaky bacon
2 bay leaves

1. Place the livers in a non-metallic bowl, pour over the port and leave to marinate for at least 4 hours in the fridge.

2. Preheat the oven to 180°C/350°F/Gas 4. In a large bowl, combine the marinated livers with the sausagemeat, black pudding, shallots and beaten egg. Add the herbs, salt, pepper and nutmeg and mix thoroughly.

3. Grease a 9 x 5 in (23 x 12.5cm) loaf tin or ceramic terrine with the fat, then line with 8 rashers of bacon. Spoon in the meat. Lay the remaining bacon rashers on top and finish with the bay leaves. Cover with foil. Place the loaf

tin inside a roasting tin and pour in hot water halfway up the sides of the loaf tin (this is a bain-marie). Bake for 1½ hours. Remove the foil and bake for a further 30 mins. Let the terrine cool in the turned-off oven. Pour off any excess juices (these can be added to a risotto).

4. Refrigerate the terrine for at least 6 hours before carefully turning out and slicing. Serve with gherkins, pickled onions, olives and *pain de campagne*. It will keep for a week in the fridge.

Fromage Blanc en Faisselle à la Crème et Pommes de Terre en Robe des Champs (Creamy Fromage Blanc with potatoes boiled in their skins)

If you cannot find *fromage blanc en faisselle* (soft cheese packed in its own strainer), quark can be used instead as the centrepiece of the dish. Serves 4.

8–12 small waxy potatoes
½ cup (120ml) crème fraîche
3 tbsp chopped fresh chives
1 shallot, finely chopped
2 tbsp chopped flat-leaf parsley
2–3 tbsp milk
sea salt and ground black pepper
1 x 500g pot *faisselle fromage frais* or 2 x 250g pots quark

1. Cook the unpeeled potatoes in salted boiling water until tender. Drain and cool until lukewarm, then peel but leave them whole.

2. In a bowl, combine the crème fraîche with 2 tbsp chives, the shallot and parsley, adding enough milk to thin to the consistency of double cream. Season, to taste.

3. Strain the *faisselle fromage frais* and place in the centre of a serving dish (if using quark, mix the two packs together and place in a bowl in the centre of the serving dish). Pour the crème fraîche mixture over the cheese, sprinkle with the remaining 1 tbsp chopped chives and arrange the potatoes around the edge of the plate. Serve with sourdough or *pain de campagne*.

October

What a Spicy Treat!

*'Life is so brief that we should not glance
either too far backwards or forwards ...
so we must learn how to fix our happiness
in our glass and in our plate.'*
Alexandre Balthazar Laurent
Grimod de la Reynière,
1758–1837,
financier and *fermier général*

Through the wide-open window, as far as the eye could see, were multitudes of trees luxuriantly covered in the sizzling colours of the Indian summer. Leaning out into the delicious warmth of the early afternoon, Charlotte suddenly yearned to dive into the tempting piles of fallen leaves. She wanted to melt into their balmy softness. Beyond, the ocean was spotless and bright, and the sky so blue: the kind of striking contrast of colours only New England in autumn could offer.

This was a special day for lost souls. For her first Hallowe'en in the States, Charlotte felt very spiritual. The college campus was very quiet. Most of the students had already left for the weekend to celebrate Hallowe'en with their friends in Salem and Boston.

Charlotte was going to a fancy-dress party that evening. Kathy had gone to pick up the surprise outfits she'd chosen. But, looking at the little clock on the wall, Charlotte saw she had a good hour before she needed to get ready.

Allez, hop! she told herself. She put on her tracksuit, a hat and some sunglasses. Taking the golden cardboard box reserved for special occasions, she left her room, eager to drink in as much of the splendour of this gorgeous day as she could.

She arrived at her secret spot overlooking the ocean, which was deserted as usual. The huge oak tree seemed to be especially welcoming, a little breeze whispering to her in its canopy, its golden leaves floating down with magical artistry. Had some spirit taken it over on this auspicious day? Charlotte loved this tree, and that afternoon, more than ever, it seemed to have a soul. The trees nearby were very lush, their brilliant colours reminding Charlotte of Fauvist paintings, but the oak tree was special. Charlotte lay down and rolled joyfully in the blanket of leaves. With a big smile on her face, she breathed deeply the aromas of Mother Nature. If this was happiness, then Charlotte was very happy entirely on her own.

'Well, Romain, sorry to say it, but I don't miss you at all!' she giggled.

Romain had broken up with her – well, fine. It was for the best since it had meant she'd made up her mind to go abroad for a year. Sure, he had exquisite manners, and money – and her mother had loved him for that, and still expected Charlotte to go back to him when she returned home – but now Charlotte felt more comfortable with the hospitable tree than she ever had with self-obsessed Romain. It would be a long time before she fell for anyone else's charms.

Leaning back against the massive trunk, she opened the golden cardboard box, her taste buds already tingling. She inhaled, and found the smell of the chocolates was as intoxicating as the beauty of the autumn day. The previous afternoon Charlotte had made a huge batch of these chocolate orangettes, using a recipe given to her by her grandmother Pauline.

Charlotte was very fond of chocolate. She'd discovered, too, that any orange-coloured food – citrus fruits, mangoes, carrots, sweet potatoes, pumpkins and smoked salmon – put her in a good mood. The warmth and vibrancy of orange was to her a source of stimulation and energy.

While the sweets were melting slowly in her mouth she started humming a song exactly in keeping with the special ambience of the moment.

'*Rêve orange, la, la, la, la, la* …'

Then she raised her head to look at the clear blue sky, and started drinking in the sight of the leaves raining down from her beloved tree.

She sat there for a while lost in a sensual dream, where everything seemed to be intensely orange. Eventually, the golden cardboard box was almost empty. She was falling asleep …

'Charlotte! Charlotte! Hi there!'

Kathy's loud, high-pitched voice woke Charlotte abruptly, bringing her back to reality, especially when she saw the huge and ridiculous costume Kathy was holding over her head.

'I knew you'd be here …' Only Kathy knew about Charlotte's secret spot.

'No way!' Charlotte exclaimed. 'I'll never wear it. You must be joking!'

'Hey, Frenchy, last year it was me in the pumpkin outfit. It's your turn now, and when you hear what the theme of the party is, you'll understand why this will suit you down to the ground.'

'But—'

'And look, I found this very cute black beret for the French touch,' said Kathy, in an exaggeratedly bad French accent.

She's obviously having fun at my expense, Charlotte thought.

'I can't wait to see my little Frenchy pumpkin!' Kathy laughed.

'I'm not going …'

And that's that!

Kathy, a tarty-looking witch dressed in black and orange, and Charlotte, a large smiling pumpkin with huge dark Betty Boop eyes, and wearing a black beret, drove to Cambridge in Kathy's car. In the end it had been, 'Either you come and experience your first Hallowe'en party, but you have to wear this costume, or you stay home.'

Charlotte had made her choice: at least she wouldn't know anyone at the party, so who else would care how ridiculous she looked?

While strolling through the pretty neighbourhood from the car to Kathy's friend's house, they both admired the elaborate Hallowe'en decorations outside so many of the houses. Then Charlotte remembered the comic-strip hero little Linus van Pelt, with his resolute belief in the Great Pumpkin, and immediately felt better about her costume. She loved that story, that ability to believe in something despite what others thought, and sometimes wished she was more naïve herself.

Suddenly the girls were stopped by a group of children. 'Trick or treat!'

Although Charlotte couldn't see anyone as innocent-looking as the characters from *Peanuts*, like little Linus, she was thrilled to be plunged into a proper Hallowe'en experience, and, smiling, she assessed the five monsters: a tiny Frankenstein's creature, two miniature Draculas, a chubby Cruella, and a petite queen who looked like Snow White's stepmother.

'Trick or treat!' the children repeated, and they evidently really meant it!

Suddenly Charlotte felt a wave of panic as she realised that she had no sweets to give them. She turned to Kathy, and was relieved to see she was laughing, as she took a paper bag out of her handbag and gave it to the trick-or-treaters.

They thanked her, and the boldest of them, the tiny Frankenstein's creature, said loudly, 'We love your costumes! Never saw anything like them before! What are your names?'

After Kathy and Charlotte had told them, the cute wicked stepmother said, 'I think, like, I get it about the pumpkin, but what about the witch in black *and* orange?'

'It's because the party we're going to has a colour theme: black and orange. We're bringing food in the same colours,' said Kathy, and the girls showed the children what they'd made: chocolate orangettes, and a carrot and blood-orange salad with black olives.

'Sounds yummy,' said the chubby little Cruella, though the others didn't seem convinced by the dishes.

After warm goodbyes, the two unlikely groups went their separate ways. Charlotte and Kathy nodded to a couple of women who they guessed were the mothers of the little monsters. Kathy explained that if children went out trick-or-treating nowadays, it was rarely without their parents in tow.

'You should have seen your face when the kids said, "Trick or treat",' she added, laughing.

'Well, it's my first time – we didn't celebrate Hallowe'en in France when I was a child,' explained Charlotte.

'Hallowe'en wouldn't make sense in France anyhow,' said Kathy. 'Not like here ...'

'People do celebrate Hallowe'en in France now, believe it or not: even if nobody knows the meaning of it, it's becoming a way to sell even more junk in our consumerist society.'

Charlotte smiled then, her mood lightening, because she felt a little less ridiculous in her heavy costume since the children had liked it.

In Lyons, she would never have dared go out wearing such an absurd outfit – especially with uptight Romain – but over here no one seemed to judge people by their physical appearance, a strong point in favour of America, where she'd been living for a couple of months. Why, there was an elderly couple coming towards them now, dressed like the stars of *The Rocky Horror Show*.

Curiously, the beautiful day had turned into a foggy evening, creating the ideal atmosphere for spirits from beyond the grave to come out and visit living souls. Charlotte felt a slight chill running up and down her spine, as if she were little Scout walking back home in her ham costume in the strangeness of the night, except that she was a pumpkin with a black beret on.

But she quickly forgot about the spooky night once she and Kathy reached the house. Straight away, they were plunged into the party atmosphere, where strange-looking carrot-coloured witches, skeletons and other diabolical creatures welcomed them cheerfully and danced to samba music.

Charlotte started dancing right away, swept up in the festive mood, even forgetting about her uncomfortable costume, despite Kathy, still at her side, having another laugh at her friend's expense.

Everything really was black and orange ... The afternoon spent surrounded by the glorious autumn colours now seemed a good omen for the evening ahead. There were spotlights illuminating the dancers, beautiful decorations – most of them carved pumpkins and garlands – and, of course, the food: black corn chips, black beans, seaweed and cuttlefish-ink pasta salad, caviar canapés, black olive tapenade, molasses bread, blackberry pies, dark chocolate cakes. And for the orange: dips, chips, Cheddar cheese, canapés with smoked salmon, salads –

like Kathy's, made of carrots and blood oranges, or with cold chicken curry and saffron rice – stuffed squashes, pumpkin and apricot pies, and candies. Someone was also making cocktails.

'Paul and Melina always give the best ever Hallowe'en parties, as it's Melina's birthday too,' Kathy explained.

Charlotte thought the two-colour buffet was a great success. The black enhanced the orange, which glowed tempting and luminous to stimulate the appetites of the guests. The table was groaning, and suddenly she realised she was very hungry. Kathy was outside by then, smoking cigarettes with some of her friends, and Charlotte decided not to wait for her.

Making her choice took a while, since she really wanted to try everything, though that would have been impossible. Eventually she helped herself, piling food on two plates: one for the canapés, salads, side dishes and bread, the other for desserts. Melina, with a creepy-looking spider on her head, made the special cocktail of the evening for her.

Then Charlotte had to find somewhere quiet to sit down. She certainly couldn't eat standing up like most of the people were doing, and she wanted to get rid of her costume, in order to appreciate her dinner more fully.

After searching for a vacant seat, trying to walk carefully through the crowd with her full plates and her glass of Hallowe'en Special cocktail, Charlotte simply couldn't take it any more – she felt as if she was about to suffocate in her cumbersome pumpkin costume. She finally found a dark alcove at the back of the room that seemed to be an office area. She put her food and drink on a chair and, with some effort, started to take off her outfit.

Aaaah! What a relief! Charlotte felt much better in just her black leotard and leggings after she'd shed the pumpkin costume. It felt good, too, to shake her long black curls free from the tight headband.

Then the magic of the night really started. Having sipped her delicious Hallowe'en Special cocktail, she ate the exquisite food slowly, appreciating every bite. As long as she had tasty food on her plate and a delectable drink in her hand, she was happy.

Who needs a man at a moment like this, especially a man like Romain?

Every mouthful of the feast was completely delicious. She especially liked the cold chicken curry salad, which went so well with Kathy's blood-orange and black olive salad.

Charlotte had always been open to the delights of international food, or fusion cuisine, despite having grown up in an extremely traditional family that ate only hearty French dishes, typical bourgeois food. That had been good and wholesome, but Charlotte had soon acquired a taste for the more exotic.

She stared at the flamboyantly dressed crowd, and saw that Kathy was flirting outrageously with a big black and orange cat that looked like Garfield.

But what about her long-time boyfriend in California? thought Charlotte. Oh, well, it's none of my business …

The big difference between the two friends was that Kathy couldn't live without a man by her side, and Charlotte could, or was trying to convince herself that she could.

The beat of the music was irresistible, and Charlotte began dancing while still seated, having put the cleared plates to one side. Holding her almost empty glass of Hallowe'en Special cocktail, she moved her legs and arms with sensuous grace to the rhythm of a merengue.

She had had a wonderful day. And feeling just a little tipsy, she even had the impression that she looked pretty fabulous!

This also seemed to be the opinion of the young man sitting at the back of the small alcove, in the darkest corner. He had been watching with delight: firstly, the pumpkin's striptease; and secondly a very attractive – and curvy – young woman really enjoying her food and drink!

This young man had always thought that there was nothing more sensual than a beautiful woman eating with real appetite. The best thing was that she was completely unaware of him sitting alone in the darkness of the office.

Ready for another cocktail, Charlotte got up to go to the bar. But before she could move away, she heard something behind her.

'Hi there!'

She was so surprised that she froze for a few seconds. Then she turned round. Her gaze met two brown eyes right in front of her, sparkling with humour.

'Where did you appear from?'

'*Du fin fond des ténèbres ...*' he said with a fake scary voice.

'Of course, from the world of darkness,' said Charlotte. 'So you speak French?'

'*Je suis de Québec*. Melina told me you're from France, *n'est-ce pas?*'

'Have you been here long?' Charlotte asked instead of answering, realising with embarrassment that he might have seen her dancing on her chair.

'For ever … I've been sitting here on the desk …'

Charlotte peered into the gloomy office area.

'In the darkest corner,' repeated the young man with a spooky voice. And he gave a loud diabolical laugh. 'Happy Hallowe'en, Mademoiselle!'

But Charlotte's celebratory mood was evaporating.

'The whole time …?'

The young man nodded with a mischievous smile.

'I'm so sorry!' Charlotte exclaimed, blushing bright red.

She set her empty glass down on her chair and flapped her hands in front of her face, trying to cool it down a little. She felt ashamed that a complete stranger – even if they did share the same native language – had been watching her as she'd been relishing her food and drink! And taking off her clothes. And dancing …

The young man was still looking at her and he laughed again, but sympathetically now.

'What have you got to be sorry for? What a spicy treat it was to just look at you! And I'm happy to see the pumpkin's real face. I've never seen such a big one – I mean such a big pumpkin costume. And the beautiful dark eyes, so sexy! And the beret! The perfect French touch!'

'Where's your costume?' Charlotte asked, looking the young man up and down, dressed as he was in jeans and a white shirt.

'Vanished!' he answered, gesturing with a wave of his hand towards the ceiling.

'That's why I was in the dark, since you have to wear fancy dress for this party.'

'Pretty much like me.'

'Actually, believe it or not, I was wearing something worse than your costume. I was dressed as a gigantic carrot with a black French moustache, a pince-nez and a dark top hat.'

Over his shoulder Charlotte was trying to see the ridiculous outfit he'd left on a chair, now hanging limply.

'You're pulling my leg?' She burst out laughing, and began to feel much more relaxed.

'It was simply for a stupid bet, but I made twenty bucks because I walked down the street wearing it.'

Charlotte couldn't restrain herself. She laughed wholeheartedly – her inhibitions cast aside at the comedy of the situation, and with the effects of the cocktail. Picturing herself as a pumpkin with a beret, and the young man as a carrot with a French moustache, was too much for her.

'Watching you – I should say, *admiring* you – has been the best thing about the whole evening.'

Well, he's definitely got some nerve for a guy this side of the pond, Charlotte thought. By then she didn't know whether or not she should stop laughing. It might be his French heritage, she decided, but nerve or not, he is so charming!

Yes, this young man was much more daring than any Americans she'd met since she'd been here. He was the first man who had ever flirted so openly with her, and she had been to quite a few parties in the last two months.

242

'Michael Deschênes,' he said, offering his hand and smiling infectiously.

'Charlotte Farisier! Let's have a toast,' exclaimed Charlotte, thrilled to meet a French native from the New World for the first time. Actually, she was dying to go to Quebec. It would be fascinating to hear and to read French in North America, land of great cold and wide expanses. She had also always admired the determination involved in keeping French as the first language in an area of the world surrounded by imperialistic English.

'Oh, but my glass is empty!' Charlotte remembered she'd been about to go for a refill when Michael had appeared.

'Mine as well.' Michael raised an empty beer glass. 'What are you drinking?'

'Just ask for the special cocktail of the evening. Melina will make one for you.'

Charlotte described what the drink was.

'It sounds incredibly exotic compared to my pumpkin-brewed beer. I'll get one for myself as well. I'll be right back.'

It took less than two minutes for Michael to return with the drinks.

'Had to be fast in order to avoid the "Where is your carrot costume" questions. It's lucky I put these ridiculous dark glasses on! I found them on the desk where I was sitting.'

'It's lucky for me that nobody knows me here,' asserted Charlotte, 'so they can't tell me I'm not following the rules of the party – except Kathy, my roommate, who is a good friend of Melina's. But she seems to have disappeared …'

'Like a ghost …'

'More like a bimbo witch, actually, and with a fat Garfield lookalike!'

Michael laughed.

'Let's have a toast to the *Je me souviens* motto, the maxim of my *belle province*!'

'To *Je me souviens*!'

'What about more food? I haven't eaten much, being too busy staring at you.'

Charlotte put the huge sunglasses on and was as quick getting the food as Michael had been with the drinks, not because she cared if people saw her without her pumpkin costume, but because she was eager to get back to Michael. She came back with three plates laden with food.

'Try the cold chicken curry salad. It's exquisite!'

'I know,' answered Michael with a big smile.

'You like it too?'

'I made it.'

He is charming and he knows how to cook! Awesome … Charlotte thought excitedly.

Sitting in the dark little office area, Charlotte and Michael had a terrific time chatting about what was on their plates, amongst many other subjects. No one could really see them, but they could see the rest of the party, which was even more amusing for them. To Charlotte, it was like sitting in the window of the little café she went in back home, watching the passers-by.

She moved on to talk about her beloved *belle France*, and Michael about his *belle province*. The place you're from often seems more appealing when you're away from it, and they really enjoyed talking about their home cities.

I'm having such a great time, I want it to last for ever, Charlotte found herself thinking, smiling up into Michael's twinkling eyes. Time should stop right here ...

Suddenly a hideous bony hand with long black nails crept over Michael's shoulder. A witch, with long orange hair, who appeared to Charlotte to be both extremely ugly and extremely beautiful at the same time, leant down to say something in Michael's ear. Her black-toothed mouth then greeted Charlotte, who frowned in reply.

What does this witch creature want? Is she Michael's girlfriend? All at once Charlotte was filled with anxiety.

The creature then left as fast as she had appeared.

Michael turned back to Charlotte. 'I'm sorry to cut short such a lovely time, but I've got to leave. You really are very attractive and it's been a real joy meeting you. I've had such a great time! Thank you so much. *Au revoir!*' He kissed her hand, then disappeared into the crowd without looking back.

Charlotte was flabbergasted. She'd hardly had a chance to say '*Au revoir*'. Everything had happened so fast! He'd thanked her, and then vanished into thin air? But she had hoped they would arrange to see each other again. They'd talked as if they had known each other for ever, and they shared a common French heritage. How long had they sat together? A couple of hours? She couldn't say. And hadn't there been a frisson of shared sensuality over the food they'd enjoyed? Such a special moment couldn't end there!

Charlotte caressed her hand where Michael had kissed her. The atmosphere of this strange party was very much in keeping with the mysteries of this haunting night. Had she been dreaming? Was she going to wake up with a Hallowe'en Special cocktail in her hand and food in her mouth, appreciating life without a man, as she'd been doing earlier? No, Michael's floppy carrot costume was still heaped untidily on its chair. Their empty plates and the huge dark glasses were resting on the floor.

Michael Deschênes … She knew his name now. She wrote it a few times on a paper napkin, as if she were afraid she might forget it even though it was emblazoned in her memory.

Charlotte threaded her way through the crowd, hoping to step outside to see if she could catch a final glimpse of Michael. But suddenly, on the edge of the dance floor, a firm hand grabbed her and halted her progress.

'Charlotte, here you are! Why did you take your costume off?' But Kathy didn't give Charlotte time to answer. 'Let me introduce you …'

Charlotte greeted the fat Garfield lookalike, who then went to get some drinks for them.

'Sorry that I didn't spend much time with you. Wait until I tell you the whole story … I hope you haven't spent the evening by yourself.'

'By myself? No.' Charlotte told Kathy about Michael.

'I don't know any Michael here tonight. Was he—'

Kathy didn't get any further because a group of wild, spooky black-and-orange creatures dragged the two of them on to the dance floor. Charlotte decided to join the dancers, making sure that she kept the paper napkin with Michael's name on it safely in her bra, as if it were the only proof of the reality of their encounter.

Well, you don't have such a great time with me and then vanish like some kind of ghost, my dear Michael. We're going to meet again and then you can explain to me who that witch was! I'll make sure of it, Charlotte vowed. Besides, I want the recipe for that exquisite cold chicken curry salad.

Orange-Coloured Recipes for a Halloween Potluck
Each recipe serves 6.

Hallowe'en Cocktail

For each cocktail, mix 1 tbsp peach or apricot brandy and 1 tbsp mango juice in a champagne flute. Top up with champagne.

Kathy's Carrot and Blood-Orange Salads

For the carrot salad:
5 carrots, peeled
1 garlic clove, crushed
2 tbsp extra-virgin olive oil
1 tbsp lemon juice
1 tsp cumin seeds
sea salt and ground black pepper
1 tsp chopped fresh coriander

For the blood-orange salad:
1 small red onion, finely chopped, sprinkled with salt
   and set aside for 10 mins
3 blood-oranges, pared and sliced thinly
1 cup (120g) black olives
2 tbsp olive oil
½ tsp cumin seeds
pinch each of ground ginger and paprika
1 tsp each chopped fresh coriander and mint, to serve

1. Cook the carrots whole in salted boiling water until just tender (about 15 mins). Drain and leave to cool, then slice thinly.

2. In a large bowl, mix together the crushed garlic, olive oil, lemon juice, cumin seeds, salt, pepper and coriander. Toss the carrots gently with the dressing.

3. Rinse the onion and dry on kitchen paper. Spread the orange slices over one half of a serving dish. Arrange the onion over the oranges, followed by the olives. Drizzle over the olive oil and sprinkle with the cumin seeds, ground ginger and paprika. Spoon the carrot salad on to the other half of the serving dish. Refrigerate for an hour. Sprinkle the salads with the coriander and mint just before serving.

Michael's Chicken Curry Salad

For the chicken:
2 tbsp flour
2 tbsp mild curry powder
½ tsp chilli powder
1 tsp cumin seeds
1 tsp ground ginger
1 bay leaf
sea salt and ground black pepper
500g chicken breasts, sliced
juice of 1 lemon

For the salad:
1 cup (200g) split red lentils
5 cups (1.25 litres) chicken stock

2 tbsp vegetable oil
1 onion, chopped
2 orange peppers, roughly chopped
2 tomatoes, roughly chopped
2 carrots, roughly chopped
½ cup (80g) sultanas

For the dressing:
5 tbsp mayonnaise
5 tbsp yogurt
juice of 1 lemon
pinch of saffron
salt and freshly ground pepper

To serve:
½ cup (60g) crushed peanuts
1 orange, pared and segmented, the segments cut into
  small pieces
finely chopped fresh coriander

1. Mix the flour, spices and seasoning in a shallow dish. Add the chicken pieces and toss to coat, then squeeze over the lemon juice. Cover the bowl with cling film and leave to marinate in the fridge for at least 2 hours.

2. Pick over and rinse the lentils. Bring 4 cups (1 litre) chicken stock to the boil, add the lentils, reduce to a simmer, and cook, covered, for 15 mins, or until just tender. Drain the lentils and allow to cool.

3. Wipe off any excess marinade from the chicken pieces and discard the bay leaf. In a deep frying pan, heat 1 tbsp oil and sauté the chicken until golden. Set aside on a plate.

Heat the remaining 1 tbsp oil in the same pan and sauté the vegetables for 5 mins.

4. Return the chicken to the pan along with the remaining 1 cup (250ml) chicken stock and the sultanas. Simmer gently, uncovered, for 10–15 mins, until the chicken is cooked through and the vegetables are tender. Allow to cool.

5. Mix the mayonnaise with the yogurt in a small bowl. Add the lemon juice and saffron. Season, to taste. In a salad bowl, gently toss together all the ingredients. Refrigerate for at least 2 hours. Scatter over the crushed peanuts, orange segments and chopped fresh coriander just before serving.

Orangettes
(Candied Orange Peel Dipped in Chocolate)

Charlotte's grandmother's recipe makes 30-40 chocolates.

3 oranges
6 tbsp Grand Marnier or other orange liqueur
1 cup (200g) caster sugar
200g dark chocolate (70 per cent cocoa), broken into small pieces

1. Cut the top and bottom off the oranges. Score through the orange peel to divide it in four before peeling the oranges. Squeeze 2 tbsp juice from one of the peeled oranges and set aside.

2. Bring a pan of water to the boil, add the orange peel

quarters and boil for 5 mins. Drain, rinse and boil in fresh water for another 5 mins. Drain and dry on kitchen paper. Cut into approx. ½ in (1cm) x 2 in (5cm) strips.

3. To make the syrup, heat ½ cup (125ml) water, 4 tbsp orange liqueur, sugar and orange juice in a small pan. Bring to the boil, then add the orange strips, reduce the heat right down and cook over the lowest possible heat for 1½ hours, checking from time to time that the mixture has not gone dry (add a drop more water if needed). Allow to cool, leaving the strips to macerate in the syrup for at least 8 hours or overnight.

4. Drain the candied orange strips and dry, spaced out on a wire rack, for about 8 hours.

5. In a bowl set over a pan of simmering water, melt the chocolate slowly with the remaining 2 tbsp orange liqueur. Do not stir until the chocolate has completely melted. Dip two-thirds of every strip of candied orange into the chocolate, leaving one-third of the peel exposed. Leave to dry, well spaced out on a sheet of baking parchment, until the chocolate hardens completely.

November

The Best Ever Turkey

'A cook, when I dine, seems to me a divine being, who from
the depths of his kitchen rules the human race.
One considers him as a minister of heaven,
because his kitchen is a temple,
in which his oven is the altar.'
Marc-Antoine Madeleine Désaugiers,
1772–1827, French composer,
dramatist, songwriter

Why was it so hard to convince people that even if I was
thirty-nine, I wasn't in the least bit worried about being
single again? Distressed? No! Relieved? Yes! Yet no one
ever seemed to believe me. And, anyway, why should I
have to explain anything? I didn't care whether or not
other people were in relationships; they could do whatever
they pleased so long as they were content, and didn't
bother me with their, *Oh, that's a pity, to still be single at
your age, Victoria – and what about children?*

Well, there I was: close to my fortieth birthday, on my
own once more and pretty pleased about it! Some say that
life begins at forty. I was looking forward with enthusiasm
to that new decade of wisdom.

As I sat on my porch, happily contemplating my future,

the ocean seemed even more beautiful than usual in the softer light of the cold season. I couldn't take my eyes off it. The big waves and the wind were raising a gentle spray that I could feel through the porch windows.

The ocean ... that grandiose and captivating expanse of water without which I could hardly contemplate living. Some diffused sunbeams illuminated its immensity and I shivered with intense satisfaction.

Hmm! The strong iodine smell of the sea was so invigorating. I breathed it in deeply while feeling the soft warmth of the pale sun on my face.

Chipolata, my beloved and faithful cocker spaniel, lay at my feet, snoring peacefully.

The fire burnt low in the fireplace I'd recently had installed in my porch – there was now a fireplace in every room except the bathroom – and I sipped my tea comfortably, warmed by the fire and a thick blanket while I read the latest issue of *Gourmet Chitchat*. The main article was about cookery classes, which, it said, might become mandatory in high schools. Good, it was about time we thought seriously about what we put on our plates and in our stomachs every day – and the younger we started, the better. Why not teach cooking at school, since so many parents didn't take the time to educate their children's palates?

The last few pages featured a piece about the trendy restaurants that had opened in New York, such as the one where you dined in the dark, or others where the menu consisted of food of entirely one colour: yellow, based on eggs, polenta, citrus fruit; or red, with lobster, rare beef, tomatoes, peppers, raspberries ... When I saw how pricey these food places were I put the magazine down impatiently and turned my attention back to the ocean waves, preferring nature's own extravaganza to the latest passing fad.

Actually, Ken would have enjoyed going to fashionable restaurants like that – it was *de rigueur* if, like him, you belonged to the rich-and-not-famous mob, as I privately called the spoilt young people who had never had to struggle to get whatever they wanted in life.

I poured myself more tea as I sighed with relief to be free of him. Ken was a real jerk, after all. I should have known that from the beginning. Chipolata had never liked him, and most of my girlfriends, married or not, had wanted to sleep with him.

I was proud of myself. I'd kicked Ken out pretty impressively when he'd shown up at my door: Ken had decided he wanted to live with me, and that my house needed a man. *My foot!*

We'd started dating only three months earlier; it had been much too soon for him to be moving in. I smiled again, picturing him arriving with his five huge suitcases a few days before. As he parked his latest-model Mercedes in front of the house, he'd looked very content and full of self-confidence – as usual.

Ken had wanted his moving in to be a surprise. Sure, he was handsome and extremely charming; his black eyes, that morning, had been brighter than usual. Knowing how much I liked them, he'd arrived clutching a bouquet of peach-coloured roses and a huge box of Cœurs Noirs chocolates. He'd tried all the arguments he could to convince me he was just what my domestic situation lacked, but I wasn't buying it.

'No way!' I shouted.

I felt the urge to slam the door in his face, but I managed to resist.

Ken might have wanted to surprise me, but in the end he was the one who was more taken aback because he certainly hadn't expected my refusal. Had anyone ever said no to him before?

We'd never really discussed our future. We'd spent most of the short time we'd been together in my bedroom or at the table, talking mainly about our work – actually, *his* work – his parents, and the latest high-tech gadgets he had acquired. Pretty boring conversations, when I thought about them. He couldn't even appreciate the beauty of the ocean from the porch as he was always too busy checking his cell phone for messages and pictures.

So when he turned up with his roses and his chocolates I didn't invite him inside. I left him standing there, surrounded by his luggage. I then explained to him that I didn't want to be his slave, as most women still were for men, even if they didn't want to admit it. He replied that I'd only have to do the cooking, since I was brilliant at that, and he'd do the shopping – except for the special groceries he knew I'd need to source for my recipes – and the laundry, the cleaning, the ironing … Ken had thought of everything.

I interrupted his inventory of domestic chores.

'Have you ever done any housework?'

'I'm ready to try for you, Victoria …'

I was silent, waiting for what I was sure would come next.

He understood.

'Or we could hire a maid!'

'Never!'

No one would ever come in to clean my home, and invade my privacy.

'Have you ever used a broom in your life?' I asked, knowing the answer.

'Come on, Victoria, you know I still live with my parents, and we have a maid …'

And that I'm a spoilt brat! Yes, I know you are.

'Then go back to your parents.'

'I can't live without your cooking,' he sighed, trying another ploy.

'You're only here for my cooking, then?'

'Of course not; you know very well I'm not.'

'Ken, I can't have a relationship with someone who just decides to come live with me without even talking to me about it.'

'I wanted to surprise you! We have a good time together, don't we?'

Puzzling over his last remark, I looked at him without saying a word. He was so handsome! But I knew I would never again be swept away by his charms.

In the face of my silence, he became apologetic.

'OK, I'm sorry. You're right. Surprising you wasn't the best idea. But you can also be pretty impulsive, can't you?'

Yes, I can – but I don't expect impulsiveness from you. It doesn't go with your self-image of perfection.

'Stop frowning like that, Victoria … OK, OK! I get your point. But at least can you think about it?'

'No!'

Infuriated, I shut the door firmly. It was all very sudden indeed but I was confident that I really was doing the right thing. It was time to end this shallow relationship that had limped along only because I found him handsome, and he liked my cooking.

Then I beamed: no intruder within these walls any more at all! My number one rule was that I had to live as I wanted, by myself, in my own house. Maybe I should have said that right away. In future, I resolved, when I met a man I was interested in, I would make it clear at once that the only way the relationship could work for me was if we each kept our own place. We'd visit each other, when invited, so that we would always be happy to see each other. Not like married people, who saw each other all the time, enduring together all the monotony of everyday life.

Outside, Ken had wisely decided not to hang around. I'd heard the sound of his car fading into the distance. Then I'd opened the door and taken the roses and the box of Cœurs Noirs he'd kindly left behind.

Thanks.

I hadn't heard from him since. Ken, who used to call me twice a day! I must have hurt his pride, since he was considered to be a very good catch, and a lot of women dreamt of tying the knot with him. Well, not me. Our relationship had been fine while it lasted, but I needed to turn the page. The only thing I would miss about Ken was those eyes I'd fallen for right at the beginning: those very dark eyes that reminded me of two shiny black pearls.

Ken wasn't the only man who had turned up on my doorstep saying he couldn't live without my cooking. I should never have cooked for men once I'd started dating them because they became crazy. But I couldn't help it. Often the dishes I made were completely new to them, and they were so funny when they pretended they were enjoying everything, when clearly they weren't, because they were so afraid that I would get angry with them.

It was their mothers I had to thank, most of whom weren't even capable of boiling an egg. Usually, anything was better than what their mothers put on their plates, so it was easy for me to seduce the sons with my food, despite the little games I liked to play with my experimental cooking. Admittedly, it had been harder when I'd dated Nino. Italians, like the French, usually worship their mothers' cooking …

Ah, how good it felt to be all on my own again with only Chipolata for company!

The tea was pretty good, and my finger sandwiches, filled with marinated raw salmon, cucumber and fresh dill, had been delicious! By then I was ready for some of the chocolate truffles I'd made that morning, and the glass of cranberry liqueur I had waiting on my little tray.

Sure, I enjoyed the sex, and Ken had been all right. I found it all worked the same, most of the time, and after a while it became routine, so why make such a big deal of it?

In my view, sex was the easiest part of a relationship. After these more or less relaxing and exciting physical connections, things always got a little more complicated. The fatal question inevitably came up: *what do we need to do in order to keep this relationship alive?* It was usually too much for me.

If a relationship became too complicated, I'd rather break up and be by myself. I would meet someone else eventually. It wasn't often that I met anyone that I found interesting, though. Was it because I liked my freedom so much that I couldn't see the appeal of most men? Why would I need a guy here, possibly telling me what to do? I'd had my parents and teachers for that! And they had been so tiresome …

And I shouldn't have to behave in a certain way in order to please a man. After all, I had to do that with my clients. But I could put up with them, since it was thanks to them that I had become what I was. Maybe it was because I used up all my energy pleasing my clients that I needed to recoup and just wanted to enjoy being alone with Chipolata.

Talking of clients, I realised it would soon be time for me to go to work. That evening, the Browns were having a special Thanksgiving dinner party to celebrate their recent adoption of twin baby girls from New Orleans, who had lost their parents in the Hurricane Katrina disaster. The previous night I had started preparing a Cajun–New England meal for the occasion.

I got up from my rocking chair feeling refreshed and energetic after my break, ready to face the evening's work. Chipolata woke up and went for a walk around the perimeter of the house because she knew she'd have to stay inside while I was away.

Things had gone well. I was pleased. Everyone seemed to appreciate my meal. I always enjoyed the challenge of creating new and unusual bi-cultural dishes.

This was the best part of the evening for me, now dinner was over. I could relax a little while my team served drinks and sweet titbits and the waiters started to clear the dining table.

I found a quiet corner in the huge kitchen, which my hosts seemed barely to use. What a pity! It was a beautiful room, and full of the latest culinary utensils and appliances. The ochre walls and the small red hexagonal floor tiles gave it an air of rural Provence or Tuscany. Very charming!

I sipped a glass of wine and nibbled some cake while admiring the scene through the window. How stylish these Victorian mansions were, especially the green one opposite. It was completely in keeping with the peaceful street setting, lit now by ancient gaslights. I tried to imagine the inside of the green mansion: the paintings, furniture, the *objets d'art*, a magnificent table with beautiful food enjoyed at the leisurely pace of olden times, all creating a picture in my mind of the residents' good taste.

Images from another time slowly filled my head, and I allowed myself a moment of respite. Mmm, this local wine was really good! I should buy a few more bottles …

'Vicky?' called Tom, my assistant, from the other side of the vast kitchen, abruptly cutting short my reverie.

'Here!' I answered, rather reluctantly.

'A certain Robin Harris is asking for you.'

Robin Harris? The name rang a bell, but I couldn't place it.

Feeling a little irked, I left my glass half full but swallowed the last mouthful of cake before going to find this person.

Robin's face was vaguely familiar: one of those young women from the rich-and-not-famous mob, who sometimes talked to me at the end of fancy dinner parties I'd cooked for.

'Victoria! I didn't see you at the cocktails before dinner because I came a little late.' She hugged me as if we were best friends. 'So happy to meet you again!' She grinned.

'Likewise,' I said, insincerely. I still couldn't really remember who she was.

'I want to introduce you to my friends Daphne and Adriana!'

I stared at the three young women, who looked so alike: same hairstyle and colour – it seemed that dark hair with red highlights was in; similar outfits showing plenty of cleavage; pointy shoes – also in vogue, I believed, but too uncomfortable for me since I didn't have pointy feet.

A quick glance around and I became convinced that everyone looked like everybody else.

The three friends were skeletal. Their skintight tops and trousers showed even more of their stringy figures, which would have looked better in looser-fitting clothes. They looked terrible! What did they eat? Or, more appropriately, what did they not eat?

After ritual hand-shaking, *so nice to meet you* and *your food was exquisite*, Robin turned to me with a serious face.

'Well, after our chat, I really did a lot of thinking …'

Our chat, our chat … What are you talking about?

'Victoria, please, have a glass of Kir Kennedy,' offered Mrs Brown, my employer for the evening, who had just come over, with Steve, one of my waiters, following in her wake. 'You deserve it!'

They all toasted my fantastic dinner. I had to admit that these little celebrations after a meal I'd cooked made me quite proud. What a difference from the reproaches I used to get from the parents of children at the school I used to work at. It had been 'kindly' explained to me that the healthy food I was cooking for their offspring was unsuitable.

'Cook them fries or pasta instead of veggies! At least then they'll eat something!' had been the strong suggestion made to me, accompanied by a broad, hypocritical smile. I had never regretted quitting on the spot.

Robin looked me straight in the eye, which was a little disconcerting as I was still trying to remember what kind of talk I'd had with her, and when, and where.

After Mrs Brown had left us to circulate among her other guests, Robin, her identical friends and I sat down on comfortable chairs with our glasses of Kir Kennedy.

'Well, I finally dumped Lancelot. And it's thanks to you!' Robin said.

I was dreading having to ad lib, but luckily the name 'Lancelot' brought it all back. How could anyone forget such a name!

'And I met Gabe, who is gorgeous and …'

Yes, just like all the others: gorgeous, smart and, of course, most importantly, loaded!

By then I'd remembered everything: that was the night in spring when the Winchesters had been celebrating their tenth anniversary on their private yacht.

Robin had caught my attention because she'd been crying her eyes out the whole time, a drink in one hand, a box of tissues in the other, looking out at the ocean on the upper deck. I'd gone up there to take a little break. It was one of those warm, dry, beautiful spring days when New England looked so special.

I'd asked her if she needed anything, and she'd started to tell me that she had just found out that her boyfriend, Lancelot, was cheating on her. Of course, she could have confessed this to anyone, but it was I who was lucky enough to be right there when she needed to talk. *Yes, lucky me!*

Lancelot – I remembered thinking – what a name! I pictured him on horseback, valiantly following a narrow woodland path that led to another Guinevere. Just then, Robin, with her packet of tissues, certainly hadn't looked much like a queen, but I'd kept my thoughts to myself. I had given her a couple of Cœurs Noirs, which I always carried with me in my bag, and then said something to her about the benefits of chocolate and that you could actually have a better time with chocolate than with men.

Robin had liked what I said, managed to smile, and even laughed. I'd then told her that I was sure she would meet someone else soon, and she'd seemed to believe me. The remainder of the conversation had been about Robin's future.

Although I liked to spend a lot of time by myself, if I saw a soul in pain I would try to offer some comfort. Since

I usually didn't know the people I gave advice to, I could be more objective and less judgemental than their friends or family would be.

My parents and my two sisters had been amazed that I'd decided to train to be a cook. They had thought I would become a kind of Mother Teresa, a sort of saviour of lost souls. 'But food has the power to comfort, doesn't it?' I'd said.

When I witnessed people in such turmoil because their relationships were going badly, it strengthened my conviction that I'd rather be by myself, eating some Cœurs Noirs with a glass of cranberry liqueur, sitting on my porch looking out at the ocean, with my devoted Chipolata at my side, than suffering with a man.

Robin and her friends Daphne and Adriana could not allow themselves to be alone, although not for economic reasons. They had to have boyfriends even if they weren't really happy because, for them, being in a relationship was all that mattered.

Robin went on to relate how she'd followed my advice: she had taken a few months off, away from everyone, and ended up in Tokyo, working part time for her father's firm, which had an office there.

'And then I met Gabe, who was also living in Tokyo for a while …'

She told us that they were getting engaged, and that she wanted me to cook for their engagement party since she believed I'd brought her good luck. I was also invited to the wedding, but strictly as a guest. I wouldn't have to cook for that.

Wow, that was fast! She didn't waste any time after our conversation on the yacht.

I should have been flattered that Robin was asking me to cook for her engagement dinner and that she'd invited me to her wedding, but I didn't really know what to say besides 'That would be lovely', since I wasn't part of Robin's social circle at all. I resolved to make the effort to attend her wedding, though, as it could be good for business.

After another toast to this news, Daphne cleared her throat hesitantly.

'Um, so tell us. You're known as someone who likes being single – is that really true?'

What *was* really true was that some chefs were as famous as Hollywood stars. I doubted I would like that. By then, I was refusing to speak to any journalist, a decision I'd made immediately after reading the only article ever written about me in a food magazine. I didn't like reading about myself in the least, or seeing the phoney picture of me in my kitchen. The article was entitled 'The Stardom of the Famous Chef who Doesn't Want to Be Famous'. Unfortunately, these women had evidently read and remembered it.

'From what we read about you,' Adriana said through a mouthful of chocolate, 'you really seem to enjoy living by yourself. A bit like a hermit really?'

I'd got the feeling that Daphne and Adriana were trying to challenge me a little. I looked at the two of them. Daphne was waiting anxiously for my answer. Adriana hadn't stopped eating sweet titbits. Robin, meanwhile, had tuned out, giving the impression that she was dreaming about her wedding to Gabe as she gazed at a gilt-framed Italian painting on the wall next to her depicting a group of jolly, plump cherubs.

'What works for me doesn't necessarily work for others,' I answered calmly.

'Of course not,' Daphne mumbled. 'I, um, I'm curious because I've never met anyone like you before.'

'Jeez, Daphne, get to the point,' Robin said, taking her eyes off the cherubs and winking at me as if we were friends sharing a great secret. 'Actually, Daphne would really like you to tell us about your everyday life by yourself, since the article didn't really say much about it,' she explained apologetically, as if slightly embarrassed for her friend.

'Your truffles are my favourite! What's in them?' Adriana interrupted loudly, helping herself to more from a new tray that Steve had discreetly brought up from the kitchen.

She looked as if she was the type of person who made sure she always had food within easy reach, no matter where she happened to be sitting. The amount she ate didn't equate at all with her thinness. Either she had the most astonishing metabolism, or she wouldn't be eating for the next week – unless, of course, she was bulimic.

'Chocolate, pecans, cranberries and Bourbon,' I answered.

'Wow! You're a genius! I'm so thrilled to meet the great Victoria Prescott!'

I said nothing.

'I'm quite amazed that you like to live by yourself.'

Daphne evidently couldn't drop the subject. 'You see, I can't spend a minute alone. But if I do happen to be by myself, I take my cell phone and work through my phonebook until someone answers, or I send emails, or chat online with strangers from all over the world.'

Oh dear, I feel so sorry for you.

Unfortunately, this was how people had begun to live, vicariously, through a myriad of communication gadgets, which seemed to give a purpose to their lives. I wondered if they were actually afraid to be by themselves, even if only for a little while.

'Daphne thinks that you're very shrewd since you advised Robin so successfully,' added Adriana, gazing at the last truffle in her hand.

Robin nodded in agreement.

Jeez, I'd had no idea my words would be so convincing that she'd take them so literally.

Adriana was beckoning to Steve to bring her another Kir Kennedy. Her glass was already empty. I'd hardly touched mine. Even though it was quite good, I didn't feel like drinking it after the wine I'd been sipping so peacefully in the kitchen until I was called upon to present myself.

'So tell us about your hermit life,' Daphne implored.

'What can I say? I guess it all started when I realised that I didn't want to be like my parents or other couples around me because they were always engaged in a power struggle. I came to the decision to only rely on myself in order to be truly independent and to try to have a peaceful life. I don't like conflict.'

'But you need a man. You know what I mean; we are

human, after all,' asserted the bold Adriana, popping the last truffle into her mouth in a very sensual manner.

'You mean, for sex?'

Robin and Daphne reddened. Adriana took a sip of her drink.

'Well, of course we're animals too, aren't we? And we all have basic instincts and needs. But I like to think that, being human, we are also very emotional – at least I am – and therefore I can find more refined pleasures in life.'

'Like eating chocolate,' Adriana exclaimed, 'or enjoying your delicious food! I don't blame you. For me that's how it works. No sex for a while, no big deal! I've just had a nice meal with champagne, and some chocolate for dessert. I don't need anything more to enjoy myself!'

I suspected she must have sex more often than food, as she was as skinny as a rake. Was she eating tonight to compensate for going without sex for a week?

They were making me feel a bit defensive with that tired old cliché: no sex, but an addiction to food. But that wasn't it at all! I didn't agree but it wasn't worth trying to explain to them. They probably wouldn't understand.

'Where do you live?' Daphne asked, willing at last to change the subject.

'In a pretty little house near the ocean, with my faithful Chipolata.'

'You have a cat. I'm allergic to them,' Adriana rushed in.

Another cliché. Single women have to live with cats, don't they?

'Chipolata is a dog, a darling cocker spaniel.'

'But what about having a family?'

I could see from her face when she asked this question that Daphne was dying to meet a man to father her future children.

'Well, when I said that I didn't want to be like my parents or other couples because they were always engaged in a power struggle, that applies to the entire family as well. I don't believe in family harmony. At least, I've never met a family that would make me want to have my own. Besides, I've got friends and relatives who have children. I see them once in a while. It's good enough for me.'

'I want three or four children,' Daphne stated.

'Yeah, sure,' Adriana laughed.

I didn't pay any attention to her.

'You know, I simply enjoy looking after my garden, and plants are much quieter than children …'

'My nieces and nephew are cute but they cry all the time!' Adriana told us all. She always had to have her say even when her mouth was full of yet more of the chocolate truffles that Steve had just brought out. 'But I heard that when they're your own, it's—'

Robin frowned and shushed her.

'I work a lot, like we all do nowadays. So when I have some free time I really want to appreciate it my own way. For example, in winter, I usually sit by the fire in my living room, just watching the flames, or if the sun is shining I'll sit on the porch where I also have a fireplace. In summer I sit on the beach and watch the ocean, and just listen to the waves and wind. I love hearing the sounds of nature. The ocean is what fascinates me the most. I love everything about it: its sounds, its smells, its colours and textures.'

'That sounds, er, interesting,' whispered Daphne the dreamer, who I was sure had never experienced such a simple existence, and who wouldn't ever have much time for one with the big family she intended to have.

'Sounds boring to me,' confessed Adriana.

Of course! Adriana was obviously like so many young people, constantly listening to her iPod or talking on her cell phone, even while walking on the beach. I'd be willing to bet she never even heard what was going on around her.

Robin was pensive again, looking once more at the gilt-framed Italian picture with the plump cherubs.

'You know, it's quite important for a cook to be able to smell the essence of what Mother Earth gives us: aromas and perfumes that I take from my garden to the table.'

'You are quite sensuous,' Robin remarked.

'And sensual as well,' added Adriana. 'That's why your cooking is so delightful, and so full of flavour. You cook with your heart and soul.'

You should try it sometime, I was tempted to say.

'Don't tell me that you don't have relationships with guys at all?'

I don't know why I even bothered to reply, since I was not in the mood to discuss my private life. I must have been very tired.

'Not often. If I date someone, after only a few weeks I start to feel the pressure of commitment, and I find that difficult. My work is tiring, and I really need time by myself to recover.'

'Right, I see,' chorused the three women at the same

time; even though they didn't really have to work for a living and just did it to fill the time.

'Well, if you'll excuse me, I think I'd better go back and see what's happening in the kitchen.'

They politely thanked me for the food and the time I'd shared with them, and made promises that they would keep in touch, that I'd cook for Robin's engagement party, and that I'd come to her wedding.

As I turned to leave I heard Adriana say, 'Daphne, when are you going to introduce me to your cousin now he's back from Sardinia?'

I was right. She needed a man. All that chocolate she had been eating was just a substitute for sex.

The other two started giggling along with her. They wouldn't change. They liked having affairs, relationships, or whatever they liked to call them. They were all terrified of having too much blank space in their precious diaries.

Mrs Brown was calling me. A friend of hers was dying to meet me.

Oh, good heavens, it was Ken!

Great!

After a smiling introduction, Mrs Brown left us.

'When I found out you were going to cook for the Browns, I invited myself over, but I had to have dinner with my parents first. You know, Victoria, everyone here is amazed at how you managed to combine food from Louisiana and New England for the menu tonight, and that you cooked the best ever turkey.'

Talking about turkey, here you are.

'Give me another chance, Victoria …'

Without thinking, I suddenly took his arm and led him to the comfortable chairs where I'd left the three women a few minutes earlier.

'Robin, Daphne and Adriana, I want you to meet Ken, who is …'

Three pairs of eyes looked up at me, then at Ken, with unabashed joy.

'… er, who is desperately interested in meeting all of you. If you'll excuse me, I have to get back to the kitchen.'

I walked away quickly without looking back.

The last thing I heard was Ken calling my name.

Finally I was able to leave, having asked Steve to supervise the remainder of the clearing up in the kitchen and dining room.

Back home I was so tired that I knew if I went to bed immediately I wouldn't sleep.

On the porch, I lit the fire, took out my blanket, made myself some nice herbal tea, poured out a small glass of cranberry liqueur, sat on my rocking chair, and looked at the white waves softly illuminated by the immaculate moon. Chipolata was panting gently, also enjoying the moment. I valued this special time, knowing that the ocean would never let me down. Every little sip of the cranberry liqueur was a drop of life: bitter, sweet, bitter, sweet …

Two Victoria's Secrets

Victoria's New Orleans Chocolate Truffles

Makes about 35 truffles, enough for Adriana *and* her friends.

250g dark chocolate (minimum 50 per cent cocoa),
  broken into small pieces
1 tbsp butter
½ cup (125ml) full-fat crème fraîche
¾ cup (75g) finely chopped pecan nuts
¾ cup (75g) finely chopped dried cranberries
2 tbsp Bourbon
sieved cocoa or icing sugar, to dust

1. Melt the chocolate with the butter in a bowl set over a pan of simmering water.

2. In a separate small saucepan, bring the crème fraîche to the boil. Take off the heat and gently stir in the melted chocolate until smooth. Stir in the rest of the ingredients and allow to cool. Transfer to a bowl and refrigerate for an hour.

3. Using a melon-baller or a teaspoon dipped in hot water, shape the mixture into about 35 truffles and place on a baking sheet lined with parchment. Refrigerate for another 15 mins. Each truffle can then be rolled in sieved cocoa or icing sugar. The truffles keep well in the fridge for a week.

Victoria's Cranberry Liqueur

This cranberry liqueur is delicious topped up with sparkling wine or champagne to make a Kir Kennedy. Makes approx 1.25 litres.

2 cups (320g) dried cranberries
1 bottle (70cl) vodka
1 cup (200g) granulated sugar

1. Place the dried cranberries in a 1.5-litre jug or jar. Pour in the vodka and cover with a lid or cling film. Leave to soak for 4–7 days in a cool, dark place.

2. When the cranberries have steeped for sufficient time, heat the sugar and 2 cups (500ml) water in a saucepan until the sugar dissolves. Bring to the boil, then simmer gently, uncovered, for 30 mins. Allow the syrup to cool, then pour it over the vodka and cranberries. Cover and leave to stand overnight.

3. The next day, filter the cranberry liqueur through a jelly strainer or muslin cloth. Pour into sterilised bottles, seal, and leave to settle overnight before drinking.

The leftover strained cranberries can be turned into a preserve to sandwich a Victoria sponge or served with ice cream. Cook gently with an equal weight of granulated sugar for an hour.

December

Food, Comfort and Joy

'Tell me what you eat and I'll tell you what you are.'
Jean Anthelme Brillat-Savarin,
1755–1826, French lawyer,
politician, epicure and gastronome

'So you're telling me that you want to sue Fifty State Burger and Cable Boon because you think that they're the ones responsible for—'

'They are the ones to blame. There's no doubt about it!'

This was said sharply and unequivocally.

I turned my eyes away from the window. I had been looking out at the slowly falling snow. Now I observed my new patient with greater attention since I had never heard anything like that before. Although he seemed comfortable lying on the blue sofa, his breathing was loud and laboured, as if he were having respiratory failure. Pen in hand, I was poised to write down whatever words came out of his mouth.

His name was Dominic.

Dominic was very obese. I had noticed immediately how uncomfortable it was for him simply to exist. His red face was an obvious sign of poor health. His vast clothes were sloppy. Dominic didn't give me the impression that he took much care of himself. It was distressing to look at him. Poor man! I hoped I'd be able to help.

His round eyes were a beautiful pale green and were fixed on the picture on the wall facing him.

'Tell me more about it,' I said gently, though I thought it both ridiculous and grotesque.

No answer.

I tried again. 'Is it new, this decision to sue the fast-food and television companies?'

A great sigh escaped from the large man. 'Two weeks ago, I guess, I came up with it after I saw a woman on TV who got one million dollars in damages from the cigarette company she'd sued. She'd been smoking cigarettes since she was thirteen, and developed lung cancer because of it. She said that if the cigarettes hadn't been on sale she wouldn't have started smoking in the first place.'

Sure, as if someone forced her to buy and smoke them.

Stories like that made me angry. Nobody wanted to be responsible for their own actions any more. We lived in an infantile society where we demanded more security but accepted no responsibility. It was always others who were to blame.

'This story made me think, you see ...' Dominic continued, his eyes still glued to the picture. 'It made me realise that I've been eating food from Fifty State Burger for more than forty years now. It's certainly the reason why I'm so overweight and unhealthy today.'

So Dominic had already started eating at Fifty State Burger when he was just four years old. Yuck! I once went to one of these restaurants just to try their food, and I was sick for almost two days! As soon as I entered the place, I could smell the grease. Everything was deep-fried, even the vegetables.

'My mother would take us there pretty often. You see, I've got three siblings, and my dad was always travelling. There was a Fifty State Burger right down the street, and since they were always saying on TV and the radio how it was the right place to take your family for good food, my mother would do like the other mothers from the neighbourhood and take us there all the time.'

It was impossible to miss these restaurants. In front of every one there was an enormous kitsch red bull, wearing a white stetson, with the American flag emblazoned across its flank.

This got me thinking about my own family when I was growing up. We didn't have much money but we always had healthy food on the table, since my mother didn't work and she had time to shop. We didn't have any choice but to eat healthily as she had problems with her cholesterol at a young age. We all had to follow her diet. With hindsight I realised how lucky we all were. And portions were smaller then, weren't they? They seemed to have become bigger and bigger over the years, growing along with people's appetites: not a very positive trend.

Dominic continued his story.

'We would go there every other day because it was so much fun! I also remember collecting the tiny bulls from the different states. I got all fifty! I displayed them in a cabinet in the family room ...'

A beautiful collection!

'Most of the time we would meet our neighbours there. In the summer we kids could play in the inflatable pool while our mothers would chat after we'd eaten. This regular gathering really seemed to reinforce our neighbourhood community.'

Right!

'At that time, it was proven that Fifty State Burger's food contained all the nutrients we needed every day. We all believed it.'

And how could people avoid the silly song? On radio, TV ... Promotional cars with loudspeakers blaring out the Fifty State Burger slogan would even drive around the neighbourhoods, drumming up customers.

After another big sigh, Dominic started singing. His voice was smooth and melodious. Surprised, I listened intently to him.

Of course the lyrics didn't mention the deep frying, the excess salt and sugar.

'Their kids' playroom, their bull collection ... Later on, when I was thirteen, when my mother wasn't at home, since by then she'd started working, I used to stop off at Fifty State Burger on my way home from school because I was always hungry.'

Dominic went on to relate a typical day when he was a teenager.

'What is it that you like about this food?'

'Come on, it's really tasty! The mixture of sweet ketchup and tangy mustard smeared over a cheeseburger, the golden French fries, and the deep-fried veggies ... And

279

it all looks great as well as being good to eat. Then you wash it down with a giant, cold, thirst-quenching cola.'

'Don't you find it too fatty, too salty and too sweet, all at the same time?'

'No,' Dominic answered simply, then upon reflection added: 'Well, I never used to think that but I guess I was being deceived all those years. That's why I'm going to sue the liars!'

Dominic had got used to the excessive flavourings, which had gradually destroyed his taste for less processed and more natural foods.

By then I was feeling more like a dietician than a therapist.

'You know, the restaurants are very clean. You'd be amazed!'

Oh, please!

I didn't say anything.

'Yes, I can assure you. Have you seen the new bottles of antibacterial mustard and ketchup they put on the tables? I can't fault them on their hygiene.'

'No, I haven't,' I replied, wondering for a moment if he was joking. But no.

So essentially they poisoned people with their salty, sweet, deep-fried food, but they countered that by putting antibacterial mustard and ketchup on the table. As long as it killed the germs, who cared whether or not the food was healthy or tasted natural?

Flavour was very important to me: the freshness and smell of fruit without sugar or ice cream on it, or a vegetable cooked without oil; the texture and savour of a perfectly ripened Vacherin cheese, the bouquet of a full-bodied wine – all were perfectly wrapped gifts straight from Mother Nature.

'And it's cheap,' Dominic continued. 'And we don't have to wait to eat. You're hungry, you want to eat right away.' He was apparently still trying to convince me – or maybe himself – about the good side of Fifty State Burger, even though he was planning to sue them.

Just as a car needed to be filled with gas to keep it running, so, for my patient, food was nothing more than fuel. He didn't seem to appreciate what he had on his plate as long as it gave him immediate satisfaction and filled his stomach.

I longed to be able to tell him that when I baked a cake, or something was simmering on the stove, a delicious, joyous aroma would permeate my apartment ... not a foul greasy odour from frying meat.

I needed to know more about Dominic's family background.

'Are you married?'

'Why, you think women today can cook?' he laughed. 'Even my mother didn't cook much.'

So it's partly her fault, then, if today you find yourself in such bad health, is it?

Whatever next? Parents being sued for not having fed their children properly?

This made me think about the latest commercial for Super Vital soup. It showed a domestic scene from the sixties when many mothers had already stopped cooking and would simply open a tin and serve a liquid substance

281

that was supposedly soup. Their slogan: 'Good soup like your mother used to serve you! From the can!' *Yummy!*

'Today, women *and* men can enjoy cooking,' I said, thinking how much my husband loved to cook.

Unfortunately, our hectic life didn't give us much opportunity to cook together, but Paul and I made the most of our time at weekends, when we prepared dishes in advance for the week ahead.

'I don't see how it could ever be enjoyable to have to feed a family. My mother used to struggle all the time in the kitchen, when we didn't go to Fifty State Burger.'

As a mother, I'd decided to work only part time in order to be home to cook most of the meals for my children, just like my own mother had done for us. Usually I enjoyed it. I was proud to have passed on my passion for cooking to my children, and always welcomed them in my kitchen. I wanted mealtimes, especially dinner, to be almost sacred daily events which the whole family enjoyed together.

In fact, we'd already agreed Paul was going to cook that evening, while I prepared my certosino and a mincemeat cake for Christmas.

'But don't you take time to eat with your family?' I asked Dominic.

'Most of the time my wife orders the kind of takeout that I don't like – sushi or bean curd, stuff like that. She and my twin girls eat together sitting on stools at the kitchen counter.'

Dominic turned his head sharply from the picture on the wall and looked straight at me.

'Do you have children, Dr Elaine?'

'Yes, but if you don't mind I'd rather ask the questions,' I answered with my special disarming smile.

I didn't talk about my family with my patients. After everything I heard in my consulting room about other families, I knew how lucky I was. It almost made me feel guilty sometimes.

'Of course … sorry!'

His beautiful pale-green eyes returned to the picture on the wall.

'No problem. You know we're here to talk about you, Dominic.'

'My wife just thinks about her life coach.'

'Her *life coach*?'

'Yes, lots of people have them nowadays because they don't have time to find solutions to their little problems.'

Why doesn't she go see a therapist? What are we here for?

'There's this guy – he looks like a model – who comes to our house regularly. He helps my wife to live a better life, I guess. She does gym exercises with him, and he gives her a list of food and drinks that she is supposed to consume if she wants to stay fit. My wife's name is Tiffany,' he went on, 'and I like her the way she is. But she has this obsession about losing weight all the time.'

'Doesn't that encourage you to do something about your own situation? I mean, um, your health condition? You seem to have difficulty breathing sometimes.'

Silence. I wondered if Dominic was pretending not to have heard my question.

'You would not believe what Tiffany buys now: drinks that block fat, or give her extra energy; pills that reduce her appetite. I'm not convinced it's good for her. I'm afraid that she might get sick, especially since she works so hard.'

Dominic had a point. Diet and energy-boosting products could be damaging to people's health if they weren't taken properly.

'And now she wants a divorce,' Dominic blurted out, 'because she's sure that she's going to meet the man she's always been waiting for. I've basically become a burden to her.'

But look at you, Dominic! Why don't you take care of yourself? You seem to be a nice man.

'Of course, I'm convinced it's the coach who's turning Tiffany's head. He's younger, good-looking and he has a decent job.'

'What do you do for a living, Dominic?'

'I don't work. I can't. I get tired too quickly.'

Oh, please!

I wondered how he and his wife managed to make ends meet. Maybe they lived on Tiffany's salary. But he didn't give me a chance to ask.

'And besides, I've got enough money to do what I want to. I'm entitled to a small disability pension.'

'So what do you do all day?'

'I mostly watch TV.'

I might have guessed.

'That's the reason I want to sue Cable Boon.'

'But you've just said that you have enough money for your needs. So why do you want to sue the cable company if not for financial reasons?'

'It's the principle of the thing. I just want to show them

– and tell the world – that Fifty State Burger and Cable Boon are bad, that they're the cause of my problems.'

'Which are …?'

I knew exactly what his troubles were, but I wanted him to say it.

'Um, well, because of my obesity, I feel tired all the time, and Tiffany wants to leave me.'

Well, it's about time you realised there's a link.

'It's also a kind of personal revenge, just to show my wife I'm capable of accomplishing something since she always tells me I'm a useless fat slob.'

'You could make an effort to try to be a little more attractive to her.'

'It's too late.'

'But physical appearance isn't always the most important thing,' I said.

'Really? What about the images that you see everywhere?' Dominic answered. 'All those anorexic models in the fashion magazines? Why do you think Tiffany wants to lose weight? To look like them! I'd be amazed if some of them ever eat at all, judging by the way their bones stick out.'

He was right. Our society defined beauty by an extreme slenderness that didn't reflect the way women – and men – really looked.

I glanced down at my curves, which Paul said he liked so much.

'That's a fair point, but what about your health and wellbeing?'

No answer. Just another big sigh.

'Do you walk sometimes?' I asked.

I loved walking, and I was lucky to live close enough to work to walk there most days. It was a pleasant route through a park and attractive neighbourhoods, and it took me only twenty minutes.

'I walk Bobo twice a day.'

Suddenly there was hope!

'About five minutes each time, and that's good enough for the old dog.' Dominic added, 'For me as well. I get tired quickly.'

My hopes vanished.

'Try walking a little bit every day. It would help.'

'There's a Fifty State Burger across the street from my house. And they can deliver twenty-four hours a day.'

'You could move away from Fifty State Burger,' I suggested.

'Believe it or not, two months after my wife and I bought the house they built that Fifty State Burger across the street!'

It was true that there seemed to be a Fifty State Burger on every corner in the city and especially in the suburbs.

'You said your wife wants to leave you. How did she tell you?'

'She just said that she was tired of me and that she wanted to meet someone else. Pretty common nowadays, isn't it?'

'Unfortunately, yes.'

True enough. Most of my clients came to me for therapy following a separation. It could be a frightening experience for many people. The person who left was often to blame, but I could feel a certain sympathy for the wife. But I wondered: had she ever tried to help Dominic?

'She was a little overweight as well. You know, working crazy hours, sitting at a desk all day and eating fast food for lunch.'

And having to live with I-am-not-working-or-taking-care-of-myself Dominic ...

'Then a woman started work at her company and talked to Tiffany about how her coach had saved her life. My wife decided to call him.'

'Do you think there's something going on between him and your wife?'

'No, I think he prefers men.'

'It's interesting to see how some people can have an impact on others,' I asserted.

'I guess that's the whole point of hiring a coach, isn't it?'

'Indeed.'

'It costs enough money, that's for sure. But I don't say anything. It's Tiffany's money, after all.'

I decided to try once again to get him to talk about his health.

'I'm concerned about you, Dominic. Um, health-wise, how are you coping?'

'OK, I guess. I don't see doctors much. For what they have to say, it's just not worth it.'

'What made you decide to come see me, then?'

'My wife. It's a part of the divorce procedure, she says. And I said to myself, well, why not, after all? I like the kind of relationship Tony Soprano has with his therapist.'

I was speechless.

'It's a good show, don't you think?'

Not really ...

I'd watched one episode when I'd been staying at a hotel, and since everyone was talking about the show I felt I had to catch it. Well, there was far too much violence, and far too many F-words for my taste.

'I don't have a TV,' I said, almost apologising.

'What?' Dominic shouted, almost falling off the sofa. 'I've never met anyone who doesn't have a TV!'

It hadn't always been that way. One evening, almost ten years previously, our son had broken our TV irreparably while he was trying to fix it. We'd got rid of it, and Paul and I just hadn't bought a new one. We read more, and often went to the movies. And Manhattan had so much entertainment to offer!

'Yeah, *The Sopranos* is not quite *proper* enough for you, I suppose. But you might have found it interesting since the therapist is one of the main characters. It's a really good show,' Dominic affirmed, nodding his large head with conviction.

I went over my notes quickly.

My patient let out another big sigh. 'Yes, it's all about personal revenge. I'm not only a big fat wimp, I also want Fifty State Burger and Cable Boon to pay for what they've done to me!'

Right ...

'Tell me about your daily routine.'

'I get up at nine. I have breakfast.'

'What do you usually eat for breakfast?'

'Bacon, sausages, fried potatoes and a cola. You know, it's really convenient, the things you can buy today. Everything is precooked, and all in the same package! You just put it all in the microwave.'

I wondered if even performing such a simple task was a major effort for him.

'Then I take a shower.'

I'm glad to hear it.

'Then, at ten, the best of my Cable Boon premium package programmes starts.'

'And you sit down for the rest of the day?'

Dominic seemed hesitant. Was he going to be able to accept the fact that he needed to make drastic changes to his lifestyle?

'Well, yes, most of the time. Except when I have to take Bobo for a walk, and when I go out to Fifty State Burger. What else do you expect me to do in my condition?'

'What more do I need? I feed my body and my mind. Nothing else matters. Of course more sex would be appreciated, but, well ...'

Let's keep that for another session.

'What's your favourite Cable Boon programme?' I asked dutifully, though I really didn't want to know more about Cable Boon, which was famous for its dim-witted drama and comedy shows, game shows, trashy movies, reality shows and incredibly biased, phoney news programmes.

Television, and especially Cable Boon, had been described as 'the opiate of the people' in the previous month's psychology journal: a scourge of society that encouraged people's tendency to live vicariously through others and to believe everything they saw on TV while being completely incapable of managing their own lives.

After Dominic had told me all about his favourite programmes, I asked, 'What about watching the healthy food channel? It might give you some ideas for healthy meals for you and your family.'

Dominic looked at me strangely, as if I'd suddenly started speaking Chinese. Then he smiled, his handsome eyes turning back to the picture on the wall.

A couple of minutes passed in absolute silence. I waited. I wanted him to think a little.

While I waited, I envisaged him as a typical couch potato, eating peanuts and potato chips, quaffing beers, and ordering greasy meals from Fifty State Burger when he was too tired even to walk across the street. Bobo, the old dog lying at his feet, probably ate the same terrible food. Poor creature!

I wasn't sure whether to feel sorry for Dominic or not. After all, I firmly believe that our destiny is mostly in our own hands. Who else was to blame for his situation if not himself?

'Tell me about your girls.'

'They're ashamed of me. They're both thin, nineteen years old. They're in their first year at college. They eat sushi and bean curd, just like their mother. I don't know much more about them than that because we hardly talk.'

Well, if Dominic didn't spend the whole day in front of the TV there would probably be a bit more conversation in the house.

After heaving another sigh, he went on, 'You know, having a father who stays home is a pretty shameful thing for the girls. Men are supposed to be the strong financial pillar in a family and bring home the money.'

'It's pretty common to see men nowadays who are unemployed or decide to work at home to take care of the kids,' I asserted.

'Not in my world, Dr Elaine.'

He was right. I must have seemed like a dreamer to him, someone from another planet. Men were still feeling the pressure to be successful at work, and bring home money to support the family.

'Would you like your wife to stay with you?'

Dominic fell silent once again. He possibly didn't know how to answer this question: he either didn't want to be left alone, or, like so many men, he needed a woman only to cook his meals, do his laundry and provide occasional sex.

'You know, Dominic, you *can* tell me.'

'Yes, of course. I've got nothing to hide from you. At this point, how could I? Besides, Dr Elaine, I can talk to you so easily. But, you see, the thing is, I don't know if I want my wife to stay.'

He looked at the picture facing him even more intently.

The phone rang. Alice told me that my next patient had arrived.

'Do you wish to come back next week?' I asked Dominic, smiling.

'Why not?' he answered immediately. 'You're the only woman I've had a proper conversation with for a long time, and I really love this picture.'

'Matisse is my favourite painter.'

No reaction.

'What are you going to do for Christmas?' I asked.

'My wife and girls will go see my mother-in-law in Tennessee, and I'll stay here. It's not a problem because I love the TV programmes at Christmas.'

'Sure,' I muttered under my breath, thinking about the cakes I had to make that evening because the children and Paul's parents were coming for Christmas. It was the best gift we could have wished for.

'But you know that the festive season is supposed to be all about love and forgiveness? Why don't you try to forget about taking your revenge on Fifty State Burger and the cable company and think about some good things you can do for yourself?'

'I know I'm not supposed to ask questions, but are you going away for the holidays?' Dominic asked rather than answering me.

I told him that it was a time of year when my patients needed me more than ever, so we usually stayed here in Manhattan, and our families came to us.

'Have a beautiful Christmas, Dominic! I'll see you next week then.'

We set a time for our next meeting, and Dominic heaved himself off the sofa and left, a broad smile on his generous features.

I told Alice to send in my next patient in ten minutes. I needed time to think over the somewhat odd conversation from my session with Dominic. I quickly wrote down a few more comments and some questions that I intended to ask Dominic next week. I wanted to help him. He was very touching, in an exasperating yet perfectly honest way. I had a feeling that he would somehow manage to extricate himself from his dreadful situation. My first impressions were rarely wrong.

For a moment I studied the painting on the wall: Matisse's *La Chambre Rouge*. In this painting I always saw my own mother placing fresh fruit on the table in a stylised atmosphere in which life and food were richly celebrated.

The phone rang again reminding me of my next patient. I checked her file: Carla, a very friendly woman whose eyes were also constantly on the Matisse. It reminded her of the still-life exhibition she'd seen in Paris in January when she'd been on a culinary tour of the French capital.

I hoped that Carla was getting over the fact that Armand and his little daughter, Juliette, were moving out and that she'd decided, as I'd suggested, to work part time, doing the shopping and cooking herself since she had learnt so much from Armand. That would also mean she'd have more time to visit Armand and Juliette, who were going to live in Brooklyn with Armand's girlfriend, Liana. There was no reason why Carla shouldn't cook a wonderful Christmas dinner for herself, her husband Rick, Armand, Liana and little Juliette. I resolved to give her my recipes for the certosino and mincemeat cake. Christmas is always such a great time for food, comfort and joy!

Elaine's Christmas Cake Recipes
Certosino

This traditional Italian Christmas cake is best made at least
three days ahead. A week is even better.

¾ cup (120g) glacé cherries, chopped, plus 8 more,
  halved, to decorate
½ cup each (80g) chopped dried apricots and chopped
  pitted dates
½ cup (125ml) dark rum
¾ cup (180ml) runny honey, plus another 2 tbsp, to
  decorate
2 cups (250g) wholemeal flour
2 tsp baking powder
2 tbsp cocoa
5 tbsp each orange marmalade and apricot jam
½ cup (100g) mixed candied peel
1 cup (120g) ground almonds
½ cup (50g) each chopped walnuts and almonds
¾ cup (100g) pine nuts
1 tsp anise seeds
butter, for greasing
½ cup (60g) toasted flaked almonds, to decorate

1. Soak the glacé cherries and dried fruit with the rum for
about an hour.

2. Preheat the oven to 180°C/350°F/Gas 4. In a large
bowl gently mix the honey with ½ cup (125ml) water. Add
the soaked fruit along with the rum and all the other cake
ingredients except the flaked almonds, and mix well.

3. Grease and line an 8 in (20cm) cake tin and transfer the mixture to the tin. Bake the cake for 45 mins. Test with a skewer that the cake is cooked right through. Turn off the oven but leave the cake in until cold, then turn out.

4. Mix 2 tbsp honey with 1 tbsp water and brush over the top of the cake. Arrange the remaining glacé cherry halves over the cake along with the flaked almonds. Store for at least 3 days in an airtight tin before cutting. Certosino is excellent served with chocolate cherry ice cream or whipped cream.

Mincemeat Cake

A quick and easy Christmas cake that busy people, like Elaine and Paul, can make at the last minute.

120g softened butter
⅓ cup (60g) soft light brown sugar
3 eggs, at room temperature
1 x 410g jar mincemeat
½ cup (60g) self-raising flour
½ cup (50g) oat flakes
½ cup (80g) polenta
1 tsp baking powder
½ cup (80g) chopped dried cranberries
1 cup (100g) chopped walnuts
grated zest of 1 tangerine
½ cup (125ml) dark rum

1. Preheat the oven to 160°C/325°F/Gas 3. In a large bowl, cream together the butter and sugar until light and fluffy. Add the eggs one at a time, beating thoroughly with each addition. Fold in the remaining ingredients.

2. Grease and line a 9 x 5 in (23 x 12.5cm) loaf tin and transfer the mixture to the tin. Bake for 1–1¼ hours. Test with a skewer that the cake is cooked right through. Turn off the oven and leave the cake in until cold. The cake keeps well for a week in an airtight tin and is excellent served with whipped cream.

See a selection of the recipes from
Freedom Fries and Café Crème demonstrated
at www.gallicbooks.com

The Gourmet

Muriel Barbery

France's greatest food critic is dying, after a lifetime in single-minded pursuit of sensual delights. But as Pierre Arthens lies on his death bed, he is tormented by an inability to recall the most delicious food to ever pass his lips, which he ate long before becoming a critic. Desperate to taste it one more time, he looks back over the years to see if he can pin down the elusive dish.

Revealing far more than his love of great food, the narration by this larger-than-life individual alternates with the voices of those closest to him and their own experiences of the man.

Muriel Barbery's gifts as an evocative storyteller are put to mouth-watering use in this voluptuous and poignant meditation on food and its deeper significance in our lives.

A delectable treat to savour.

ISBN 978-1-906040-31-4
£6.99

Where Would I be Without You?

Guillaume Musso

Over 1 million copies sold worldwide

Sometimes, a second chance can come out of nowhere…
Parisian cop Martin Beaumont has never really got over
his first love, Gabrielle. Their brief, intense affair in San
Francisco and the pain of her rejection still haunt him
years later.

Now, however, he's a successful detective – and tonight
he's going to arrest the legendary art thief, Archibald
Maclean, when he raids the Musée d'Orsay for a priceless
Van Gogh. But the enigmatic Archibald has other plans.
Martin's pursuit of the master criminal across Paris is the
first step in an adventure that will take him back to San
Francisco, and to the edge of love and life itself.

ISBN: 9781906040345
£7.99

The Girl on Paper

Guillaume Musso

Just a few months ago, Tom Boyd was a multi-million-selling author living in LA, in love with a world-famous pianist. But after a very public break-up he's shut himself away, suffering from total writer's block, with only drink and drugs for company. One night, a beautiful, naked stranger appears in Tom's house. She claims to be Billie, a character from his novels, who has fallen into the real world because of a printer's error in his latest book.

Crazy as her story sounds; Tom comes to see that this must be the real Billie. And she wants to strike a deal with him: if he writes his next novel she can go back to the world of fiction; in return she will help him win back his beloved Aurore.

What does he have to lose?

Guillaume Musso's latest romantic adventure is a story of friendship, love and the special place that books have in our lives.

ISBN: 978-1-906040888
£7.99